PENGUIN BOOKS

The Templar Throne

'Oh, crap,' groaned Holliday, putting it together. The hairs on the back of his neck rose in warning, giving him a split-second advantage as the flimsy cabin door burst outward and Antonin Pesek hurtled through the opening, a dark flat automatic already raised in his hand.

Instinctively, Holliday threw the wheel hard over and the flat-bottomed boat slewed drunkenly to port, throwing the assassin off balance, the pistol flying out of his hand as he fought to stay on his feet. The weapon spun across the deck, lost in the clutter of equipment around the transom.

The killer barely paused, a broad-bladed knife appearing almost magically in his right hand. Pesek lunged and Holliday backed against the gunwale as the lethal instrument slashed across his belly . . .

The Templar Throne

PAUL CHRISTOPHER

PENGUIN BOOKS

PENGUIN BOOKS

Published by the Penguin Group

Penguin Books Ltd, 80 Strand, London WC2R ORL, England

Penguin Group (USA) Inc., 375 Hudson Street, New York, New York 10014, USA

Penguin Group (Canada), 90 Eglinton Avenue East, Suite 700, Toronto, Ontario,
Canada M4P 2Y3 (a division of Pearson Penguin Canada Inc.)

Penguin Ireland, 25 St Stephen's Green, Dublin 2, Ireland (a division of Penguin Books Ltd)

Penguin Group (Australia), 250 Camberwell Road, Camberwell, Victoria 3124, Australia
(a division of Pearson Australia Group Pty Ltd)

Penguin Books India Pvt Ltd, 11 Community Centre, Panchsheel Park,
New Delhi – 110 017, India

Penguin Group (NZ), 67 Apollo Drive, Rosedale, Auckland 0632, New Zealand
(a division of Pearson New Zealand Ltd)

Penguin Books (South Africa) (Pty) Ltd, 24 Sturdee Avenue,
Rosebank, Johannesburg 2196, South Africa

Penguin Books Ltd, Registered Offices: 80 Strand, London WC2R ORL, England

www.penguin.com

First published in the USA by Signet, an imprint of New American Library,
a division of Penguin Group (USA) Inc. 2010
First published in Great Britain in Penguin Books 2012

003

Set in 13.5/16.5pt Garamond MT Std
Typeset by Jouve (UK), Milton Keynes
Printed in England by Clays Ltd, St Ives plc

B-format ISBN: 978-0-241-95119-4
A-format ISBN: 978-0-241-95253-5

www.greenpenguin.co.uk

MIX
Paper from
responsible sources
FSC
www.fsc.org
FSC™ C018179

Penguin Books is committed to a sustainable
future for our business, our readers and our planet.
This book is made from Forest Stewardship
Council™ certified paper.

ALWAYS LEARNING   **PEARSON**

The very word 'secrecy' is repugnant in a free and open society; and we are as a people inherently and historically opposed to secret societies, to secret oaths, and to secret proceedings.

John F. Kennedy

The Assyrian came down like the wolf on the fold,
And his cohorts were gleaming in purple and gold;
And the sheen of their spears was like stars on the sea,
When the blue wave rolls nightly on deep Galilee.

Lord Byron, 'The Destruction of Sennacherib'

I

Colonel John 'Doc' Holliday, US Army Rangers (retired), most recently a professor of medieval military history at the United States Military Academy at West Point (retired from that, too), sat on the glassed-in terrace of La Brasserie Malakoff, an upscale café in the prestigious six-teenth arrondissement of Paris. His companion was Maurice Bernheim, director of the Musée National de la Marine, the National Maritime Museum of France.

Both men were eating a lunch of salad and croque monsieur, the Parisian version of a Reuben sandwich that might as well have come from an entirely different universe. The Parisians looked down their noses at everyone else on the planet, but when it came to food they were right. Even a *Royale avec Fromage* at a Paris McDonald's was vastly superior to a Big Mac sold anywhere else in the world. Bernheim had been lecturing him on the subject for the better part of an hour, but a good lunch on a spring day in Paris made up for a lot of things.

Holliday had crossed paths with Bernheim previously when he was in the midst of tracking down the secret of the Templar sword. The chubby little historian who smoked the foul-smelling cigarettes called Boyards had helped him then and Holliday was hoping he'd help him again.

'I must say it is too bad that your charming niece could not be with you today,' said Bernheim. He finished the sandwich and hailed a waiter, ordering crème caramel and coffee for both of them.

'Cousin,' corrected Holliday. 'She's too busy being pregnant in Jerusalem.' Peggy and the Israeli archaeologist Rafi Wanounou had married last year shortly after their adventures in the Libyan desert, the same adventures that had eventually led Holliday to his high-cholesterol lunch with Maurice Bernheim.

'Such a pretty young woman,' sighed the middle-aged man.

'Her new husband thinks so.' Holliday smiled. 'Speaking of which, how's your wife and kids?'

'Pauline is well, thank you. Fortunately for me her dental practice keeps me in the style to which my little hellions and I have grown accustomed. The twins of course must also have the latest running shoes. *La vie est tres cher, mon ami.* Life is very expensive, yes? Soon it will be makeup and matching Mercedes.' Bernheim flicked an invisible bit of fluff off the lapel of his very expensive Brioni suit.

The crème caramel arrived and the museum director stared at it reverently for a moment, as though it was a great work of art, which, to Bernheim, it probably was. Holliday ignored the dessert and tried the coffee. As with everything else at Malakoff's, it was excellent. At least with the ban on smoking in Paris restaurants he didn't have to endure Bernheim's Boyards.

'So,' said the nautical expert. 'What brings you to Paris and my humble little museum?' He took another bite of the crème caramel and briefly closed his eyes to savor the flavor.

'Have you ever heard of a place called La Couvertoirade?' Holliday asked.

Bernheim nodded. 'A fortified town in the Dordogne. Built by the Templars, I believe.'

'That's right,' Holliday said and nodded. 'A while back an archaeologist, a monk named Brother Charles-Étienne Brasseur, discovered a cache of documents from there relating to the Templar expedition to Egypt.' Holliday paused, trying to remember it all. 'The texts were written by a Cistercian monk named Roland de Hainaut. Hainaut was secretary to Guillaume de Sonnac, the grand master who led the Templars at the Siege of Damietta in 1249.'

'Of course. The Seventh Crusade,' said Bernheim. 'They couldn't get upriver because of the Nile flooding so they sat around for six months and had their way with the Egyptian women.'

'They also played at being tourists,' added Holliday. 'Guillaume de Sonnac's personal ship as grand master was a caravel called the *Sanctus Johannes* chartered out of Genoa from a ship owner named Peter Rubeus. De Sonnac provided his own captain, a fellow Frenchman named Jean de Saint-Clair.'

'A common enough name in France, I'm afraid,' said Bernheim. 'Rather like John Smith in America.' He smiled. 'A name used to sign hotel registers with.'

'Well, while this particular Saint-Clair was in Damietta he traveled a little way to Rosetta, where the famous stone was found a few hundred years later by Napoleon's archaeologists.'

'And stolen by the British, I might add,' snorted Bernheim.

'Take it up with the queen,' said Holliday. 'Anyway, while Saint-Clair was on his little visit to Rosetta along with de Sonnac's secretary, they stumbled on some old Coptic documents in a monastery there. The documents described something they referred to as an Organum Sanctum.'

'An Instrument of God,' translated Bernheim. 'It generally refers to a person. Moses was an instrument of God, for instance.'

'Not this time,' said Holliday. He opened the floppy old-fashioned briefcase on his lap and took out two ten-inch-long strips of wood. One of the strips was slightly thicker than the other and had a square hole halfway down its length. The narrower of the two pieces was clearly meant to fit into the hole, forming a cross. Both strips were notched at regular intervals.

'A Jacob's Staff,' Bernheim said and nodded. 'A sixteenth-century navigational instrument.'

'Except the documents were discovered by Saint-Clair and de Sonnac's secretary two hundred years before that,' said Holliday. 'Stranger still, the documents described the device from which that model was made as being even older – from the time of the pharaohs, in fact.'

'Ridiculous,' scoffed Bernheim.

'I found the original of the device you hold in your hand in the mummified hand of the pharaoh Djoser's vizier. The mummy was entombed at least twenty-five hundred years before the birth of Christ and four thousand years before Jean de Saint-Clair was in Rosetta. The original is now in the safekeeping of the Metropolitan Museum of Art in New York. The copy you're holding is an exact duplicate made by their model department.'

'There can be no mistake about the age?'

'Spectroscopic analysis is accurate within a margin of error less than ten per cent for African juniper. There's no doubt about it, Maurice: the instrument is forty-five hundred years old.'

'*Merde,*' breathed the man, his crème caramel forgotten. 'You know what this does to the basic paradigm of modern nautical history?'

'Destroys it,' answered Holliday flatly.

'This device would be as much a secret weapon as the atomic bomb,' said Bernheim. 'A seafaring nation that had it would have an incredible advantage over a nation that lacked it.'

'At least for the two hundred years or so between Saint-Clair's discovery and the Jacob's Quadrant being invented in the fifteen hundreds,' said Holliday.

'Columbus goes out the window.'

'And it almost certainly means that those fairy tales about the Templars going to America are true. Or could be,' said Holliday.

'Saint-Clair, Sinclair,' mused Bernheim. He ran his thumb along the notches along the sides of the two strips of wood, then fitted the two pieces together. He held up the cruciform instrument. 'Have you ever seen the ancient coat of arms of the Saint-Clairs?' Bernheim asked. 'The original, as it was used in France?'

'Sure,' answered Holliday. 'A scalloped cross.'

'*Pas escallope, mon ami*. In France it is called *La Croix Engraal*,' said Bernheim. 'An "engrailed" cross.'

'Which means?' Holliday asked.

'In heraldic terms *engraal* means "protected by the Holy Grail," the Grail being indicated by what, in that silly *Da Vinci* book, was referred to as the V of the sacred feminine, not sangraal, the blood of Christ. But what if, on the Saint-Clair crest, the *engraal* notches on the cross referred to

7

something else? Something much more prac-
tical.' Bernheim ran his thumbnail along the
notches in the wood. Holliday suddenly under-
stood.

'The gradation indentations on a Jacob's
Quadrant,' Holliday said and grinned. 'The sim-
plest explanation is most often the truth. Occam's
razor.'

'*C'est ça,*' said Bernheim happily. 'The mystery
is solved.'

'Not until I find out more about this Jean de
Saint-Clair, whoever he was.'

Bernheim had gone back to his crème caramel. He put down his spoon and wiped his lips
with a napkin. He shrugged.

'Historically the Sinclairs of Scotland came
from a little place known as Saint-Clair-sur-Epte.
The Epte River once served as the border between
Normandy and Ile de France; that is, between the
English possessions and the rest of the country.
It is also the river diverted by Claude Monet to
create his famous water-lily pond.'

'What on earth does any of this have to do
with maritime history?' Holliday laughed, impressed by Bernheim's fund of knowledge on
such an obscure subject.

'Your interest, your expertise is in medieval warfare, correct?'

'I'd like to think so.'

'Mine is ships and the sea. Before ships there must be wood; before wood there must be trees. Have you ever heard of the Beaulieu River in England?'

'No.'

'Then you've never heard of the village of Buckler's Hard.'

'Not a name I'm familiar with.'

'Anyone involved in French maritime history would be,' said Bernheim. 'HMS *Euryalus,* HMS *Swiftsure* and HMS *Agamemnon* were all built there, ships that were key during the Battle of Trafalgar in which the British defeated the French fleet in 1805. It was wood from the surrounding New Forest that built Nelson's entire fleet.'

'You're saying the Epte River had the same function?'

'Since the time of the Vikings,' Bernheim said with a nod. He scraped the last of the crème caramel from the sides of his dish. He smacked his lips and sighed. 'If the Saint-Clair you seek was a seaman he almost certainly came from Saint-Clair-sur-Epte.' He stared mournfully down at his empty dish and sighed again. 'There is an old abbey nearby, the Abbaye de Tiron. Speak with the librarian there, Brother Morvan. Pierre Morvan. Perhaps he will be able to help you.' He glanced over at Holliday's untouched crème caramel. 'Not hungry?' Bernheim inquired hopefully.

2

The average student thinks the best synonym for 'research' is 'Google.' Real, original research, however, has more to do with pinball than search engines; it's usually a matter of hit and miss, with a lot more misses than hits. You ricochet around the table gathering points as you go, eventually finding out a direction before eventually reaching your destination.

Discovering the whereabouts of Pierre Morvan turned out to be a long-distance game of pinball, ricocheting northwest for a hundred miles from Paris to the monastery of the Abbaye de Tiron in the town of Saint-Clair-sur-Epte, then seventy miles south to the tiny village of Le Pin-la-Garenne and its even smaller eleventh-century church, and finally a hundred miles due west to the town of Dol-de-Bretagne near the Brittany coast and the cathedral there.

It was time well spent. Holliday discovered that the Abbaye de Tiron was reputedly the birthplace of Freemasonry, which usually allied with the Templars. The little church in Le Pin-la-Garenne had a lot of Saint-Clairs buried in its crypt, and Dol-de-Bretagne was reputedly the original home of the Stuart kings of Scotland, also closely associated with the Templars, especially after the official dissolution of the order in A.D. 1312. It was also the birthplace of the ancestors of William Sinclair, First Earl of Caithness, Third Earl of Orkney, Baron of Roslin and the builder of Rosslyn Chapel, in Midlothian, the supposed location of the final secret in the book *The Da Vinci Code*.

The Cathedral of Dol was a grim-looking Gothic structure, black with a thousand years of soot and grime. The original church was built in A.D. 834 and added on to for the next six hundred years. According to legend, St Samson, in the midst of building the cathedral, infuriated Satan, who threw a gigantic rock at the cathedral, destroying the north tower, which no longer exists. Holliday found Brother Morvan on his hands and knees taking a rubbing of a Latin inscription on the floor of the nave. Morvan was wearing the white habit and black scapular 'apron' of a Cistercian, the sect of monks the Templars were most frequently associated with.

Holliday cleared his throat. 'Brother Morvan?'

The gray-haired monk glanced up at him and smiled. He was a grandfatherly man, complete with twinkling eyes and old-fashioned rimless spectacles perched on a large hooked nose.

'You must be Mr Holliday,' said the monk. 'Do people ever call you "Doc" like the famous western gunfighter?'

'All the time,' answered Holliday. 'I came by it honestly, though; I do have a Ph.D.'

'In what?'

'Medieval history.'

'Which explains why you're looking for me all over France.'

'How did you know I was looking for you?'

'I may wear a monk's robe, Mr Holliday, but that doesn't prevent me from having a cellular telephone. Your reputation precedes you, courtesy of Société Française de Radiotéléphone.' Morvan stood up and dusted off his robe. He appeared to be in his early to mid-sixties. 'How did you lose the eye?' he asked, nodding at the patch over Holliday's right eye.

'A piece of gravel on a back road in Afghanistan.'

'So presumably it wasn't always just plain "Mister" Holliday.'

'What makes you say that?'

'Afghanistan from the twelfth century to the fifteenth was effectively under the rule of people like Genghis Khan and Tamerlane. Not much to interest a medievalist. Also you have an officer's bearing.'

'You're good,' said Holliday, laughing.

'My cell is a BlackBerry,' answered the monk. 'I Googled you, Colonel Holliday. Your specialty is medieval arms and armor. What brings you to a cathedral? There are a few dead knights entombed here, but any swords are carved in stone.'

'I use a BlackBerry, too,' Holliday said with a smile. 'Maybe I should have Googled you first. Anyway, I'm looking for one knight in particular. A Templar named Jean de Saint-Clair.'

'Interesting,' said the monk. 'Walk with me.'

Morvan didn't wait for an answer. He headed back down the nave and then turned toward an open side door. A few moments later Holliday found himself in a small graveyard, an alleyway of ancient granite mausoleums, the stones old and worn, most of the inscriptions faded away to nothing.

'There are a great number of artisans buried here,' said the monk. 'The man who crafted the Abraham Window in the cathedral, for instance, the so-called Abraham Master.' He stopped at a simple square mausoleum and rested his large gnarled hand on the old gray stone. There was the indistinct image of some strange beast over the door. A cat perhaps? 'The image is the lion of St Mark, the patron saint of stained-glass painters,' explained Morvan. 'It is the only means we have to identify him, but six hundred years after his death we still see his work as though it was created only yesterday. It is living history, the very imagination of a single human being.'

'I know what you mean,' Holliday said and nodded. 'I can go to some places that seem soaked in history. You can almost breathe it in like perfume. Some battlefields are like that. There is graffiti on the walls of a brothel in Pompeii that's two thousand years old.'

'Art endures is the lesson, I think. Businessmen are rarely remembered much past their time. No one remembers Michelangelo's patrons, but they remember the man. The *Mona Lisa*'s smile endures, the pyramids still stand. It's the reason I joined the Tironensian Order.'

'Because of their association with Free-masonry?'

'Not just the Masons,' said Morvan. 'It was a community of artisans. ShipWalkers, or ship-wrights, glassblowers, goldsmiths, stonecutters, craftsmen of all types. Creators of things that lasted. It seemed to me the greatest expression of God's immortality, what he had given man to express infinity:

> To see a world in a grain of sand
> And heaven in a wildflower
> Hold infinity in the palm of your hand
> And eternity in an hour

'William Blake wrote that two hundred years ago but it's still quoted today.'

'I'm not sure why that makes my question about Jean de Saint-Clair interesting,' said Holliday.

'Jean de Saint-Clair, also known as John Sinclair, was born in Saint-Clair-sur-Epte, the son of a master shipwalker. He ran away to sea, became a knight, joined the Templars, carried men and supplies to the Crusades and disappeared during the dissolution of the order in 1312. He returned to France and specifically to Saint-Clair-sur-Epte in 1332 with a dispensation from Pope Gregory IX, the man who introduced the world to the Inquisition, by the way. Saint-Clair was one of a very few Templar knights to survive the dissolution. Most of the others were simply murdered or burned at the stake. He joined the monastery at the Abbaye de Tiron and spent the next twenty years in seclusion. When he died, a group of monks from the Abbey of Mont Saint-Michel appeared, pickled him in a barrel of Calvados apple brandy and took him to the island abbey, where he was then interred. His tomb bears the inscription *et in arcadia ego,* which has a number of translations, the most popular being "I lived in Arcadia." Both *The Da Vinci Code* and *Holy Blood, Holy Grail* use the phrase in relation to the blood-line of Christ, which of course is utter nonsense on a par with the discovery of Piltdown Man. But that's not why your question was interesting.'

'Do tell,' said Holliday.

'What is truly interesting is the fact that you

are the second person this week who's asked me about Jean de Saint-Clair.'

'Really?'

'Really,' Morvan said, nodding.

'Who was he?'

'Not a he at all. A she. A nun from the Convent of St Agnes of Prague. Her name is Sister Margaret Emily.'

'Not a very Czech name.'

'From her accent I'd say the American South. Mississippi or Alabama.'

'Why is she interested in Jean de Saint-Clair?'

'Apparently she's writing a definitive history of the convent for a Ph.D. thesis at Notre Dame. Saint-Clair's name came up in her research.'

'Apparently?'

'In my experience a great many people lie,' said Morvan, trying to keep his voice neutral.

'You think she was lying?'

'I didn't say that.'

'But you must have thought it or you wouldn't have mentioned it.'

'Perhaps.'

'A lying nun. Now *that's* interesting.'

3

Mont Saint-Michel is a Walt Disney-style Fantasyland Castle, monastery and abbey on a tiny, rocky island half a mile off the Normandy Coast close to the mouth of the Couesnon River, not far from the town of Avranches. Once upon a time the narrow causeway connecting the island to the mainland was covered by the exceptionally high tides, but over the centuries the causeway has been built up so that the little island is always accessible.

The eleventh-century fortress and Benedictine refuge has been commercialized in direct proportion to its elevation. The lower levels of the island are crammed with overpriced souvenir shops, mediocre family hotels and expensive restaurants serving second-rate foods. By the time you reach the abbey and the top of the *grand degré*, the main staircase, you are back in the land of the pure and holy. There is one exception to this rule.

On the back of the island, away from the crowds and facing the sea, is a single-roomed chapel, nothing more than four stone walls and a slate roof. It is the Chapel of St Aubert, named after Saint-Michel's founder and one of the oldest existing structures on the island.

The exterior walls are crusted with barnacles, the stones battered by seventeen centuries of pounding storms. It is only a few yards away from the original stone breakwater that once served as the island's port of entry. There is nothing between the chapel and the sea. Worn to near anonymity, a small granite statue of Bishop Aubert stands on the simple peaked roof, his back to the empty ocean.

The old wooden door of the chapel sagged outward, allowing a long drift of sand and dirt to creep in across the stone floor. It looked as though no one had been there for a very long time.

Holliday stepped into the chapel, his feet crunching on the sand and small shells blown in through the entrance. The new Nikon D3 he'd picked up for the trip to France hung from his shoulder. He'd been guided there from the abbey by several black-robed monks.

She stood at the far end of the bare room,

contemplating the stone effigy of a knight that stood as the cap on a simple stone sarcophagus. Even in her simple gray skirt and jacket and black head covering she was striking, not quite beautiful in the classic sense but extraordinary-looking just the same, a hint of bright red hair peeking out from beneath the head scarf, a scattering of freckles across the bridge of her elegant, finely sculpted nose and a wide, full mouth. Holliday approached her and she looked up as he came nearer. Her eyes were pale-lashed and large, the irises a strange gray-green color. She looked as though she was in her late thirties, faint crow's-feet only just beginning to show.

He smiled, trying to put her at ease. She looked back at him curiously.

'May I help you?' she said. He bristled a little at the question. She made it sound as though the chapel was her private preserve.

'Just looking around,' he answered. He stood beside her at the foot of the sarcophagus. The knight's effigy was a little strange; the figure was half turned, the right knee bent as though he was climbing a stair, the shield held to one side. On his surcoat was the clear design of a Templar cross, engrailed. The figure itself was covered in detailed chain mail from head to toe. At the feet was a stone plaque that read *In Arcadia Est*.

'There's not much here in the way of photo opportunities,' said the woman, eyeing the big camera.

Just to annoy her, Holliday slipped the Nikon off his shoulder and clicked off a few shots of the knight. Then he turned quickly and took a shot of the woman herself. Her expression darkened and she frowned, her hands balling into fists at her side.

'I *beg* your pardon?'

'Afraid I'm going to steal your soul?' Holliday grinned.

The woman scowled. 'Certainly not. You took my photograph without permission. That's an invasion of privacy.'

'So this is your private chapel?'

'I'm not a tourist. I'm doing historical research.'

'Who says I'm not doing the same?'

'I have a master's degree in the history of religion from Harvard,' she snapped. 'What's your degree in?'

'Medieval history. I have a doctorate from Georgetown University. Ph.D. trumps M.A. Beat you,' Holliday said and laughed.

The woman turned beet red. 'Is that true?'

'Would I lie to a nun?' Holliday answered, still laughing. 'If I did, my old teacher Sister Claudille would come down from heaven and whack me across the back of the head with her special whacking-over-the-head ruler.'

The gray-green eyes widened. 'How did you know I was a nun?'

'Elementary, my dear Watson, you're wearing a modern "Urbanist" Clare habit, black and gray. From the cut of the skirt I'd say it was one of the eastern European convents. Agnes of Prague, perhaps. *Korektní?*'

She looked totally flabbergasted.

'That's impossible!' she blustered. 'You couldn't know all that!'

'And I couldn't know that this was the grave of Jean de Saint-Clair,' said Holliday blandly. 'Or that your name is Sister Margaret Emily.'

The nun stared at him. After a moment her expression hardened.

'Brother Morvan,' Sister Margaret Emily said, finally figuring it out.

'Bingo.'

'Exactly who are you?' Sister Margaret Emily said frostily. 'And what were you doing talking to Brother Morvan?'

'You've got quite the proprietary tone going for you there, ma'am,' said Holliday. 'Do you own Brother Morvan as well as the chapel?'

'I'm not a ma'am and I spoke to Brother Morvan in confidence.'

'Your name is a state secret?' The young woman was getting under his skin. She was beginning to remind him of 'Hot Lips' Houlihan on *M.A.S.H.*, at least as far as her haughty attitude was concerned.

'I'm usually called Sister Meg,' said the woman primly. 'And you are?'

'John Holliday, US Army, retired. My friends call me Doc.'

'I wasn't aware that the army employed historians,' said Sister Meg.

'Quite a few of them, actually,' replied Holliday. 'You know the old saying, "those who ignore history are doomed to repeat it."'

'George Santayana,' said the nun.

'The army takes it quite seriously. Ignoring history leads to things like invading Russia in winter or taking big hollow horses into walled enemy cities. In my case, I taught the history of warfare at West Point.'

'One of my ancestors went to West Point,'

said the nun, a hint of pride in her voice. 'He was a general.'

'Which one?' Holliday asked.

Sister Meg waved a dismissing hand. 'It doesn't matter.' She pointed down at the effigy of the knight. 'Why are you interested in Jean de Saint-Clair?'

'He discovered a nautical instrument that gave the Templars a great advantage at sea. He may well have traveled as far as North America.' He smiled. 'I'm not quite sure why a nun would be interested in a man like him.'

'The Convent of St Agnes was founded in 1232 by Princess Agnes, a niece of the king of Bohemia,' explained the nun. 'She died in 1282. Before she died she entrusted a relic to the care of her own niece, the Blessed Juliana. The relic is known as the True Ark.'

'As in Noah or the Ark of the Covenant?'

'Neither,' said Sister Meg. 'In Latin the word for "chest" is *arca*. Over time the word has been invested with far more meaning than it really should. It simply means "box." The True Ark is the single most important religious relic in the world with the exception of the bones of Christ himself. I'm going to find it.'

'Presumably there's something inside this ark of yours,' suggested Holliday.

'There is,' said the nun. 'Historically the contents of the box were thought to have been the Holy Grail, the Crown of Thorns, the Holy Shroud, and the Ring of Christ.'

'The main event,' said Holliday.

'The fourteenth century was the age of relics,' said the nun. 'The True Cross, the Shroud of Turin, the bones of various saints. Whatever was in the box was felt to be significant.'

'So Juliana gave it to Saint-Clair?'

'Yes. Juliana had been married to a member of the French royal family. When he died she was betrothed again, this time to a man she did not love, a cousin of King Philip who was also a bishop. Part of the dowry was the True Ark. Rather than marry the bishop and lose the ark she fled, with Jean de Saint-Clair's help. According to the stories he was the greatest navigator of his time. They vanished for a number of years. From 1307 to 1314.'

'Interesting,' said Holliday. 'Saint-Clair was a Templar. The order was proscribed by King Philip in 1307. Saint-Clair would have been on the run from the king's men.' Holliday paused. 'Was it some sort of elopement? Were this Juliana and Saint-Clair lovers?'

'There is no evidence of that,' said the nun coldly.

'What happened when they came back?'

'Jean de Saint-Clair reappeared in December of 1314, at the monastery of the Abbaye de Tiron in the town of Saint-Clair-sur-Epte. The Blessed Juliana joined the Convent of St Agnes in Prague on Christmas Day of the same year.'

'Good timing,' said Holliday. 'The Templars' two greatest enemies, Pope Clement and King Philip, both died in 1314; the Pope in April, the king in November. What about the ark?'

'There is no record of either Jean de Saint-Clair or the Blessed Juliana ever mentioning it again. Jean de Saint-Clair lived out his life as a monk and the Blessed Juliana became mother superior at the convent.'

'They never saw each other again?'

'Not according to the convent archives.'

'And the ark?'

'No one knows.'

'A mystery then.'

'It would seem so,' said Sister Meg primly.

'Interesting,' murmured Holliday, looking down at the sarcophagus.

'What is?'

'He's buried as a knight, not a monk. The wording on the plaque at his feet doesn't tally with the monastery at Tiron, either. It would have been more likely to have had a Mason's symbol – a compass and a square maybe – not an inscription in Latin. *In Arcadia Est.*'

'In Arcadia I am,' said the nun, translating literally.

'Very Yoda-ish,' said Holliday. 'But what does it mean, exactly?'

'Arcadia was the romantic ideal during the Renaissance,' replied the nun.

'But not in 1314,' answered Holliday.

'Originally it was a Greek province,' said Sister Meg. 'It still is.'

'Unlikely Saint-Clair would mention it on his grave.'

'Then what?' Sister Meg said.

'It was the original name for the maritime provinces of Canada,' said Holliday. 'The first French settlers there – from around here actually – were referred to as Acadians. When they were thrown out by the English in 1775 a lot of them went to Louisiana. It's the origin of the name Cajun – Acadian with the *A* knocked off.'

'Making history fit into your theory,' said Sister Meg, the expression on her face not quite a sneer.

'If the shoe fits,' Holliday said with a shrug.

'I'm not sure that it does.'

'And I'm not sure that it doesn't,' snapped Holliday. 'Have you got a better idea?'

'Maybe it doesn't mean anything at all,' said Sister Meg. 'I'm certainly not going to Canada on a silly whim and a story about Cajuns.'

'How about Prague?' Holliday responded.

'Excuse me?' Sister Meg said.

'You said your convent had archives,' replied Holliday.

'Very complete ones, as a matter of fact. Although the old convent itself is now part of the National Gallery.'

'Can you get us into the archives?'

'Us?'

'Why not? We both want to know what happened. I want to know where Saint-Clair went and you obviously want to know what happened to the ark, right?'

'I'm not sure it would be proper,' said Sister Meg. She flushed again. Holliday couldn't help smiling. Innocent women didn't blush that easily. Either Sister Margaret Emily had a very fertile imagination for a nun or she had a past. She saw the smile and the blush became even darker. She scowled again angrily. 'What are you smiling about?'

'You're blushing,' said Holliday.

'I most certainly am not!'

'Could have fooled me, Sister.'

'You're a boor,' answered the nun.

'But you're still blushing.'

'Go away!'

'France is still a relatively free country,' said Holliday. 'Liberty, Equality, Brotherhood . . . or in this case sisterhood. You go away first. I'll follow you all the way back to Prague. The Czech Republic is a free country now, too.'

'You're insufferable!'

'Maybe, but that doesn't change the situation.' Holliday held up a placating hand. 'Listen, Sister, let's call a truce here. We both want the same thing. We're both historians. I know why Saint-Clair was considered to be the greatest navigator of his time and you're determined to find the

True Ark. Why not share our knowledge, join forces?'

'I'm not sure I want to join forces with a man like you. I don't even like you.'

'I'm hurt,' Holliday said and grinned. 'But we don't have to like each other to reach a common goal. We didn't much like the Russians during World War Two, either, but they were still our allies.'

'I barely know you.'

'It's a long drive to Prague,' answered Holliday. 'Your rental car or mine?'

4

Most movies, books and television shows refer to Central Intelligence Agency Headquarters as being located in Langley, Virginia. Appropriately enough, however, there is no such place; Langley was simply the name given to the old woodlot estate purchased by the federal government for the CIA's new offices back in the 1950s. The actual location is in the suburban district of McLean, Virginia.

The original CIA campus is now half a century old and looks it. Even the 'new' addition is heading into its fourth decade of use. The huge computers, once state-of-the-art and requiring their own power lines, could now be replaced by a no-name knockoff PC from Wal-Mart. The most common physical ailment at the CIA is food poisoning and the cafeteria has been cited for more food and hygiene violations than any other government food service operation in the Washington area. The workers there simply cannot learn to wash their hands after using the toilet facilities.

The director of operations was in his seventh-floor office and regretting his choice of the hamburger platter at lunch. Joseph Patchin was a career CIA man and had been in the clandestine services for the better part of thirty years, serving in stations from Berlin to Kuwait. He spoke half a dozen languages fluently and could get by in half a dozen more. He was married and had three grown children he had barely spent any time at all with while they were growing up. His wife put up with him for the security of his large salary, his pension and the mortgage-free, equity-heavy house they owned in Chevy Chase. He knew that when a heart attack finally killed him, she was going to move to Florida. She'd had a regular string of lovers for the past twenty years and he hadn't really cared for the last fifteen.

There was a sharp double tap on his office door, like the sound of a professional killer giving his victim two to the back of the head. The fact that he thought in terms like that sometimes bothered him, but not too often. It came with the territory. He kept a bottle of expensive Johnny Walker Blue Label in one desk drawer and an old Ruger Single Six .22-caliber revolver in another desk drawer specifically for killing himself if it ever became necessary. He kept it loaded with long rifle mushroom bullets, which would turn his brains into frappuchino but which didn't have the velocity to exit the skull and wouldn't make a mess. That was the kind of person he was: always thinking about the other guy.

'Come,' he said to the tap at the door.

His DDO stepped into the room. Deputy Director of Operations Mike Harris had the seamed, squinty-eyed face of a Charles Bronson and the lanky, shuffling body of a professional boxer. He looked like everybody's idea of a bad guy and he played up to his looks, wearing rumpled suits and Peter Falk trench coats. He had a surprisingly smooth baritone voice that made him sound like Al Martino, the Johnny Fontane character in *The Godfather*.

'You called?' Harris said, sitting down in the comfortable chair on the visitor's side of his boss's desk.

'I did,' said Patchin. 'What do you know about Rex Deus?'

'They're the ones who think they're the direct descendants of Christ. Most of them are supposedly descended from the ancient kings of Europe or something. They're supposed to be allied with those excommunicated anti-Semitic types who think all of those photographs of Auschwitz and Buchenwald were faked. Nut jobs, basically.'

'What about domestically?' Patchin asked.

'Here in the States?'

'That's what domestically usually means.'

Patchin's second in command shrugged. 'I have no idea. Why?'

'I'm hearing murmurs.'

'What kind of murmurs?'

'White House murmurs.'

'About Catholic fringe groups?'

'About people with a great deal of money and power. In the final analysis their religious affiliation is irrelevant.'

'So what does it have to do with the Agency?' Harris asked.

'More murmurs,' said Patchin obscurely.

'About what?'

'Little birds are telling me there is a Rex Deus mole in Operations.'

'Dear God, not another mole hunt,' groaned Harris. 'The last one had the whole place tied up in knots for years.'

'The last one led us to Aldrich Ames,' answered Patchin dryly.

'Except the Cold War is over now.'

'This isn't about war, hot or cold. This is about a power grab.'

'I don't get it.'

'For the moment you don't have to. Just find the mole.'

'How am I supposed to do that?'

'According to my source our mole is interested in a pair of historians who are snooping in places they shouldn't.'

'Snooping for what?'

'We're not sure. Find out. Do we have any assets in Prague?'

'Sure,' said Harris. 'Why?'

'Because that's where they're snooping next.'

'So these historians are bait?'

'Something like that.'

'Who are they?'

'One's an ex-colonel in the Rangers who used to teach at West Point. The other's a nun.'

'Anything else I should know?'

'We're not the only ones interested in these two.'

'Who else, the FBI?'

'The Vatican,' answered Patchin.

'Oh dear,' said Harris.

Cardinal Antonio Niccolo Spada, Vatican Secretary of State, and like the Holy Father himself once the prefect of the Congregation for the Doctrine of the Faith, better known as the Holy Inquisition, sat on the private dining terrace of the Hotel Splendide Royal in Rome and looked out over the twinkling lights of the city. Spada was dressed in the red-buttoned 'ordinary' cassock of a Catholic cardinal complete with its scarlet cummerbund, marking him as a Prince of the Church. He was a man in his mid-seventies, lean, dark and hard, betraying his Sicilian peasant heritage. The look was deceptive; Spada had a mind like a steel trap and a temper to match. Priests who crossed him, or caused him any kind of grief, usually found themselves trying to convert obscure Indian tribes somewhere up the Amazon.

Across from him at the table was a dark-haired priest with heavy, gray-specked five o'clock shadow. He was known as Father Thomas Brennan, but Spada doubted that was really his name. Brennan was the head of Sodalitium Pianum, the organization that passed for the Vatican Secret

Service. It had been initiated by the ultraconservative Pope Pius X before the First World War, and although officially disbanded in the early 1920s it still quietly went about its business, as much a watchdog of the Vatican's own piety as an outside espionage agency. Brennan had been a fixture at the Holy See for years and predated Spada's own climb through the ranks by a decade or more. The pale, cadaverous Irishman was more than happy to play the simple priest while others wore the gaudy robes of state. Brennan's power lay in his vast knowledge of the Vatican's darkest secrets, not in his position within the Church.

The cardinal sliced his *bistecca all' erbe* with the precision of a surgeon, blood from the rare tenderloin leaking into his *patate alla griglia*. He tucked neat, small pieces of the expensive meat into his mouth, staring across the starched tablecloth in the five-star private dining room as he chewed, his pale blue eyes watching Brennan, always the Irish peasant plowing through a large serving of 'bisna' polenta made with beans, sauerkraut, and onion. His breath would stink when the meal was over, but those sorts of niceties never bothered Brennan.

'I gather you've had dealings with this man

Holliday before,' said Cardinal Spada, taking a sip of Barolo from the generous tulip glass by his plate.

'I have indeed, Your Eminence, and a right bastard he is.'

'This involved the problem we were having with the bullion deposits, did it not?'

'Yes. Earlier he was part of the situation regarding the Templars. Apparently his uncle had been part of their inner circle since before the Second World War.'

'A longtime member, as I recall.'

'Yes.'

'Does he present a problem?'

'He is very resourceful and he has the power of the order behind him.'

'The order doesn't really exist. It hasn't existed for more than seven hundred years,' argued the cardinal with an exasperated sigh. 'The Order of the Temple of Jerusalem is a fantasy kept alive by a few old men and conspiracy theorists on the Internet.'

Brennan shrugged. 'Orders come and orders go, but assets remain. Money never disappears, it simply changes hands. Holliday has access to a great deal of power if he wishes to use it.'

'Is he using it?' Spada asked.

'It has come to our attention that Holliday has become involved with the political machinations of Rex Deus.'

Spada laughed. He patted his lips with a starched napkin, his lips curving up in what passed for a smile.

'It really is extraordinary how things take hold,' said the cardinal. 'A man writes a silly novel based on the premise that a homosexual Italian artist from the sixteenth century would have the slightest interest in the concept of the divine feminine and would waste his time encoding obscure references to it in an obscure fresco in an even more obscure church in Milan. Da Vinci's drawing of Vitruvian Man is just that – a man, not a woman. The idea is farcical but the book sold tens of millions of copies.'

The cardinal shook his head. 'Rex Deus and the idea that there is a family tree for Jesus Christ is just as silly as the plot for *The Da Vinci Code,* but people still believe it, just like Shirley MacLaine and her followers believing they're all descendants of Cleopatra. Have you ever wondered why none of them find out that in a past life they were one of the slaves who built the pyramids? It's always Cleopatra, or Napoleon, or Jesus, never the plumber from down the street. Rex Deus is like the Templars: wishful thinking.'

Brennan shoveled another mouthful of food into his mouth, then washed it down with a slug of wine. He dug into the pocket of his jacket and took out a crumpled pack of Macedonia cigarettes, fished one out and lit it with a kitchen match he'd taken from his other pocket. He dropped the dead match into what was left of his polenta.

'You may well be right, but the reality is that this man Holliday is capable of causing us a great deal of trouble.'

'So what would you have me do? Sanction his murder?' The cardinal let out a barking laugh. 'Unleash the Vatican's secret army of albino monks on him?' The man in the red silk skullcap shook his head. 'Assassination is bad for the Church's image, especially with a German Pope occupying Peter's throne.'

'It's not Peter's throne that concerns me,' grunted Brennan.

'What's that supposed to mean?' Spada asked irritably.

'Rex Deus is having a convocation of its

members sometime later in the summer. Kate Sinclair is involved.'

The cardinal suddenly looked concerned.

'The senator's mother?'

'The presidential candidate's mother,' corrected Brennan. 'There's a rumor about the True Ark going around. Sinclair's looking for it.'

'The True Ark is a myth.'

'Maybe not.'

'And Holliday?'

'He's one of the people looking for it.'

'Hired by Sinclair?'

'I have no idea, but we need to find out. If Holliday's connections to the new Templars ever join forces with Rex Deus it could give us serious problems. Financial ones. Since the global economy took a turn for the worse the Vatican Bank has become stretched very thin. It can't be allowed to be stretched any thinner.' Brennan took a deep drag on the cigarette. Below the terrace the sounds of heavy nighttime traffic could be heard.

'What are you proposing?' Cardinal Spada asked.

'Nothing more than a watching brief for now. Find out why Kate Sinclair is looking for a relic that probably doesn't exist and find out what Holliday's involvement is. Apparently he is on his way to Prague in the company of one of ours – a Clare Sister from the Agnes of Bohemia convent.'

'What do we know about her?'

'Nothing.'

'Find out,' suggested Cardinal Spada.

5

They crossed the Czech border at Rozvadov. Before the Soviet Union fell apart, Rozvadov had been a gloomy place in the forest with a no-man's-land of tree stumps, barbed wire, land mines and guard towers full of armed men. Now it was a modern waypoint with lines of bored truckers waiting for their bonded loads of Mercedes parts and beer to be passed through customs.

As they were waved over the line after showing their passports, Holliday glanced to his left. The no-man's-land was still there, a healed gash like the path of a whirlwind through the dark trees, but the stumps were gone and so was the barbed wire and the guard towers. It was like the old Civil War battlegrounds back home – rolling green sod. Picnic parks where the blood of thousands and sometimes tens of thousands had been spilled, and for what? Emancipation? Breaking the Southern cotton cartels? A difference of attitude? A hundred and fifty years later whatever it was didn't really seem to matter anymore and the hundreds of thousands of soldiers were still just as dead and gone.

He drove the big rental VW sedan through the pleasant rural countryside beyond the forest and thought about soldiers and wars and dying for your country. They'd asked him to pose for a recruiting poster once because he looked so romantic with his weathered, outdoor, Marlboro Man face, not to mention the rakish look of adventure the patch on his eye gave him. He turned them down because it was all a lie.

The army wasn't a ticket to travel and adventure and anyone with a brain in his head knew it. The army was a gamble. You got a free education if you wanted it, in return for the strong possibility of having your legs or your arms or your head blown off by an Iraqi or an Afghani or a Pakistani with a stick of dynamite, a RadioShack detonator, and a bag of rusty nails for a payload.

The truth of it was most people who joined the army or the navy or the air force or the marines *didn't* have a brain in their heads; they were too young and wet behind the ears. And they didn't join up to protect their country or make the world safe for democracy – they joined up because they couldn't get a job anywhere else, or they were trying to get away from something the way Holliday had been trying to get away from his drunk, abusive old man when he joined up.

And there certainly wasn't anything romantic about his eye, or lack of it. Like an idiot he'd been riding with his head up out of the hatch of a Humvee on a road outside Kabul, and like a forgetful idiot he hadn't been wearing his protective goggles. A piece of gravel thrown up by the tires had scratched his cornea and it became infected and eventually he'd lost the eye.

'A penny for them,' said Sister Meg, sitting primly in the passenger seat, hands folded in her lap.

'You don't want to know,' said Holliday.

'It's still a hundred and fifty kilometers to Prague; we have to talk about something.'

Holliday knew she was trying to be friendly but he wasn't in the mood.

'I was wondering why soldiers become soldiers,' he said finally. 'And I couldn't come up with one good reason.'

'I expect it's the same reason priests become priests and nuns become nuns,' answered Sister

Meg instantly. 'Because they believe in what they're doing.'

'Bull,' snapped Holliday coldly. 'You're talking about heroic gestures. Heroes are generally pretty stupid, in my experience. And on a battlefield the last thing you're thinking about is belief in anything beyond your own immediate survival. If you're thinking about anything other than pissing your own pants and saving your own skin maybe you're thinking about the buddy you're sharing your foxhole with, but that's about it. In war the operative emotion is fear, believe me.'

'You're a very cynical man, Mr Holliday.'

'I've been in a lot more wars than you have, Sister. True believers and heroes make the worst soldiers. They take foolish unnecessary risks and they get people killed.'

The red-haired nun gave him what was probably her most withering look.

'If everyone thought that way there never would have been an American Revolution,' she argued. Her hands were balled into fists on her lap now and there were red, flushed circles on her cheeks.

'And maybe there shouldn't have been,' Holliday said and shrugged, beginning to enjoy baiting the young woman. 'Canada became a nation on its own quite peacefully. They never had a crippling civil war and they abolished slavery thirty years before we did without killing more than half a million young men in the process.'

'You're not much of a patriot, are you?' Sister Meg responded.

'"The people can always be brought to the bidding of the leaders,"' quoted Holliday. 'That is the easy part. All you have to do is to tell them they are being attacked, and denounce the pacifists for lack of patriotism and exposing the country to danger. It works the same in any country.' He glanced at the nun seated across from him. 'Sound like a familiar policy? A bit of Fox News?'

'Who said it?' Sister Meg sighed.

'Hermann Göring,' answered Holliday. 'Commander of Hitler's Luftwaffe.'

'Maybe we should stick to medieval history,' suggested the nun.

'Maybe you're right,' said Holliday.

They drove on in silence.

They followed the Autoroute east, bypassing Pilsen, where Pilsner beer had been invented, and reached the outskirts of Prague an hour later. It hadn't changed much since Holliday had been there last – it still looked like a poster for Stalin-era architecture, block after dreary block of concrete high-rise slabs filled with hundreds of tiny apartments. Looking carefully you could see the differences, though – there was no laundry drying on the balconies now and the cars in the parking lots were mostly Japanese instead of the ubiquitous twenty-horsepower East German Trabants or the locally manufactured Skodas with their infamously faulty brakes. Funny how bad Soviet cars had been, Holliday thought. They'd made excellent tanks and machine guns during World War Two.

'Presumably you'll want to go to the convent,' said Holliday as he navigated his way through the unfamiliar cloverleafs and the equally unfamiliar blue and white signage.

'No,' answered Sister Meg quietly. 'The only accommodation is at the monastery next door. The convent has been entirely converted into a museum now.'

'All right, the monastery then.'

'I've only been doing research here. The Convent of St Agnes isn't my Mother House. This is the high season for the monks. They make most of their income from renting out the cells in the monastery to young travelers. I have my own source of private income. I was renting a room in Andel, but they are tearing the building down to put up another condominium. I'm really quite homeless.'

'Don't worry, I know just the place,' said Holliday.

He guided the big Volkswagen off the D5 and on to the narrower E50, coming into the city from the southeast. They drove into another clutch of function-before-beauty apartment blocks. He turned off on Slavinskeho Street. The fuselage and tail section of an old Tupolev airliner in Czech Airlines red-orange livery stood pancaked and wheels-up in a vacant lot beside a long window-less building.

'Good Lord,' said Sister Meg, staring. 'What on earth is *that* doing there?'

'It's a prop,' explained Holliday. 'The Barrandov Film Studios are down the way about half a mile. I think the building there is a special effects lab.' Holliday turned onto Geologika Street and pulled into a parking lot beside a three-storey barracks-style building with a curved glass extension along the front that looked like a greenhouse.

On the other side of the street was a row of apartment blocks.

There was a familiar Best Western sign on the scruffy lawn in front of the glass extension that read HOTEL SMARAGD.

'Smaragd means Emerald,' explained Holliday. 'When they built all those high-rises across the street during the Soviet era the hotel was a barracks for the foreign workers they brought in. After the Soviet Union collapsed a couple of brothers bought the building for next to nothing and turned it into a budget hotel. They didn't have much money to work with and the only paint they could get was an awful government green; that's the reason for the name. Everything's white now. It's not the Ritz but it's comfortable and it's cheap.'

'It looks fine,' Sister Meg said. They climbed out of the car, got their bags from the trunk and went into the small, low-ceilinged lobby of the hotel. An open archway on the right led into the curved glass extension – the hotel restaurant and bar. On the left was an enclosed counter with something like a sitting room behind it. A balding man in a T-shirt was leaning on the counter reading a newspaper. At the rear of the lobby a wide staircase led to the second floor. There was a scattering of seventies Swedish Modern armchairs beside the reception counter and a rack of postcards. A fat man in a bad suit came into the hotel and sat down in one of the armchairs and opened up a copy of *Czekhiya Sevodnya*. His head looked like a shiny cue ball.

They booked in, taking a double room, and climbed the stairs to the second floor. The rooms were oddly laid out, reflecting their barracks origins. Each double room had a small tiled foyer with a shared bathroom against the outside wall and a door leading into a bedroom to each side. The rooms were square, utilitarian, and equipped with twin beds, one lamp, one child-size desk with a telephone and a television. Nothing had changed since Holliday's last stay; there were two channels in English, British Sky News and CNN. Everything else was in Czech or German.

Holliday dropped off his bag, washed his hands and then went across the room to Sister Meg's room. She'd changed into a man's white shirt, jeans and sneakers, but still wore the obviously religious head covering. Apparently there was no middle ground for Sister Meg; a nun was a nun was a nun.

'Settled in?' Holliday asked. He gave her his best smile, feeling a little guilty for baiting her in the car the way he had.

'As well as can be expected.' She glanced around the bleak little room. 'Not much in the way of ambience, is there?'

'It has a certain ascetic *je ne sais quoi*,' answered Holliday in a la-de-dah voice.

The nun laughed, which seemed to be a step in the right direction.

'I thought we could go down to the restaurant and have something to eat. The last time we did was in that awful place on the Autobahn.'

'Nordsee?' Sister Meg said. She made a face.

'You should have known better than to order curried prawns and fries in the middle of Germany,' Holliday said with a grin.

'Is the food any better here?'

'They do a good goulash and their veal cutlets and dumplings are good.'

'As long as the chef hasn't changed.'

'He's one of the brothers who owns the hotel,' said Holliday.

They went downstairs to the restaurant, a long narrow room looking out on to the scrappy lawn with tables on the right and a bar on the left.

A man in an apron sat on a stool behind the bar reading a newspaper. There were only two other people in the dining room, a gray-haired man with a van Dyck beard drinking Bacardi and Coke and a lean and quite handsome middle-aged man who was vaguely familiar, drinking a long-necked Staropramen beer. The familiar-looking man spoke only English and the older man with the beard spoke accented English, but ordered in Czech.

'E.T.,' Holliday said finally.

'E.T.?'

'The Extra-Terrestrial. He was in the movie, the guy at the back of the room. One of the kids. Tyler, I think. He's been in all sorts of things since.'

'The dark-haired one or the man sitting with him?'

'The dark-haired one.'

'That's quite a memory you have,' commented Sister Meg.

'C. Thomas Howell,' said Holliday, getting it at last.

'Never heard of him.'

'That's because you aren't a film buff.'

'I assure you, nuns watch movies,' the woman answered curtly.

'Nun movies?'

'There's such a classification?'

'Sure,' Holliday said and nodded. '*The Nun's Story*, *Sister Faustina*, *Agnes of God*, *Song of Bernadette*, *The Singing Nun*, *Lilies of the Field*, *Two Mules for Sister Sarah*, *The Bells of St Mary's*, *Dead Man Walking*. I could go on.'

'Please don't,' said Sister Meg. A young waiter appeared and they ordered. Meg asked for the goulash and Holliday chose the breaded veal with French fries.

'I had a Czech friend who once told me the only two words I need to be able to speak in Czech: *hranolky* and *pivo*. French fries and beer. At least that way you wouldn't starve to death or die of thirst.'

'So what's next?' Sister Meg asked.

'After dinner?' Holliday replied. 'After dinner we go outside for a nice walk in the evening air and see if there's a green late-model BMW in the parking lot with Austrian license plate MD 337 CA.'

'Pardon?'

'Do you remember a man who came into the hotel after us when we checked in? He sat down and started to read the paper.'

Sister Meg thought for a moment and nod-ded. 'Vaguely. He had a shaved head. He was fat.'

'That's the one.'

'What about him?'

'He was in the Nordsee restaurant outside of Nuremberg. He had fish and chips and a Coke. Twice. Once in the restaurant as well as a take-out order.'

'You're sure?'

'Positive.'

'Maybe it's just a coincidence?'

'Somehow I don't think so.'

6

The following morning they came down to the lobby and Holliday bought all-day transit tickets from the sleepy desk clerk. They went into the restaurant, ate breakfast, then left through the back exit by the bathroom rather than the way they'd come in through the lobby. They found themselves on Slavinskeho Street, the far side treed with scrubby cedars, the near side laid out in allotment gardens behind the hotel, each with its own little shed.

'What about the car?' Sister Meg asked.

'We're taking the bus instead,' answered Holliday. 'Make it a little harder for our bald friend.' He checked the schedule beneath the protective plastic covering on the bus stop post and then looked at his watch. There was one due in less than five minutes. While they waited he looked back down the street, back toward the hotel.

'I still think you're being paranoid,' said the nun. 'Just because you saw the same man on the

Autobahn doesn't prove anything. Why on earth would anyone want to follow us?'

'I don't know about you, but I've made a few enemies in my time.'

'This is just silly. We're not in a James Bond movie,' snorted Sister Meg.

'Do you always argue this much?' Holliday asked. The woman was like everyone's idea of a younger, smarter sister – a Lisa Simpson from hell.

The red and white bus appeared a few minutes later, pulling up so that they could get on through the middle set of doors. In Prague, Holliday knew, the front doors were only used as an exit. When the doors hissed open they stepped up, slipped their tickets into the time stamper, then waited for them to be spat out again. Holliday walked to the very rear of the bus and sat down as they moved off. Sister Meg dropped down beside him with a sigh.

'This really is idiotic,' she muttered.

'Really?' Holliday asked. 'If you check behind us you'll see a green late-model BMW with Austrian license plate MD 337 CA, am I right?'

Sister Meg turned her head to look. She paled.

'Dear God,' she whispered.

'Told you,' said Holliday.

The bus went down Slavinskeho Street, the gray-blue Art Deco bulk of the Barrandov Studios main building and the soundstages directly ahead of them. At the traffic circle they swung to the left past the guard kiosk and the barrier, then eased on to Filmarska Street, then Barrandovska. The houses on the left were set on large lots in an urban pine forest, most looking as though they dated from the 1930s, all looking expensive.

To the right the lots hung at the edge of the famous Barrandov cliffs, and in between the houses they could look to the northeast across the Vltava River, snaking through the smoggy haze far below. As they swung left and began to move down the steep hill, the houses on the cliff side became enormous stone and stucco mansions. Once upon a time they'd been built for executives of the enormous film studios, Prague's version of Beverly Hills.

'The whole area including the film studios was developed in the twenties and thirties by the Havel family for local bigwigs. During the war the Nazis took over and those big houses were the summer residences for all the party bigwigs, including Hitler. Then it was KGB bigwigs for a while, and now it's capitalist bigwigs again.'

eg wasn't paying any attention.

'...s that man?' Meg asked, her voice tense ...host accusatory.

'...he bald fellow? He looks like a cop,' said Holliday. 'At a guess, I'd say he was contract help.'

'What on earth is that supposed to mean?'

'He's not official. Some organization has hired itself a local pair of eyes. He's been following us across Germany. He was probably in France before that. He's probably following one of us or the other, not both.'

'Because of a knight who died almost a thousand years ago? Ridiculous.'

'I agree, but he's on our tail nevertheless.'

'It has to be you. Something from your military past.'

'I had some trouble with a neo-Nazi group a while back; almost two years ago now. It could be them, or what's left of them.'

'There! You see? I knew it!' Sister Meg said triumphantly.

'On the other hand, it could also be the Vatican Secret Service.'

'The Vatican doesn't have a secret service,' said the nun, promptly and with conviction. 'I should know.'

'The Vatican certainly does have a secret service, and I *do* know, Sister. It's called Sodalitium Pianum. The friends of Pius X, the Pope it was named after. In France it's called La Sapinière. It's been around since the beginning of the last century. It's a covert arm of the Vatican secretary of state's office.'

'That sounds like some sort of stupid urban myth,' scoffed the red-haired nun.

'Whatever the case, that guy in the BMW is no myth; he's real enough, isn't he?'

The nun didn't answer, crossing her arms in front of her, spots of color blooming on her cheeks.

The bus continued down the hill to the main four-lane expressway at the bottom. On the left, carved into the yellowish rock of the rugged cliff side, Holliday could see the man-made niche that had served as a guard booth during the war. Back in those days access to the big houses on the Barrandov hill had been restricted to the very few and there had been a barrier here. It was one of the few places in the city that still showed physical evidence of the Nazi occupation between 1939 and 1945.

The bus swung left and slipped on to the

broad multi-laned highway, threading through a couple of ramps and cloverleafs until they came out on Strakonicka Street. To the right Holliday could see intermittent views of the river, and to the left were railway yards, graffiti-covered rail and subway cars lined up waiting to be shunted in one direction or the other. Here and there they passed dark stucco buildings with either blue curtains or red.

'I always wondered what those places with the colored drapes were,' said Sister Meg as the bus rolled past yet another red-curtained building. 'They always seem so dark.' A red neon sign in the front yard read PANSKY KLUB.

'A *pansky* club is a brothel,' explained Holliday. 'A *pani* club is a brothel for women. Red for men, blue for women.'

'I don't believe it.'

'Prostitution isn't legal here, but it's not illegal, either. They've even got a brothel called Big Sister that's online, like a reality show.'

'That's disgusting,' said Sister Meg.

'That's free-market capitalism.' Holliday shrugged and glanced over his shoulder. The BMW was still on their tail about three cars behind. Meg followed his look.

'What are we going to do about him?' she asked.

'We'll get off at the Smichov terminal and get on to the Metro. He'll have to park his car. Maybe we can lose him if we get lucky and catch a train right off.'

The bus turned left down a side street and then right on to a wider roadway set with streetcar tracks. They passed a war surplus outlet in an old brick warehouse, a banner advertising genuine KGB fur hats strung across the grimy front entrance. They finally pulled up under a fibreglass canopy.

They climbed off the bus and dodged across several sets of streetcar tracks, cutting through the streams of sleepy-looking late commuters. There was no sign of the BMW or the bald man. They went through the glass doors, then down a wide set of steps to a Stalin-era platform, the letters of the station formed out of sheet steel and bolted to the concrete slab wall. There were two choices, the one side of the platform and the two. The trains arriving on the left side of the platform went to the last station at Slicin, and the ones on the right went to Cerny Most.

'Which way?' Meg asked.

'Two,' said Holliday. 'Cerny Most.'

A train pulled in on the Cerny Most side of the platform and whined to a pneumatic stop. The trains were silver-sided with red doors, and like subways around the world the cars were slathered with graffiti of varying quality.

Holliday looked back up the stairs as the doors hissed open.

'Shit,' he muttered.

'Pardon?' Sister Meg said, a little shocked.

'Our large bald friend,' said Holliday.

Puffing hard, the man from the BMW was charging down the stairs to the platform.

Holliday and the nun stepped into the car. Holliday leaned out until there was a bonging chime and a mellow, almost sedated female voice spoke over the public address system.

'*Ukoncete nastup a vystup dvere se zaviraji.*' Finish embarking and disembarking, doors are closing. Holliday ducked his head back into the car. The doors slid shut against their rubber bumpers and the train droned into motion.

'Did he get on?' Sister Meg asked, gripping the bar beside him.

'The car behind us.'

'Now what do we do?'

Holliday glanced up at the schematic system map above the doors. Four stops to the junction point of the A and B lines at the big Mustek station on the other side of the river. About eight minutes. The station they really wanted was one station farther on at Namesti Republiky.

'We'll do a Charnier,' said Holliday.

'A what?'

'Alain Charnier, Popeye Doyle. Gene Hackman, Fernando Rey.'

The nun looked at him blankly. 'I have no idea what you're talking about.'

'*The French Connection*?'

The nun shook her head. She was much too young, of course. Holliday sighed, suddenly acutely aware of the age difference between them.

'It's a scene in a famous movie. A French crook fools a cop into getting off a New York subway, then hopping back on at the last second.'

'And we're going to do the same thing?'

'We're going to try.'

A minute later they moaned smoothly into the next station, Andel. The doors slid open and Holliday started counting softly to himself.

'One Mississippi, two Mississippi, three Mississippi . . .' At fifteen the sleepy voice of the announcement was heard; at twenty the doors slid shut and the train moved off again. The same happened again at Karlovo namesti and Narodni trida, the next stations on the B line.

'Get off at the next stop and walk forward on the platform and slightly away,' instructed Holliday. 'When I say "go" turn around and get back on the train as fast as you can.'

The nun nodded silently. The train moved off.

'You've done things like this before, haven't you?' Sister Meg said quietly.

'Once or twice,' admitted Holliday. A few moments later they pulled into the junction station at Mustek and the doors slid open. Holliday stepped out, putting his hand on Meg's back and propelling her on to the platform ahead of him. The lower-level platform was as bland as the one at Smichov, a set of stairs leading up to a flyover to the escalators taking you up to the A line level. There was a line of plain oval pillars running down the center of the platform.

Holliday started counting as they joined the herds of commuters heading toward the stairs, keeping his hand on Sister Meg's back, guiding her toward one of the pillars and circling behind it briefly. He watched as cue ball head blundered forward toward the stairs, searching the crowd for any sign of Holliday and the nun. He reached the stairs then stopped, turning his head left and right, looking more and more panicked with each passing second.

'Fourteen Mississippi, fifteen Mississippi . . .'

The chime bonged its *ding-dong-ding* three-note refrain.

'Go!' Holliday urged, pushing Meg back toward the waiting subway train. She gave him a single, over-the-shoulder nasty look then did as she was told. Holliday followed. Out of the corner of his eye he caught sight of the bald man as the man spotted him. The fat man surged forward against the flow of the crowd as the announcer went through her recorded advisory. Meg stepped through the doors of the car ahead of the one they'd been traveling in with Holliday right behind her. Cue Ball didn't stand a chance. The doors closed with the bald man lumbering forward, elbowing people out of the way. He was still ten feet away when the train began to move.

He stood impotently on the other side of the doors as Holliday gave him a smile and a little finger-waggling wave, just the way the French crook had done in the movie.

'Bye-bye,' Holliday said and grinned.

They headed into the tunnel and disappeared.

7

Cardinal Secretary of State Antonio Niccolo Spada sat in the ornate carved oak throne behind his equally ornate fourteenth-century Spanish desk. Across from him Father Thomas Brennan, head of the Vatican Secret Service, Sodalitium Pianum, paced back and forth across the immense silk rug that covered the floor in Spada's office.

The cardinal's workplace was located on the top floor of the Governatorato, the Vatican Civil Administration Building located directly behind St Peter's Basilica. The lavish fourth-floor corner office also looked out across the Viale Osservatorio to the San Pietro Monument and the walled enclosures of the Papal Gardens. Next to the Pope's own audience chamber there was no more important place in the Vatican.

The voice of God might well whisper orders directly into the Holy Father's ear, but the orders were interpreted and carried out by Antonio Spada. The Pope was God's emissary on Earth;

Spada was His enforcer. The baker's son from the village of Canneto di Caronia on the road to Messina had come a long way, and not just from Sicily.

'I think it's a mistake,' said Brennan, pacing. As he walked back and forth he puffed on his inevitable foul-smelling Macedonia cigarette, spilling a continuous shower of ash across the carpet, even though the cardinal had a conspicuously placed crystal ashtray on the desk for his guests.

'Why?' Spada asked.

'Because Holliday is too far above the horizon. He has friends in high places, he knows people.'

The cardinal shrugged. 'Accidents happen.'

'Accidents that happen to men like Holliday are investigated,' argued Brennan.

Spada allowed himself a small, knowing smile. 'You're frightened of this man.'

'You're bloody right I am, begging your pardon, Eminence,' Brennan said and nodded, continuing his pacing. 'He's dangerous. He upsets the balance of power, he interferes where he has no business.' Brennan paused. 'Not to mention the fact that he's caused a great deal of trouble for us in the past. And a great deal of money as well, I might add.'

'All the more reason for us to rid ourselves of him now,' murmured the cardinal.

'But why?' Brennan insisted. 'He and the woman are looking for a box of relics that probably don't even exist.' The priest eyed his superior. 'Besides which the Church forbids the worship of such things. The twenty-fifth session of the Council of Trent, I believe. As are the purchase or sale of such relics.'

'Don't presume to teach me about Church dogma, Father Brennan,' the cardinal said coolly.

'Then tell me why we're interested in this so-called True Ark or whatever it is.'

'A relic is as a relic does, Father Brennan,' said the cardinal obscurely.

Brennan frowned. 'You'll have to explain that, I'm afraid,' said the priest.

'The True Ark is said to contain the Holy Grail, the Crown of Thorns, the Holy Shroud, and the Ring of Christ.'

'The fecking jackpot then,' snorted Brennan.

'Nevertheless,' said Spada.

'You can't believe it's true,' said Brennan, astounded.

'It doesn't matter what I believe, Father Brennan,' the cardinal answered. 'Perception is everything. It's like the story of the emperor's new clothes: if enough people *say* the emperor is wearing silk, then he might just as well *be* wearing silk. If enough people *say* Paris Hilton is beautiful, then she *is* beautiful – even though it's patently untrue. She's far too skinny, she's flat-chested, her nose is too large and her ankles too small.' The secretary of state paused. 'Whatever they find, we must have. That rag in the cathedral in Turin has been scientifically proven to be a fraud, but that doesn't stop tens of thousands coming to see it.'

'If they find anything,' grumbled Brennan. He butted his cigarette in the ashtray and lit another. Cardinal Spada let out a long-suffering sigh. He was tired of discussion. Why didn't Brennan just do as he was told?

'The best way to guarantee that they find nothing is to stop them looking,' the cardinal said. 'Besides that, if what you told me earlier is true, then this man Holliday has been entrusted with the true secret of the Templars – the numbers for their bank accounts. A bonus, although the money rightfully belongs to the Church, anyway.'

'If we do this thing we can't have this coming back on us,' warned Brennan.

'I understand that,' Cardinal Spada said and nodded. 'Hire outside help if you wish.' The man in the scarlet skullcap stared across the desk. 'Holliday is important, but remember who the woman is, as well.'

'They're in Prague. I know just the people.'

'Then get on with it,' said Spada.

It was a dismissal.

Brennan left Spada's office and went down two flights of marble stairs to his own, much smaller office on the second floor. It was a plain square room with bare wooden floors, a metal desk, some black metal filing cabinets and a plain cross on the wall.

The only other decoration was a photograph of his long-dead sister Mary, a Magdalene nun, standing in front of St Finnbar's in Cork City, smiling into the camera, squinting in the sunlight. The picture was from the late sixties, faded to sepia.

She'd worked as a supervisor of the indentured girls at the Magdalene Laundry on Blarney Street, above the North Mall and the River Lee with its famous swans. She'd so loved to feed the swans. She'd imagined they were the souls and spirits of ugly girls come back to the world as something beautiful. She'd died of some terrible respiratory sickness a year after the photo was taken, coughing her lungs out and praying to a heedless god.

The priest sat down at his desk, flipped through his old-fashioned Rolodex and came up with a number with a 420 prefix. He dialed and almost immediately the Vatican switchboard broke into the call. He gave the male operator the number, and then a name. There was a pause and then the double tone of the call ringing through in Prague. The phone rang three times and then was answered.

'*Prosim?*' The voice was a slightly phlegmy baritone.

'*Pan* Pesek? Antonin Pesek?'

'I am Pesek,' said the voice. 'Who are you?'

'This is Romulus,' said Brennan, staring blankly at the photograph of his sister as he ordered the killing. 'I have a job for you.'

The Convent of St Agnes of Bohemia is located on Milosrdnych Street in the Josefov, or Jewish Quarter, of Prague, the eleventh-century center of the original city that had grown on the banks of the Vltava River a thousand years before. The convent, now part of the National Gallery of Prague, was a collection of meticulously refurbished fourteenth- and fifteenth-century Gothic buildings centered around the old vaulted cloisters that now contain one of the finest collections of Baroque and Renaissance art in the world.

Holliday and Sister Meg got off the Metro at the Namesti Republiky stop and climbed up into the sunlight. The square was crowded with tourists and local shoppers, and there was a festive feeling in the air. People were eating cotton candy and popcorn as they strolled along, talking and laughing. Uniformed cops walked in pairs, doing as much window-shopping as the people around them. There was a line out of the door at McDonald's.

Holliday and the nun walked north up Avenue Revolucni, a wide thoroughfare noisy with rumbling streetcars and lined with shops of all kinds, interspersed with ATMs every hundred yards or so just to make sure you had lots of Czech crowns in your pocket.

They turned west a block short of the river and took a shortcut through a government building parking lot to Rasnovka Alley, a narrow cobbled lane that led them down to the main entrance to the old convent. They paid their hundred and fifty koruna, roughly six dollars, and went into the thousand-year-old building.

The cloisters that made up the gallery were almost empty, and except for an old man dozing on a bench and a young couple more interested in each other's anatomy than the paintings on the wall, Holliday and Sister Meg had the place to themselves.

'I came for the archives, not the art,' said Holliday. 'Shouldn't we be next door at the monastery?'

'There's something here I wanted to show you,' said the nun, eager excitement in her voice. 'Something I remembered last night.' After their escape from their bald pursuer Holliday was willing to indulge her. The paintings, the religious statuary and the extraordinary carved wooden altarpieces were certainly worth looking at, even if they had nothing to do with their objective.

They went up a narrow set of steps to the upper floor of the cloisters and down a long arched hall. Meg led Holliday to a large gilt-framed painting hanging on the plain, off-white plaster wall.

A man in armor stood on the left, a veiled woman on his left wearing a cowl on her head, throwing her face into shadow, a long black gown obscuring her figure. The man was wearing a full-length chain mail hauberk that came down to his ankles. He had a long sword sheathed at his waist and an overshirt with the familiar Saint-Clair engrailed cross coat of arms, while his shield bore the red Maltese cross of the Templar order.

The knight was holding what appeared to be a wooden engrailed cross in his free hand. Behind the two figures was a heraldic portrayal of a winged gold lion with a sword held in its right front paw and standing on a rippling blue field of water. In one corner, like the illustration from an ancient tarot card, six monks in their white habits prayed as they stood around a well. In the opposite corner of the painting was a stamped symbol of a heart with a cross in it.

Sister Meg read the description of the painting on a small plinth next to it. 'The Blessed Juliana With Her Protector, painted by Lucas Cranach the Elder, 1427.' She stared up at the near life-sized figure of the woman in the painting. 'She always appeared veiled so men wouldn't be distracted by her great beauty,' said Sister Meg, awe clear in her voice. She turned to Holliday. 'Does her protector remind you of anyone?'

'It's Jean de Saint-Clair,' said Holliday. 'And that's a Jacob's Quadrant in his hand. The navigation instrument I told you about.'

'Do you know the significance of the lion with the sword?' Sister Meg asked. 'I couldn't figure it out, or the six monks around the well.' She shrugged. 'I even ran it through Google. There are lots of lions with swords but none that quite match up. The closest was the old imperial crest of Persia.'

'I don't know about the well and the monks but a golden lion with a sword standing on water is the coat of arms of Venice,' said Holliday. 'It's also a quadrant on the coat of arms on the Zeno family crest, the shipbuilders who leased the Templars most of their fleet during the Crusades. According to this I'd say your Juliana and Jean de Saint-Clair went to Venice together, probably to rent a ship.'

8

They found a little terrace restaurant on the other side of the Jewish Quarter and sat at a shaded table out of the direct sunlight. The restaurant was called U Vltavy, probably because it was only a block from the river. They had an odd menu – part Mexican, part Austrian and part Czech. Sister Meg had gazpacho and some sort of pork dish with freshly ground horseradish, while Holliday settled on beef stroganoff with rice and some of the same horseradish. They ate in silence for a while, enjoying the summer warmth and watching the tourists go past.

For some reason he didn't quite understand, Holliday had always enjoyed Prague more than any other city in Europe, east or west, even during the Soviet era. The locals had a sense of humor and seemed innately curious about everyone and everything. They'd use any excuse to engage tourists in friendly conversation, and a favorite game on the subways was to trade language – a few words of Czech in exchange for a few words in English. There was even a television channel that showed nothing but English movies with Czech subtitles as a language teaching aid.

Perhaps it had something to do with a few thousand years of being the western end of the Silk Road. With a few rare exceptions the city had been remarkably tolerant and welcoming to people of all races. It came as no surprise to Holliday that the Czechs were the first to rise up against the Soviet regime in 1989.

Thinking about that year always brought a smile to his face. After seventy-odd years of Soviet hegemony and the Iron Curtain, it had all turned out to be smoke and mirrors. The vaunted power of the Soviet army with its thousands of tanks turned out to be invested in so many inert chunks of rusting, immobile steel, silent for want of enough gasoline to run them a hundred feet, let alone a thousand miles into the heart of NATO territory.

The guidance systems in half their intercontinental ballistic missiles were years out of date, the people of Moscow were running out of toilet paper and the armed forces hadn't been paid in a year. It was all a lie, and the United States' supposedly all-knowing intelligence community hadn't seen it coming. Not even close. It was just as much a crock as the Russians'. Apparently you certainly could fool all of the people all of the time.

'What are you smiling about?' Sister Meg asked, patting her lips with her napkin, her face pleasantly flushed by the fresh horseradish. His smile broadened; maybe that old paranoid story was true; maybe we never really did land astronauts on the moon; it was all a story cooked up on a back lot somewhere by Richard Nixon and his cronies.

'Things never work out the way people think,' answered Holliday. 'Reality gets in the way or something comes flying in from left field and upsets the apple-cart.'

'Nice mixed metaphor,' the nun said and smiled.

'There's an old Jewish saying – Man plans, God laughs.'

'You're talking about the painting?' Sister Meg said.

'It changes everything. It proves that Saint-Clair really did have the Quadrant and Lucas Cranach thought it was important.'

'There's nothing in the archives about the Blessed Juliana going to Venice; not a mention.'

'Someone knew,' said Holliday. 'Cranach must have known or he wouldn't have painted them like that two hundred years after the fact.'

'But how?' Sister Meg asked.

'It's not hard to figure out. Dig deeply enough into history and you can always find the degrees of separation between people. Cranach was a painter with a number of important patrons, including kings. Royalty during the Renaissance was a tight little group. Contemporaries boasted about their patronage. Cranach could have easily known a Venetian painter. Some of his early work looks a lot like Domenico Ghirlandaio, for instance. Maybe they shared stories looking for subject matter.' Holliday shrugged. 'Maybe one of Ghirlandaio's patrons was a member of the Zeno family. They were rich enough.'

'So now you're an art expert?'

'Not really, but paintings were the Middle Ages equivalent of news footage or photographs. A lot of information about battles and tactics can be found on the walls of major art galleries.'

'Do you have an answer for everything?'

Holliday sighed and put down his fork, his appetite gone.

'Only to snotty questions from arrogant nuns.' He stared at her across the table. 'You've been riding me since we met,' he said. 'Why? What did I do to you?'

'You've been patronizing me from the beginning,' she answered.

'If that's true I certainly didn't do it on purpose,' said Holliday.

'That doesn't make it any better.'

'I've been teaching eighteen-year-old wet-behind-the-ears cadets for the last few years. Maybe that's why I seem patronizing. Before that I was ordering soldiers around.'

'I'm not a cadet or a soldier and I'm not wet behind the ears or eighteen either.'

Something caught Holliday's eye and he glanced over her shoulder.

'Don't look now but Cue Ball is back.'

Sister Meg froze. She stared at Holliday, eyes wide.

'You're joking,' she said coldly. 'If this is a joke then all bets are off. We go our separate ways.'

'No joke. He's leaning on a lamppost at the

end of the block reading that stupid newspaper of his.' Holliday shook his head. 'He's going to get skin cancer on that chrome dome if he stays out in the sun without a hat the way he does.'

'How did he find us?'

'He must have figured we'd head for the convent. He had to be waiting for us to come out and then followed us here.'

'What should we do?'

'Why don't you decide,' said Holliday. 'I wouldn't want to sound patronizing or anything.' He sat back in his chair and waited.

'Maybe we shouldn't do anything,' she said. 'He knows we'll eventually go back to the hotel.'

'What if we don't?'

'Pardon.'

'You have your passport on you?' Holliday asked.

'Always.' She nodded, patting the plain canvas bag in her lap.

'Me too,' said Holliday. 'Anything you'll miss back at the hotel?'

'Just some clothes, a few toiletries. What are you suggesting?'

'Hang on,' said Holliday. He took out his BlackBerry and thumbed the keys.

'What are you doing?' Sister Meg asked.

Holliday looked down at the little screen.

'There's a train to Vienna with connections to Venice leaving *Praha hlavní nádraží* at five o'clock this afternoon. It gets into Venice at eight tomorrow morning. If we can give Cue Ball the slip until then we should be okay.'

'We have to get out of here first.'

Holliday casually twisted around in his chair.

'That's Listopadu Street up ahead, which means the Starenova Synagogue is a couple of blocks south of us,' he muttered, trying to orient himself. 'That means the restaurant has to back on to the top end of the Jewish Cemetery.'

'So?'

'That's our way out.'

Holliday dug into his wallet, pulled out a fifty-koruna note – coincidentally the one with a picture of Agnes of Bohemia on it – then dropped it on the table to cover their bill. He took out another koruna, this one an orange-brown two-hundred-crown note, worth about fifty American dollars. He stuck his wallet back into his pocket.

'I'm going to get up and go into the restaurant. Cue Ball will think I'm going to the bathroom. Count to sixty, then get up and do the same. At a dead run it'll take him a couple of minutes to get down here. Got it?'

'Of course,' snapped the nun irritably.

Holliday stood and disappeared into the restaurant. Sister Meg waited as long as she could, then followed him inside. He was waiting at the rear of the dining room, standing beside a young dark-haired waiter in a long apron.

'*Sledujte mne, prosím,*' said the young man, motioning with one hand. Follow me, please. He led them through a pair of swing doors, into the kitchen and through another door that led to a narrow courtyard. At the back of the cigarette-butt-littered space was a low stone wall that looked very old. It was made of small stones mortared together and topped with curved, half-pipe terracotta tiles to facilitate drainage. Holliday boosted himself up on to the wall and the young man cupped his hands into a stirrup for Sister Meg. A few seconds later she was on top of the wall with Holliday.

'*De'kuji,*' said Holliday, thanking the waiter.

'*Za malo.*' The waiter shrugged. *No big thing.* He lit a cigarette and stood watching as Holliday and the red-haired nun jumped down on the far side of the wall.

The Josefov cemetery is the oldest existing Jewish burial ground in Europe, dating back to 1439 and used up until 1787. It is small as cemeteries go, taking up less than an acre made up of the courtyards of a long, L-shaped block, but more than a hundred thousand people are buried there, some in spots twelve coffins deep, the headstones only marking the people buried in the top layer.

With most of the stones less than a foot apart, there is almost no space for grass to grow. The roots of the big overarching shade trees have moved the worn and almost indecipherable headstones every which way and there is a ruined, abandoned sense to the place that is far from true. Countless visitors flock to the cemetery each year, paying their ten crowns and their respects to the dead. Rabbi Low, the creator of the forerunner of Frankenstein's monster, the golem from Vlatava mud, is buried here, as are other Jewish notables.

Dropping down into the cemetery, Holliday and Sister Meg found themselves hemmed in by headstones and had to pick their way slowly and carefully between the markers until they reached one of the main paving-stone pathways that wound around the property.

The pathway was crowded, mainly with tourists, some of them carrying cameras, some reading the old Hebrew inscriptions. The only thing they had in common was the fact that none of their heads were bare. For a few moments as they threaded their way through the crowds, Holliday wasn't sure why everyone seemed to be glaring at him. Then he remembered that it was considered disrespectful to enter a Jewish cemetery without some kind of head covering.

Less than a minute later they reached the exit, an old gatehouse, and bullied their way out on to a narrow street lined with souvenir carts selling postcards, paper hats and little plastic golems. The whole thing was so crass Holliday almost expected one of the carts to be selling Rabbi Low action figures.

'Now what?' Sister Meg said. It was hot and a thin line of sweat had formed on her forehead where her headpiece was tight.

'I've got an idea,' answered Holliday. He took a quick look around to make sure that Cue Ball wasn't anywhere in sight, then turned down Stroka Street, heading for the river. They reached the open plaza of Jan Palach Square and crossed to the statue of Antonin Dvorjak. Jan Palach

Square had once been known as *Náme˘stí Krasnoarme˘jcu˚*, or Square of the Red Army Soldiers, but had changed after a twenty-year-old student named Jan Palach covered himself with gasoline and set himself alight to protest the Soviet occupation in 1969.

Skirting the statue, they went down a few steps to the park that ran beside the river. Directly in front of them, in the shadow of the Manesuv Most, or Lesser Town Bridge, was a large floating dock with an outdoor café and several tour boats tied up.

A boat with a Staropramen beer ad on the side named *Vltava Královna*, Vlatava Queen, was loading passengers. Holliday and Sister Meg joined the lineup. Holliday paid thirty dollars for each of them and they went aboard. The boat was not much more than a barge with rows of seats and a fiberglass canopy. A few minutes later they cast off and headed downriver. Holliday had kept his eyes on the gangplank and there'd been no sign of Cue Ball. It looked as though they'd lost him for the second time.

The boat slipped under the bridge and continued downstream, the immense looming fortress of Prague Castle on the high bluff on the far side of the river to their left, with the Lesser Town laid out below it. They rounded a bend, making their way through a near traffic jam of tour boats and sport fishermen, and then went under the low gray span of the Cechuv Bridge.

'Just exactly where are we going?' Sister Meg asked. 'Or is this some kind of mystery tour?'

'No mystery,' answered Holliday. 'We're going to the train station without Cue Ball knowing where we're going. If he managed to follow us we'd know it. I was watching the gangway after we got on. He's not aboard.'

Stavice Island lies slightly off center in mid-river about a mile downstream from the Lesser Town Bridge where they had embarked. Although awkwardly located, Stavice had been home to Prague's first professional hockey rink and grass tennis courts. The island was also where there had once been a series of dangerous rapids, now smoothed to a simple weir with no more than a three-foot drop and with a lock installed between the island and the nearside riverbank to make downstream navigation possible and as an aid to flood control, a perennial problem in the spring.

Their tour boat entered the long lockway and

waited for the enclosure to empty before the lock doors opened to let them through.

'Come on,' said Holliday. He grabbed Meg by the hand and pulled her over to the gunwale on the right-hand side of the boat, elbowing chattering passengers out of the way as he did so.

'What are you doing!?' Meg yelped as Holliday quickly climbed up on to the broad steel gunwale. An older woman in a large floppy hat and enormous lime green sunglasses let out a squeaking shriek of alarm.

'Getting off the boat,' answered Holliday. He leaned out, grabbed an iron rung bolted into the stone wall of the lock and began to climb. Meg had no choice except to follow, acutely aware of the heavyset German in the Hawaiian shirt and his apple-dumpling wife who were getting a perfect view up her skirt.

Using swear words she hadn't uttered since high school, she clambered up the iron ladder after Holliday. A furious-looking lockmaster came charging out of his little control booth yelling as Holliday hauled her up on to the walkway at the top of the ladder. He turned and yelled back at the man.

'*Policiye!*' Holliday bellowed.

Down in the lock the captain of the tour boat sounded his air horn. Confused, the lockmaster turned and ran back into his control booth to activate the big swing doors.

'Run,' said Holliday.

They headed up a wide set of concrete stairs. At the top of the steps was a paved road, and on the far side a series of fenced-in clay tennis courts, all in use, the *pock-pock* hollow sound of tennis balls sounding like a metronome. Behind the open courts were the bloated science-fiction sausages of several canvas inflatable domes.

'Where are we?' Meg asked.

'Stavice Island. It's a big public sports complex.'

'Why here?'

Holliday pointed to the left. Through a stand of trees Meg could see the approaches to a bridge.

'That's Hlavkuv Most,' said Holliday. 'The Hlavek Bridge. Cross that and you're on Wilsonova, which is where the main Prague train station is. Satisfied?'

'Wasn't there an easier way of getting here than by playing Tarzan?' Meg asked.

'Just being careful,' said Holliday. 'When you're tailing someone you usually use more than one person. If there was a second tail on the boat we lost him, too.'

They began walking down the road toward the bridge.

'Do you honestly think all this cloak-and-dagger stuff is necessary?' Meg asked, her tone sour. 'It really does seem a little over the top, you know, climbing over walls into graveyards and jumping off boats. Bald spies skulking about looking suspicious. People following us halfway across Europe. Come on now, Colonel.'

'Come on, yourself,' Holliday answered. 'This ark you're looking for, how valuable would you say the contents are, if they exist?'

'They'd be priceless, of course,' she replied.

'Right, and I've seen people killed for a lot less than "priceless," believe me, Sister.'

The Prague Hilton was located just off the multi-laned, elevated Wilsonova on Porezni Street, only a block away from the river. It was a huge place with a glass-pyramid-enclosed atrium and everything a well-heeled international traveler could want. It took less than ten minutes for Holliday and his companion to reach the hotel from the island and half an hour more to shop for the things they needed, including a couple of small designer suitcases for their purchases.

It was three in the afternoon by the time they finished, so they took a taxi for a short ride to the station. They picked up tickets in the new below-ground station and then walked down the long concourse to the original Art Nouveau station, which had been turned into a large *kavarna*, or café.

They sat in the big stained-glass-domed restaurant drinking excellent coffee and snacking on jam-filled *palac'inky*, the Czech version of crepes. At four fifteen the early boarding call for sleeping car passengers on the through train to Venice via Vienna was called and they went back down the concourse to the main station and boarded.

Neither Holliday nor Sister Meg had noticed the slight, neatly bearded man and his attractive companion seated on the concrete bench next to the waiting train, and they wouldn't have recognized them even if they had noticed, although Holliday had once seen them from a distance in front of a hotel on the Côte d'Azur more than a year ago.

Like Cue Ball, the bearded man and the woman

had been waiting outside the convent that morning and had followed them to the Vlatava restaurant as well. They'd seen Holliday and the nun do their little vanishing act and had watched, amused, as Cue Ball panicked.

The man and the woman hadn't bothered to keep up their surveillance. The man had already correctly deduced Holliday's eventual destination and the woman concurred. They might go back to their hotel, but from the look on their faces it was clear that they'd discovered something in the gallery-convent, and it was equally clear that they'd assume that the airport at Ruzyne just outside the city would be under surveillance as well.

The train station was the most likely answer. They'd arrived well before Holliday and Sister Meg, and they'd been behind them in the line when the ex-Ranger and the nun bought their tickets to Venice. They followed suit, purchasing a double berth two doors down from Holliday's compartment. The bearded man then bribed a porter to let him wait for the train to be called at trackside and they watched as the couple boarded the train.

Calmly, Antonin Pesek, Father Thomas Brennan's chosen arm's-length assassin, and his

Canadian wife, Daniella Kay, got up from the bench and stepped aboard themselves. A few minutes later amid a flurry of horns and clanging bells the lumbering overnight train to Venice left the station.

9

Venice stinks like an open sewer. Although rarely mentioned in the brochures, this is a simple, smelly fact of life in that otherwise beautiful city; household waste is flushed out with the tide every day, but some of the backwater canals remain stagnant and repulsive. Serenely beautiful Venice is not quite as romantic as it's cracked up to be.

Holliday and Sister Meg arrived at the Venice Mestre train station on the mainland just after eight in the morning and took a double-decker commuter train to the Santa Lucia station on the far side of the Liberty Railway Bridge. The day was already blisteringly hot by the time they arrived and the vaporetto they hired had no canopy. By the time they reached their hotel Holliday had a flaming headache and Meg was showing the first flushed sign of sunburn.

They booked two single rooms at the Rialto, the only hotel Holliday knew in Venice. He'd been to the city only once before, honeymooning with his late wife, Amy; married at Schofield Barracks in Hawaii, where he'd been based at the time, honeymooned in Italy.

They'd laughed when it had rained throughout their precious ten days – while Hawaii was having perfect weather – but they didn't really care. It had been hideously expensive fifteen years ago; it was a nightmare now. Almost sixteen hundred dollars a night for two junior suites overlooking the Grand Canal and the Rialto Bridge after which the hotel was named, the only available accommodation in the hotel.

But it was familiar and that was all that counted right now.

'I can't afford a place like this,' whispered Sister Meg, looking around the ornate marble and wood-paneled lobby. The floor was laid out in black and white marble squares like a chessboard and polished to a brilliant sheen. It made you want to take off your shoes.

'Neither can I, at least not for long,' Holliday whispered back. It wasn't entirely true, but Holliday wasn't about to reveal that he had access to the various Templar numbered accounts he'd discovered in Switzerland, Lichtenstein, Malta, and Cyprus.

Their suites were side by side on the fifth and top floor of the pink stucco hotel; the decor was something out of a Merchant Ivory film with lots of dark furniture and gauzy curtains on four-poster beds blowing in the breeze coming in from the balcony, except for the fact that the arched doors leading to the narrow balcony were closed and the only breeze was coming from the air conditioner, which was set at arctic levels and was making Holliday's headache even worse.

He pulled the heavy drapes closed, blotting out the view, and kicked off his shoes. Twenty minutes flat on his back with his eyes closed would fix him right up. He dropped down on to the gigantic bed and was sound asleep within seconds of his head hitting the soft down pillow.

Holliday heard a faint knock on his door and opened his eyes. It was dark in the room and for a moment he was disoriented. Then he realized the drapes had been drawn shut.

'Coming,' he said groggily. He yawned, then stood up and half staggered to the door. Probably the nun wanting to rant at him about something. He yawned again and cracked open the door an inch. It was Sister Meg. She was dressed in jeans and a man's white shirt, although she'd kept on the idiotic head covering.

'I was getting worried,' she said.

'About what?'

'You.'

'Why?'

'Do you have any idea what time it is?'

Holliday glanced at his watch. Eight fifteen; that couldn't be right.

'Eight?' He frowned. 'Time for dinner?'

'Breakfast. Eight in the morning. You've been asleep for almost twenty-four hours.'

'You're kidding.'

'I am not.'

Holliday stared at her for a moment, blinking away sleep.

'Give me a few minutes,' mumbled Holliday.

'I'm going down to the dining room,' she said. 'I'll order you some coffee.'

'And an orange juice,' added Holliday. 'A big one.' His mouth tasted like the bottom of a bird-cage. His breath had to be atrocious.

The nun nodded, still looking worried, and turned away. Holliday retreated into his suite and headed for the bathroom, stopping briefly to get his toothbrush and toothpaste out of his bag. He splashed water on his face and began brushing his teeth, staring at himself in the mirror. If he didn't know better he might have thought someone had drugged him, but in his heart he knew that it was simply age catching up on him.

There was a scattering of gray at his temples now and his one good eye had dark circles beneath it. He didn't have a chicken neck yet, but the caliper lines around his mouth were getting deeper every year. You didn't fight as many battles as he had without bringing home a few scars, both on your body and in your heart.

He had a brief flashing image of Helder Rodrigues, the Portuguese monk, dying in his arms in the rain on that tiny island in the Azores and then he thought about West Point and the classes he'd taught. A few years ago he'd wondered if he was going stale, and he was certainly bored with being off the battlefield; now he wasn't so sure.

He'd left the Point almost a year ago, packing his life away into boxes that were now entombed in a self-storage locker in New York. He'd considered rebuilding his uncle's house in Fredonia, reduced to ashes shortly after his death, but in the end he felt the old wanderlust tugging at him.

He'd spent part of his time in England but

most of it half freezing to death in Edinburgh, rummaging through the Scottish National Archives. He'd rented a room in an old stone house on nearby Cowgate Street, run by a certain Mrs McSeveney, although there was no sign that a Mr McSeveney had ever lived there or existed at all. Mrs McSeveney had a son named Tommy, unfortunately stricken with cerebral palsy and confined to the little house.

In the evenings Mrs McSeveney smoked unfiltered Players cigarettes, drank gin and watched reruns of *Rab C. Nesbitt*, an odd, dark, Scottish sitcom about an unemployed man who did his best to stay that way. Holliday often read to Tommy aloud, usually classic stories like *Treasure Island* and *The Count of Monte Cristo*. Tommy could barely speak, but by the gleam in his eyes and the tug of a smile on his face Holliday knew he was hanging on every word.

Late in the spring, working at the archives, he'd stumbled on to the story of Jean de Saint-Clair and his dimly recorded voyage into the unknown. Holliday had traced the tale to Rosslyn in the Midlothians, seat of the Saint-Clair family for more than five hundred years, and from there he'd found his way to France. Then

Prague, now Venice, and once again he found himself involved with a mystery, and by the looks of it, a dangerous one.

He finished brushing his teeth, put on a fresh shirt and then headed down to the hotel restaurant. He spotted Sister Meg at a table on the far side of the room and joined her. As promised there was a silver carafe of coffee on the table and a large tulip glass of freshly squeezed orange juice. He took a long slug of the juice, poured himself a cup of coffee and sat back in his chair.

'Sorry,' he said. 'I guess I'm getting too old for leaping off tour boats and catching night trains to Venice. I was truly pooped.'

'I *was* getting a little worried,' said Meg. A waiter approached, gave a little bow and offered them enormous menus. There were about ten different egg dishes available. Holliday chose *asparagi Florentine* and Meg settled for cantaloupe and yogurt.

The food arrived and they began to eat. The muted conversations of a few other hotel guests served as a vague, comfortable backdrop, like the bubbling of a passing stream, punctuated by occasional and discreet laughter; it was Venice, after all, not Sioux Falls, Iowa.

'So what were you up to while I snoozed?' Holliday asked as he wolfed down the delicious meal.

'Scouting the territory,' said Sister Meg, carving a slice of melon into bite-sized pieces. 'I found the archives. It took most of the day; this city is not big on signs.'

Holliday smiled faintly. He and Amy had spent most of their time in Venice getting lost. He never did get a real sense of the city; the narrow, badly numbered streets and winding canals made that almost impossible.

'Is it far?' he asked.

'Miles if you're walking. About a ten-minute ride in one of those vaporetto motorboat taxis. There's a canal that takes you within fifty feet of the front door.'

'Did you check it out?'

She nodded. 'It's open to the public during regular business hours. There are miles of stacks. It used to be a convent attached to the cathedral next door. It's all computerized apparently, and if what we're looking for isn't available in the original you can probably access it on microfilm. Everyone I talked to there spoke English.'

'Sounds good.' He'd cleaned his plate, mopping up the last of the béchamel sauce with half an English muffin from the basket in front of them on the table. Sister Meg clearly didn't approve. Holliday poured himself a second cup of coffee and sat back in his chair, sighing with approval.

'Tit for tat, Colonel. Tell me about this Zeno family we're digging for.'

Holliday gave the nun a magnanimous smile. 'Not until you stop calling me Colonel. It's Doc, or John, or Holliday, or even hey you, but not Colonel. Not anymore. I'm retired.'

'All right . . . Doc.'

'Much better.'

'The Zeno family?'

'Ah, yes, the mysterious Zenos. Mention of them usually refers to the Zeno brothers' map of the world, which they supposedly concocted in the late thirteen hundreds. The family was part of Venetian aristocracy and had the transportation franchise for bringing Christian knights to the Crusades. They basically leased ships to the Templars, who then provided captains and crew. There's some question of their origins; I suspect they were Greek or Turkish from the name. It means "stranger" or "foreigner." It's where the term "xenophobia" comes from. There's always been some question about the vanishing of the Templar fleet, but there's no mystery – the ships simply went back to the Zeno family.'

'What about this map?'

'A lot of people think it's a fake, although why anyone would fake a map in the fourteenth century is beyond me. It's not as though they were trying to convince a king or a queen to send out an expedition like Columbus and Queen Isabella.'

'Do you think it's fake?'

'Yes, but not for the reason most people do. The accepted view among historians is that the map is a preposterous hoax. I think it was a hoax that was concocted by later Templars to cover up rumors of the real Atlantic voyage made by Jean de Saint-Clair – John Sinclair, the knight in the tomb in the chapel where you and I met. Pure obfuscation. You start an argument among historians about the validity and provenance of the map and you stop right there and don't dig any deeper. It's sleight of hand, covering up one thing with another.

'A map like that is exactly what you'd get if

you were using an old-fashioned Jacob's Cross, the navigation instrument I told you about: a series of sightings showing foreshortened distances based on time spent at sea and no relative sizes of land masses – latitude without longitude.'

'I always get them mixed up, like stalactites and stalagmites.'

'Latitude are lines that go up and down; longitude goes left to right.'

'So the map is real?'

'One like it. The biggest flaw most people give as proof that the Zeno map is a fake is the fact that the place names are wrong and some of the islands simply don't exist. I think the names were changed on the Zeno map and a few islands were drawn in to make the map *look* like a phony.'

'Sort of like a double blind,' Sister Meg said, nodding.

'Exactly. Cover up the truth with a well-articulated lie. What's that old proverb about the devil? "The greatest trick the devil ever played was convincing people that he didn't exist"?'

'So where does that leave us?'

'The Zeno family was in business as ship brokers for a hundred years before the Crusades and a long time afterward. They kept meticulous books, which will be in the financial and business fonds of the State Archives. We do a little grunt work and find out if they leased a ship to a knight named Jean de Saint-Clair between 1307 and 1314.'

10

The State Archives of Venice are located in an old convent appended to the Basilica of Santa Maria Gloriosa dei Frari at the end of the Rio di San Paulo Canal, itself a right-angled intersection of the Rio di Maddonetta, which runs off the Grand Canal. The archives, a thousand years and ninety miles of shelving's worth, have been there for the better part of two hundred years, having been consolidated within the abandoned convent shortly after Napoleon's sudden departure in 1814. The convent was formed from two very large cloisters around a central courtyard, which had been subdivided into dozens of individual rooms and small research 'studies.'

Holliday and Sister Meg took a vaporetto water taxi from a small dock on the Grand Canal almost directly in front of the hotel. The vaporetti in the movies are always portrayed as classic wooden speedboats from the twenties and thirties, but the reality is a little different. Most of the water taxis were simple open dinghies or lifeboats equipped with fifty- or seventy-five-horsepower outboard engines clamped to the transom. There were larger 'water buses' that followed specific routes around the city, but none of them went even close to the archives.

They sat in the center of the boat while their driver, wearing a Guns N' Roses T-shirt and smoking a reeking pipe, cruised southwest down the Grand Canal to the Palazzo Maddonetta, where they swung right on to the much narrower Maddonetta Canal. They turned west again on to the sludgy and very narrow brown water of the Rio di San Paulo, toward the Campanile, or tower, of the Basilica of Santa Maria Gloriosa dei Frari, known by the locals simply as Frari. They arrived at the set of wide stone steps that served as a dock, the huge brick basilica only fifty feet or so away.

Holliday gave the boatman a ten-euro note.

'*Aspettare mi?*' said the boatman.

'*No, grazie,*' said Holliday, shaking his head. The vaporetto driver nodded, pulled a paperback out of his pocket and settled back in his seat, reading and puffing on his pipe. The title of the book was *Il Giovane Holden* by J. D. Salinger. It took Holliday a second but then he got it; the book was the Italian edition of *The Catcher in the Rye*. Trust the Italians to change the title. They probably called *Moby-Dick Una Balena Bianca* to make it sound like one of their own.

They crossed the *campo* and turned down a narrow side street on the right, then walked a hundred feet or so to the plain entranceway of a large, heavily stained and slightly down-at-heel-looking Romanesque four-storey building. The inner tympanum of the simple pediment capping the roofline was inscribed with the words 'Archivo Di Stato,' deeply carved in classic Roman letters three feet high.

'This must be the place,' said Holliday.

They opened the simple wooden door and stepped inside. There was a small glass-enclosed foyer with a uniformed and armed guard on the other side. Holliday noticed that he had a heavy-looking Beretta 93R automatic pistol poking out of the holster on his highly polished Sam Browne belt. It was the same weapon carried by Italian antiterrorist forces and could empty its twenty-round magazine in under a second; essentially it was a pistol-sized machine gun. The guard looked as though he was about twenty-five years old and extremely fit. He also had a permanent look of suspicion on his face. Apparently the Venetians valued their history.

They waited for a few seconds and then the glass door swung open. They stepped out and the guard beckoned them forward through an archway that Holliday presumed was a metal detector. They stepped through the arch.

'Do you speak English?' Sister Meg asked.

'Some, yes.' The guard nodded, but he turned and pointed to a poster-sized sign on the wall behind him, written in English:

NO CAMERAS, NO SCANNERS, NO BRIEFCASES, NO PARCELS NO SMOKING.

'No problem,' Holliday said and smiled, wondering what precautions they'd taken against people bringing in the hundred and one brands of ceramic fountain pen knives, key ring knives, credit card knives and assorted plastic box cutters being manufactured and which were impervious to magnetometers and even X-rays. Presumably the sign and its warning were to prevent the theft of valuable documents from the archives, but without any trouble Holliday could think of a dozen ways to sneak things out of the building.

Another sign on the wall read *Informazioni* with an arrow pointing down a short hallway. They followed the sign to a pleasant-looking woman dressed in a blazer and skirt combination that made her look like an airline stewardess. She was sitting behind a desk with a placard like the sign on the wall, *Informazioni*, this time repeated in several languages, including a single large question mark.

The stewardess flashed a smile as though she was terribly happy to see them.

'May I help you?'

The English was perfect, with a flat mid-Atlantic accent, probably learned in a Swiss finishing school or a Berlitz course.

'We're looking for information about the Zeno family,' said Holliday, trying to match the young woman's smile. 'They were ship brokers in Venice in the eleventh and twelfth centuries, perhaps even later.'

The young woman consulted a computer monitor on her right and tapped at the keyboard for a few seconds.

'Third floor reference,' she said. 'You'll find

several workstations in the front room at the top of the stairs. When a workstation becomes available you may begin your search. Identify the language you would like to use then type "Nautical, Business, Genealogy" into the search box. It will ask for the family name. The resulting fond number will give you the location of the fond in question and tell you if the documents are available either as original works, facsimiles or have been transferred to microfiche. One of our researchers will be happy to bring the material to you at your workstation. There is a nominal fee for this service. We accept most major credit cards or cash. We do not accept personal checks.'

'How nominal is the fee?' Sister Meg asked.

'Twenty-five American dollars, or nineteen euro for each request.'

'How many languages can you do your little speech in?' Holliday asked.

'Nine,' said the young woman, clearly pleased to have been asked. 'English, French, German, Spanish, Russian, Polish, Czech, Serbian and Japanese. Presently I am working on Mandarin. I have a facility.'

'You certainly do,' said Holliday. 'Where do we go to find the way to the third floor?'

'There is a stairway at the end of the hall. There are no elevators, I'm afraid.'

The hallway was old, plaster over stone, the wide pine floors worn and scarred by time. Holliday and Sister Meg walked toward the stairway.

'Do you always flirt like that?' Meg asked, a note of censure in her voice. Holliday wondered when the red-haired nun had last laughed at a joke.

'Always,' answered Holliday. 'It's fundamental to my philosophy of life.'

'You have a philosophy of life?'

'Absolutely,' he said and nodded. 'Whenever possible say something nice to the person who's helping you. What's wrong with that?'

'But only if it's a pretty girl helping you.'

'I like looking at pretty women.' He shrugged. 'What's wrong with that? You can't have something against pretty women since you're one yourself.'

'You're insufferable,' snapped Sister Meg, her face reddening. She was even prettier when she blushed.

Holliday smiled.

They reached the end of the hall and began to trudge up the narrow flight of stairs. Like the floors the steps were worn, especially in the center. At each landing there was an arched narrow window that looked out on to a courtyard in the cloister below. There was obviously access from the main floor because there were people sitting on benches, smoking, eating, drinking coffee or simply sitting on the scattered benches and looking at the plantings in the flower beds as they soaked up the dappled sunshine filtered through the trees.

They reached the top of the stairs and went through an archway into another small foyer. Sunlight poured through another arched window. A young man in a white shirt and wire-framed spectacles was tapping furiously at a computer keyboard. Behind him were four computer workstations, each one with its own partitioned carrel. It was like being back in the library at Georgetown, thought Holliday.

Holliday and Meg stepped up to the desk but the young man kept typing, ignoring them.

'*Mi scusi,*' said Holliday. 'But can you help us?'

Irritated, the young man looked up briefly, then gestured to his right.

'*La Stazione a sinistra,*' he said.

'*Grazie,*' said Holliday.

The young man went back to his typing.

'He's not very polite,' said Meg as they walked over to the carrel on the far right.

'Ah, well,' sighed Holliday. 'They can't all be pretty girls.'

Meg glared at him but said nothing; glaring seemed to be her most common expression, like a grade school teacher whose class is in a constant uproar.

'Did you ever teach grade school?' Holliday asked.

'For a short time, as a novice,' answered the nun. 'Why do you ask?'

Aha!

'Just curious,' answered Holliday mildly, sitting down on a hard plastic chair in front of a Zucchetti brand computer. He followed the instructions given to him by the multilingual information lady downstairs, chose the little Union Jack flag for his preferred language and began navigating through the system.

'Find anything?' Sister Meg asked after a few moments.

'I'm afraid so,' Holliday said.

'What?'

'Zeno Nautica – financial records: 1156–1605.

Fifteen thousand pages, a hundred and fifty-seven ledgers.'

'Maybe they break it down ledger by ledger, or year by year,' suggested Sister Meg.

'So I should try 1307 to 1314?'

'Makes sense, don't you think?'

'Let's give it a shot,' said Holliday.

He typed in the appropriate dates and waited. A moment later he had his answer.

'What does it say?' Sister Meg asked.

'One thousand and eight pages and fourteen ledgers. Busy people, these Zenos.' Holliday sighed. 'It would take forever.'

'We know they came back in 1314, or at least the Blessed Juliana did. Wouldn't there be a notation when they brought back the ship?'

'I knew there was a reason for having you here,' said Holliday, smiling.

'I'm not taking the bait,' said Meg disdainfully. 'So just get on with it.'

Holliday typed in the date.

'One hundred and sixty-four pages, one ledger. Available in facsimile.'

There was a pen on a chain and a pad of scratch paper at the workstation. Holliday jotted down the fond number for the ledger and took it to the young man at the desk, who was still typing furiously. He looked up at Holliday, pushed his glasses back up on to the bridge of his nose and scowled.

'Cosa c'è?' said the young man petulantly. What do you want?

'I want you to do your job instead of sitting there on your fanny writing romantic poetry to your girlfriend, or maybe it's your boyfriend. Pal,' snapped Holliday, using his best West Point bracing tone. He dropped the slip of paper on to the boy's keyboard.

'Diciannove euro,' muttered the young man without looking Holliday in the eye. Holliday brought out his wallet and dropped a twenty-euro note on the desk. *'No denaro,'* said the young man, sweeping up the money with one hand and putting it into his drawer.

'Keep it,' said Holliday.

The young man ostentatiously locked the drawer, picked up the slip of paper and went through a closed door at the other side of the room. Holliday went back to Sister Meg and the workstation.

'Now what?' Meg said.

'We wait,' answered Holliday.

11

'Where the hell is he?' Holliday said, looking at his watch. The sour-faced young man at the desk had been gone for forty-five minutes. 'This place is big, but it's not *that* big.'

'Maybe he's having a nap somewhere,' said Sister Meg, standing at the window and looking down into the courtyard below.

'More likely a smoke in some stairwell,' grunted Holliday. Stairwells were always the cadet favorites at the Point. He frowned a little, surprised at himself. He missed teaching a lot more than he thought he would. West Point had been his first real home in a lot of years, and now it was gone and he was a wanderer again, plagued by an incurable and inevitable restlessness.

'Maybe you should go and look for him,' said Sister Meg. 'Give him a demerit point or whatever it is you do at West Point.'

'You sound like you're on his side,' said Holliday.

'You were awfully mean to him.'

'I told him what he needed to hear.'

'He's very young.'

'He won't be any different fifty years from now. He resents the job he has to do too much to do it well. He thinks he's better than the work. You can bet your last dollar he thinks his boss has it in for him and is preventing him from getting a promotion. Nothing is ever his fault. I've heard it all a million times.' Holliday shook his head. 'He's probably a budding movie director or a novelist just waiting for his big break.'

The door at the end of the room opened and the boy reappeared, lugging an enormous cardboard slipcase. He carried the heavy box over to the workstation and dropped it heavily on the table.

'Mi dispiace, Signor,' apologized the archive attendant, his cold, unpleasant expression at odds with the words coming out of his mouth.

Holliday shrugged. *'Per me va bene,'* he answered. He handed the young man another slip of paper, this one with the number of the next fond in the series on it. Then he took out his wallet and gave the archive attendant another twenty-euro note.

'Mi dispiace,' said Holliday. *'Realmente.'* His expression was a model of sincerity.

The young man looked at the twenty-euro note, looked at Holliday, and looked as though he was about to say something and then thought better of it. Holliday might seem like a grizzled old man in the boy's eyes, but he was a grizzled old man who stood six-two in his bare feet and could still do an easy hundred one-armed push-ups without breaking a sweat. Not to mention the slightly intimidating patch over his ruined eye. The kid wisely kept his mouth shut. He turned on his heel and went back through the door on the far side of the room.

'What was that all about?' Sister Meg asked. 'He looked furious.'

'I sent him back to get the next ledger in the series,' explained Holliday. 'The one for 1315.'

'That was cruel!' said the nun angrily. 'You're just punishing him!'

'It has nothing to do with punishment!' Holliday barked, annoyed. 'After the little twerp went off the first time it occurred to me that they'd probably been using the Julian Calendar back then. The Gregorian Calendar was instituted in Venice sometime during the sixteenth century. The dates would have been way off by the year 1315 – Christmas would be sometime in February.

If your Blessed Juliana or whatever her name was didn't get back until late in the year it might be in the ledger as 1315, not 1314. The answer may well lie in the next ledger, not this one. We really do need to see it.'

The nun looked at him, still angry, but said nothing. She rejoined Holliday at the workstation as he pulled the facsimile ledger out of its slipcase. Unlike a regular accountant's ledger, each entry was written in longhand across the entire page, beginning with the number for the transaction and the date of the entry, followed by the name of the person making the entry, then the name of the person the entry was about, then the name and destination of the ship involved and finally the amount paid and the expected date of return.

The name of the entrant, the lessor, the ship and the dates were all underlined. Each entry was effectively a longer or shorter paragraph according to the complexity of the transaction. An odd way of doing things, but efficient enough. Scattered through the entries were notations on separate lines for the return of ships and the final disposition of payments. The last notation on the final page of the facsimile was one of these. The handwriting was archaic and the Italian was obscure, but Holliday's command of Latin made it comprehensible. It read:

Thirteenth December, 1314. Giorgio Zeno. Seen at Gibraltar, the Barca *Santa Maria Maggiore*, leased to Cavaliere Jean de St Clair, en route from St Michael's Mount.

'Do you think they mean Mont Saint-Michel?' Sister Meg asked, reading over Holliday's shoulder.

'Why would they translate the name into English? The notation is in Italian,' said Holliday.

'So he stopped at St Michael's Mount in Cornwall on their return?' Sister Meg said.

'Apparently,' said Holliday. 'It may have been a staging base for the outward leg as well.'

'Why would that be the case?' Sister Meg asked. 'Jean de Saint-Clair was French.'

'What was France and what was England back then is a toss-up,' explained Holliday. 'Eleanor of Aquitaine didn't speak a word of English but she was the mother of Richard the Lionheart. Brittany and Aquitaine were both British possessions in France. He could have very well been English and with a previous alliance with Mount St Michael rather than with Mont Saint-Michel. There's no way to know without going there.'

'Then we don't need to see the next ledger,' said Sister Meg.

'I'd like to see it anyway,' said Holliday. 'The closing entry might have some more information we could use.'

They waited for almost a full hour but there was no sign of the young man.

'This is ridiculous,' fumed Holliday.

'You sent him on a wild-goose chase and he knows it,' said Sister Meg.

'Wild-goose chase or not, he should do his job,' answered Holliday stubbornly. Another twenty-five minutes went by but still the young man was a no-show.

'Maybe we should just go,' suggested Sister Meg.

'Not until I see that ledger,' answered Holliday. 'I paid to see it.' He looked at his watch. It was past noon.

'There has to be another way out of here. Maybe he's gone to lunch,' said Meg.

'Then I'll get the damned ledger myself,' said Holliday. He fiddled with the computer, found the number he wanted again and jotted it down. He stood up and headed for the door leading back into the archive stacks. Sister Meg followed.

'Nobody's forcing you to come,' said Holliday brusquely. 'If I see the little punk I can wring his scrawny neck on my own.'

'That's exactly why I'm tagging along,' answered the nun.

'Suit yourself,' said Holliday. He pulled open the door and stepped through. Sister Meg was right on his heels.

Beyond the doorway the long cloister was a labyrinth of floor-to-ceiling racks of documents and papers, some loose and some in slipcase binders. Other fonds were in boxes and crates, some plastic, some wood and some cardboard. The shelves themselves were made out of wood or steel and were of varying lengths, creating little alleyways through the stacks at intermittent points like dead ends in a garden maze.

There were also varying numbers of aisles, some abruptly ending, others looking as though they went on forever. There seemed to be no order to any of it – codes on one section of shelves appeared to be alphabetical, while the next set of shelves was divided numerically, or even by date or with some Italian version of the Dewey decimal system.

'This is nuts,' said Holliday. 'I used to think the

British Library system was a nightmare – this is truly insane.'

'It is confusing,' agreed Sister Meg.

'It looks like there's elements from every era of the archives' existence, bits and pieces that were popular at the time. It's incoherent.'

'Just like Italian politics, from what I understand,' said Sister Meg.

'Don't go wandering off,' cautioned Holliday. 'It would be like getting lost down *Alice in Wonderland*'s rabbit hole.'

Sister Meg smiled at the reference.

'"Oh my ears and whiskers, how late it's getting!"' quoted the nun.

'Pardon?' Holliday said.

'It's from *Alice in Wonderland*,' she explained. 'The White Rabbit who leads Alice down the rabbit hole.'

'I never read it actually,' confessed Holliday. 'I saw it on my friends the Corbett twins' TV when I was seven or eight. They had the only TV in the neighborhood, color too; a twenty-one-inch RCA Aldrich model. Teddy loved *Alice*, Artie hated it. They were like that about everything. The only other thing I remember is the Jefferson Airplane song, "Feed your head" and all that.'

'You should be ashamed of yourself,' chided Sister Meg. 'It's a literary classic.'

Holliday clasped his hands in front of himself, bowed his head and recited the entire Mea Culpa 'apologia' in droning Latin.

'Impressive,' said Sister Meg, 'and in Latin no less.' She paused. 'Although it lacked something in the way of sincerity.'

'I was an altar boy. Have you ever met an altar boy who enjoyed having the priest box his ears when he flubbed his lines?'

'Your experience with the Church wasn't the best, was it?'

'Nuns who whacked you, priests who whacked you and sometimes worse, various Popes who told you your genitalia would rot if you had pre-marital sex or masturbated, going to confession and having voyeuristic old men listen to your most private thoughts, and to top it all off, being forced to watch Bishop Sheen instead of Milton Berle on Tuesday nights at eight. Yeah, you might say my experience with the Church was pretty lousy.'

'Nothing more anti-Church than a lapsed Catholic,' sighed the nun.

'Being a lapsed Catholic has nothing to do

with it,' snorted Holliday. 'I dislike any religion that believes it's the only true word of God. Catholic, Muslim, Jew and Evangelist alike.' He shook his head. 'This isn't the time for theological discussion. Let's find the little jerk and get out of here.'

They found him in the N 24 stack under a sign hanging from the ceiling that read simply *Navi* – Ships. He was sitting on his knees in front of the bottom Z21 shelf looking down at a ledger he'd laid out on the floor, its slipcase neatly put to one side. The young man's glasses had slipped down on to his nose. If it weren't for the trickle of blood dripping steadily from his right ear down on to the ledger, everything would have looked quite normal.

Beside Holliday, Sister Meg made a gentle noise in the back of her throat. When she spoke there were tears in her voice.

'The poor boy!' she whispered quietly. 'A cerebral hemorrhage?'

'A hatpin,' answered Holliday, who'd seen a wound just like it once before. The ear that time had belonged to a gold smuggler named Valador. 'Plastic, so it goes through airport metal detectors. She pushes it into the middle ear and then through the temporal bone to the brain via the internal auditory nerve canal.' Holliday squatted down for a better look. 'Apparently it takes a great deal of skill.'

'She?' Sister Meg said.

'Her name is Daniella Kay, the Canadian spouse of a Czech assassin-for-hire named Antonin Pesek. They're a husband-and-wife team.'

'The boy was murdered?'

Holliday pushed his hand into the open neck of the young man's shirt and pressed his palm against the bare skin over his heart. It was still warm to the touch. He withdrew his hand, forcing himself not to reach up and close the kid's staring, still bright eyes. The dulling and shrinking of the eyeballs hadn't even begun yet.

'Murdered, and not too long ago. Ten minutes, maybe fifteen.'

Sister Meg stood there, stunned, staring at the kneeling corpse.

'Why would anyone want to kill an archive clerk?'

Holliday leaned forward and looked at the ledger on the floor. Blood had pooled into a sticky mass in the center of the page, staining the spidery handwriting on the facsimile, but it was still easy enough to see the ragged tear running down the spine.

'Someone's torn out a page,' said Holliday. He pushed himself up.

'They killed him for a ledger entry?'

'It's about the third or fourth page in the next Zeno ledger,' said Holliday. 'It's almost certainly the entry for the return of the *Santa Maria Maggiore* to Venice.'

'Someone knows what we're researching?'

'Not someone. The Peseks. They got the kid because he was in the wrong place at the wrong time, but someone hired them to kill *us*. We're the target.'

'We have to tell the police.'

'Not on your life, Sister. We'd be in the glue for days, maybe weeks if we call the cops. They generally follow the line of least resistance in an investigation, which means us. We've got to go back to the workstation, wipe it down for prints, then find a back way out of here and a taxi to the airport. When they find this kid it's going to hit the fan with a bang. I want us on a plane to London before nightfall.'

12

They barely got out of the building undetected, let alone to the airport. Eventually Holliday and the nun found what must have been one of the original winding narrow stairways in a distant corner of the big rambling convent cloister. The dust on the worn stone steps had been recently disturbed. A woman wearing low-heeled shoes; Holliday could see the outline of the square heel and the pointed oval of the sole clearly in the dust. The shoe prints were coming and going. She'd left the way she'd come in.

Holliday could visualize it easily enough: a young man sees a good-looking woman where she really shouldn't be, but he doesn't get angry because her smile is so friendly. It wouldn't have taken her much to get close enough. They would have talked for a moment, standing over the ledger he'd pulled from the shelf.

Daniella Kay would have flirted with him mercilessly. She'd be good at that, hypnotic as a snake. The young man would have barely noticed her slipping the deadly plastic stickpin from her hair, and by then it would have been too late. He'd have died almost instantly, the stickpin skewering into his brain, his head full of the glorious fantasies of older women that only young men believe in.

Holliday and the nun reached the bottom of the narrow spiral staircase. It ended in a tiny dusty alcove and a door that had obviously been recently jimmied, the old wood around the latch splintered and white. Pushing out through the doorway, they found themselves in a small over-grown patch of garden between the wall of the cloister and the building next door.

'Which way?' Sister Meg asked.

To the left, through the trees, Holliday could see the end of one of the canal branches, or *ramo*. To the right a pathway led out to the plaza around the Church of San Rocco. Either way was dan-gerous; the water route meant they would be trapped in a motorboat being piloted by some-body else, and to go out through the San Rocco plaza meant crowds of people.

'This way,' said Holliday, gripping Sister Meg by the arm and guiding her down the path toward the plaza. If the Peseks were waiting for them they'd have a better chance of escaping through a crowd. He frowned. On the other hand, if the alarm went up about the murdered archivist, the plazas of San Rocco and the Frari would be the first place the cops would look. He was fairly sure the guard on duty at the entrance to the archives would recognize them, and so would the girl with all the languages. 'We have to get as far away as we can in the least amount of time.'

They headed down the pathway through the high, broad plane trees and finally stepped on to the small plaza, the church the square was named after on their right along with the Scuola di San Rocco beside it, once a private religious fraternity and now a municipal building famous for its Tintoretto paintings. The rear of the looming brick Frari was on their left. The only way out lay directly ahead, straight across the plaza at the end of a narrow street, where a tour boat was loading passengers at the foot of a set of stone stairs.

'Head for the tour boat,' said Holliday, craning his neck, checking the crowd on the plaza. There was an undeniable sense of imminent danger ringing alarm bells in his head; they were being watched. As they stepped out on to the neatly flagstoned *campo* Holliday reflexively looked upward, checking for open windows and rooftop sniper positions.

The escape route across the relatively small open space reminded Holliday of Matar Baghdad Al-Dawli, the Baghdad airport road, once an eight-lane boulevard processional route between luxury hotels and high-rises. The war had changed all that. Now it was a gauntlet to be run holding your breath and praying not to be blown to bits by an IED or turned into a target for someone in the shadows with a hate-on for Americans and a Russian-made RPG.

The danger there was to look too far down the road and lose your concentration. In Baghdad, death was always in the details, and Holliday had that same skin-crawling feeling now.

Five steps into the plaza the sky overhead opened and it began to rain, a sudden downpour that seemed to have caught everyone off guard. Holliday breathed a sigh of relief. Gripping Sister Meg's arm even tighter, he urged her forward, squinting through the deluge.

'Run!' Holliday hissed in her ear; the rain made a perfect excuse. He was careful to keep them close to groups of other tourists running for cover; if the Peseks were out there watching, he wanted to offer the smallest target.

They reached the far side of the *campo* drenched but unharmed and kept on going down the street to the canal. They were the last ones to board the canopy-covered tour boat. A plastic banner drooped from the canopy: 'Brooklyn Italian-American Hospital Workers Auxiliary Annual Cruise.'

'*Biglietto, per favore,*' said a tired-looking man in a very old officer's cap with a gold anchor stitched into the crushed and stained peak.

'Uh, we left them at the hotel,' muttered Holliday. '*Albergo*, hotel? Do you understand what I'm saying? *Capisci quello che sto dicendo?*'

The man in the sailor's cap shrugged. '*Quarantasette euro,*' he said. '*Per uno.*'

It took him a second but Holliday finally figured it out. Forty-seven euros each. He dug into his wallet and took out two fifty-euro notes. He handed them to the tired sailor.

Tiene il resto,' said Holliday, hoping he'd got it right.

The man looked down at the two bills, then up at Holliday.

'*Grazie,*' the man grumbled sourly, clearly not

impressed with what he perceived to be a measly tip. He wearily hauled in the little gangplank, slammed the boarding gate shut and blew a bosun's pipe within a foot of Holliday's ear. The shrill note was earsplitting. A few seconds later there was a rumbling cough from somewhere in the rear of the big bargelike party boat and they began to move ponderously away from the stone dock. The ticket taker in the sailor's cap sat down on a stool and lit a cigarette. He leaned back and stared at the striped canvas canopy a few feet above him. From the front of the tour boat somebody started talking incoherently into a bullhorn. Rain tapped on the canopy loudly. People milled around on the deck, chattering happily in the rain, sipping complimentary drinks with umbrellas and eating soggy canapés arranged on a table forward of where Holliday and the nun were standing.

'Where are we going?' Sister Meg asked.

'Away from here, that's all that counts,' answered Holliday.

His sense of direction completely vanished as the boat lumbered through the sheeting rain along the narrow canal. The vessel was so wide it forced several soaking stripe-shirt gondoliers to give way, the slim, elegant vessels squeezing past them, rocking heavily in the tour boat's backwash. Holliday was fairly sure the flat-bottomed craft had no business being in such a narrow thoroughfare but he wasn't about to complain. There had been danger in the plaza of San Rocco, he was sure of it, and it was only luck that had saved them.

With half a lifetime spent in critical situations, Holliday knew a great deal about luck, good and bad, and either way it never lasted. The only thing you could be sure of was that the needle was always in motion; the trick was to know the difference between the upswing and the down. The Peseks were pros of the first order; if their contract included himself and the red-haired nun beside him, then the assassin couple would be relentless. The biggest problem was that his only sight of them had been a brief glimpse across a dark road in Le Suquet, a collection of narrow twisting streets in the old section of Cannes on the west side of the famous yacht basin. He vaguely remembered Antonin Pesek as a well-dressed man with a graying, neatly trimmed goatee and Daniella as a good-looking woman in her fifties with the slightly aristocratic strut of a woman who rode horses. He doubted that he'd recognize either one if they were standing right beside him.

The tour boat slowed as it made a wheeling turn out into the broad reach of the Grand Canal, and even in the rain Holliday got his bearings straight; they were heading east and slightly north, a course that would take them to the Rialto Bridge and their hotel. He was tempted to bribe the man in the sailor's cap to let them off at the dock beside the bridge, but Holliday followed his better judgment and said nothing; there was nothing at the hotel they couldn't live without, and whoever was on their trail was almost sure to have the place under surveillance.

That was the question of the day: Who was on their tail and why? The Peseks didn't kill people just for the hell of it; someone was paying them. Holliday was on the trail of an obscure Templar knight who was using an even more obscure navigation instrument; it might upset a historical applecart or two, but it wasn't earthshaking. Sister Meg was filling in the blanks in the life of a mother superior at a relatively obscure convent of Irish nuns in a Czech convent; hardly the stuff of James Bond and Jason Bourne.

At first he'd thought it was the Vatican Secret Service, Sodalitium Pianum, but that didn't make sense either. The bald guy in Prague was clearly a contract investigator, and the Peseks were hirelings, as well, and as Holliday knew from personal experience, the Vatican had plenty of assassins of their own. Somewhere in the lives of two dead lovers from four hundred years ago there was an answer.

The tour boat and its well-oiled partying passengers made another turn, this time to the right on to a narrower canal that ran alongside the elegant façade of a massive old palazzo, its half-submerged foundations stained a crumbling, putrid brown by the effluent in the water and a thousand years of twice-daily tidal fluctuations.

Sister Meg tugged at his arm.

'What?'

'I just overheard a conversation; I know where we're going.'

'Where?'

'Some place called the Isola di San Michele. That's the third reference to Saint Michael that's come our way.'

'Maybe it's an omen,' Holliday said and smiled.

'You're making fun of me,' said the nun, color rising in her cheeks.

'I'm making a joke,' said Holliday, exasperated.

'At my expense.'

'Don't be so sensitive,' said Holliday. 'We don't have time for it. There's a dead kid back there with a hole in his head, remember?'

Sister Meg lapsed into silence. Overhead the rattling of the rain on the canvas canopy slowed and then stopped altogether. As quickly as the storm had come it vanished, the clouds rolling back and letting in broad, slanting beams of sunlight. On their left the canal widened considerably and a forest of masts appeared – a large marina, and beyond it the sudden sweep of the Venice ship channel between the islands of the archipelago and the mainland.

'*Sacca della Misericordia,*' said the tired man in the sailor's hat, still slumped on his stool.

'*Sacca,*' said Holliday. 'What the hell is a *sacca*, a bag of some kind? That doesn't make any sense.'

'Cove, I think,' said Sister Meg. 'Cove of the sheltering virgin.'

The man in the hat pointed to an island to their right about half a mile out into the broad ship channel. 'Isola di San Michele, *una isola del muerte.*'

Holliday squinted. The island looked almost artificial, a wall surrounding it with towers at the corners. A prison?

'Cimetero di Napoleon,' the tour guide explained.

'It's a cemetery,' said Holliday. 'We're going on a tour of a cemetery.'

13

At one time in its history the Isola di San Michele had actually been two islands divided by a canal. During Napoleon's brief occupation of Venice he decreed, quite rightly, that the mainland cemeteries were unsanitary, their swampy 'vapors' almost certainly the cause of the endless rounds of cholera and plague epidemics that regularly visited the tiny republic on the shore of the Adriatic. If there was one thing Napoleon was good at, it was cemeteries. He'd moved dozens of local cemeteries during the reconstruction of imperial Paris and he did the same thing in Venice.

Thousands of bodies were exhumed, packed in ossuary boxes and taken to the islands. The canal was filled in, making the two islands into one, and a wall was built around the entire perimeter.

Within a few years new burials took precedence over the old and special funeral gondolas plied the waters between the city and the island with the regularity of a bus route. Napoleon's prim, gardenlike cemetery with its parks, lines of tall trees and statuary became a cluttered slum of headstones and monuments that ranged from the simple and plain to the ornately vulgar.

Over time the 'Island of the Dead' attained a certain romantic cachet and it became the final destination for a broad spectrum of the famous and the infamous, from Joseph Brodsky, the exiled Russian poet; Ezra Pound, the exiled American poet; Igor Stravinsky, the composer; and Sergei Pavlovich Diaghilev, the dance impresario and founder of the Ballets Russe. A little more than two hundred years from its beginnings the island had apparently now become a tourist attraction.

The boat edged around to the near side of the island and a small wharf. With the sun shining brightly out of a clearing sky, the passengers obediently trudged off the barge and headed through a gate in the wall that led to the cemetery.

'Now what?' Sister Meg asked.

'We have to get to the mainland,' said Holliday as they followed some stragglers along a broad gravel pathway. The cemetery had been subdivided into immense neat squares, each square crammed with hundreds of headstones, new and old. From the looks of things there were only a few real mourners; the rest were tourists taking photographs and peering at inscriptions.

'I think the tour is heading back to the city when we're finished here. I heard people talking about getting to the hotel in time for dinner.'

'There has to be another way off the island,' said Holliday. 'They're almost certain to have found the kid by now.'

'It looked like there was another little dock farther along the wall,' suggested Meg. 'Maybe we can find someone to rent us a boat or something.'

The path they were on ended at the façade of San Michele in Isola, an early Renaissance church fitted into one corner of the island. There was a redbrick cloister attached to one side of the church. Sandaled, dark-robed Franciscan monks were tending the flower beds around the church. More Franciscans, thought Holliday, the male counterparts to the Poor Clare nuns of the St Agnes convent in Prague. A Franciscan conspiracy? That was right up there with *The Da Vinci Code* on the religious conspiracy paranoia scale.

The Vatican might be a hotbed of conspiracy, but all of them were inevitably and invariably about money.

He shook the feeling off and looked for a way around the church. In the far corner, against the brick wall of the cemetery, they found a simple wooden door. Checking to see if anyone was watching, Holliday gently tried the latch. The door creaked open on rusty hinges. Just beyond the doorway he caught the ripe smell of rotting wood and seaweed.

'Come on,' he said, and stepped through the doorway.

They found themselves standing on a narrow breakwater. The only thing between them and the dark waters of the ship channel was a row of tarred beams creating an artificial barrier against erosion.

To their right was the rear façade of the church, to the left a small brick boathouse. In front of the boathouse was an old cabin cruiser that looked almost homemade – sheets of ply-wood painted flat, robin's egg blue for the stubby hull, with more painted plywood for a simple deckhouse.

The tired-looking craft was powered by a big

Mercury outboard clamped to the frail-looking transom. The boat was hugely overpowered. An engine that size at full throttle would tear itself off the transom. The name on the stern identified the ramshackle boat as the *Casanova III* and its home port as Venice. There were half a dozen long fishing poles scattered on the roof of the deckhouse, and the afterdeck itself was cluttered with more fishing equipment, most of it obviously untended for a long time. A wooden five-spoked wheel was positioned on the cabin bulkhead and a set of controls was bolted to the port gunwale. A narrow door led into the cabin proper.

'Our chariot awaits,' said Holliday.

'Where's the owner?' Meg asked. 'We can't just steal it.' She paused. 'Can we?'

'I'm not about to look a gift horse in the mouth,' said Holliday. He went quickly along the narrow seawall and jumped down into the boat. There were bow and stern lines looped around cast iron rings set into the blackened, railway-tie-sized beams. 'Cast off the lines,' he said.

Meg didn't hesitate. She undid the twin lines, tossed them inboard and jumped into the deck well herself. While Holliday figured out how to start up the *Casanova*, she picked up a long gaff hook and pushed them away from the wooden breakwater.

Holliday examined the rudimentary controls. There was a single throttle connected by a cable to the outboard. The ignition switch looked as though it had come out of an old car, but instead of a key there was a yellow-handled Phillips screwdriver jammed into the mechanism. It was a wonder that the boat hadn't been stolen long before this, thought Holliday.

He twisted the screwdriver. There was a preliminary whine and cough from the engine and then it caught, the full-throated sound of the big outboard shattering the somber calm and quiet of the church and the cemetery beyond.

Holliday notched the throttle into the forward position and spun the wheel, taking them away from the island. Directly ahead of them was the much larger island of Murano. To the port side Holliday could see the dark line of the train bridge connecting Venice to the mainland.

He closed his eye briefly, trying to recall the simple map he'd seen back at the hotel. On the far side of Murano was open water and Marco Polo Airport. Twenty minutes across the bay and they'd be home free. He ratcheted the throttle a little farther forward and the decaying old boat started bouncing over the small waves, the deck beneath his feet as springy as a trampoline.

As a child he'd often gone fishing with his uncle Henry on Canadaway Creek a few miles inland from Lake Erie in upstate New York. Every now and again, just for the hell of it, his uncle would take their flat-bottomed rowboat down to the lake and let the little twenty-five-horsepower trolling engine rip. They'd go flying over the lake, skipping like a stone across the water, the bottom of the boat thumping and jumping just like the *Casanova* was now. Remembering his uncle and missing him, Holliday let out a whoop of pleasure to his memory as they pounded across the bay; luck was with them once again.

It was a wonder that the boat hadn't been stolen long before.

Holliday had a sudden, vivid image of the shower scene from *Psycho*. He'd had recurring nightmares for weeks after he'd seen the film one afternoon while playing hooky from the Christian Brothers Parochial School.

For a while he'd even believed his confessor,

who'd told him the nightmares were divine retribution for the sin of cutting classes.

The screwdriver in the ignition.

Casanova III had been stolen.

'Oh, crap,' groaned Holliday, putting it together. The hairs on the back of his neck rose in warning, giving him a split-second advantage as the flimsy cabin door burst outward and Antonin Pesek hurtled through the opening, a dark flat automatic already raised in his hand.

Instinctively, Holliday threw the wheel hard over and the flat-bottomed boat slewed drunkenly to port, throwing the assassin off balance, the pistol flying out of his hand as he fought to stay on his feet. The weapon spun across the deck, lost in the clutter of equipment around the transom.

The killer barely paused, a broad-bladed knife appearing almost magically in his right hand. Pesek lunged and Holliday backed against the gunwale as the lethal instrument slashed across his belly. Another quarter inch and Holliday would have been gutted like a fish.

Somehow Pesek had been one step ahead of them. He'd seen Holliday and Meg get on the tour boat and managed to get to the Misericordia marina before them. He'd stolen the cabin cruiser and reached the cemetery island before the lumbering tour boat, lying in wait, knowing that Holliday and the nun would be desperate to get off the island and to the mainland. The *Casanova* had been a baited trap and Holliday had stepped into it like an amateur.

The *Casanova* was swerving wildly now, reacting to the slightest swell or wave, the wheel spinning freely. If they weren't thrown overboard they'd be swamped or they'd hit another boat.

They were in the middle of the shipping lane from the east, and out of the corner of his eye Holliday could see a massive red-and-black-hulled oil tanker bullying its way across their bow less than a quarter mile ahead, the sheer side of the ship tall as a cliff and getting closer with each passing second.

Pesek lunged again. Behind him, Sister Meg thrust the gaff hook toward his ankles. The assassin's feet went out from under him and he stumbled forward, cursing and giving Holliday a chance to spin out of his way, one hand clamping the killer's wrist and dragging him into a close embrace, probably the safest move in a knife fight.

The boat lurched across another wave and Holliday rammed his knee into Pesek's groin. The killer twisted to one side, taking the blow on his hip, and brought the knife up again, slashing at Holliday's eyes, forcing him back against the gunwale again.

The oil tanker now completely filled Holliday's field of view; another few seconds and they'd be nothing but splintered plywood wreckage spread across the water. An earsplitting air horn blasted as someone on the tanker's bridge saw the approaching cabin cruiser.

As Pesek came after him again, Holliday dropped to the deck, then rolled back toward the transom, scrabbling for the gun.

'Grab the wheel!' Holliday bellowed to Sister Meg. His fingers found the hard weight of the weapon and he rolled on to his back just as Pesek's boot smashed down toward his face.

Suddenly the *Casanova* went into a wide lurching turn, the hull hammering into the enormous wave thrown up by the tanker's bulbous, half-submerged bow. Pesek's foot came down into a tangle of rope and Holliday squeezed the unfamiliar trigger of the compact, Czech-made 9mm automatic, firing upward. The round took Pesek under the chin and drilled up into his brain, killing him instantly. He folded silently, like a suit of clothes without a body to hold it up.

Holliday clambered to his feet and lurched toward Meg as the boat virtually surfed along the hull displacement wave of the tanker. High above them a small group of spectators had gathered at the ship's rail to take a look at the idiots who'd almost powered into them.

Holliday reached around Meg and took the wheel, his hands covering hers. She turned her head, eyes wide and flashing. They broached the churning wake of the tanker and headed into open water. Directly ahead of them a mile or so distant Holliday could see a jumbo lifting off from one of the two runways that ran parallel to the water.

'Is he dead?' Meg asked, turning to look over her shoulder.

'Very,' answered Holliday.

'Good!' said Meg, a savage note in her voice. She sagged back against Holliday, slipping her hands off the wheel, glad to give up control.

'An eye for an eye?' Holliday said, enjoying the feel of her body against his, every altar boy fiber of his adult body screaming 'sacrilege!'

'Something like that,' said Meg. She wasn't making the slightest attempt to wriggle out of Holliday's embrace. He stepped back, taking one hand off the wheel to let her go before the situation got too complicated.

Suddenly embarrassed, Meg ducked out from beneath Holliday's enclosing arm. She stared at Pesek, crumpled on the garbage-strewn deck a few feet away. Holliday followed her glance. The entry wound under his chin was totally hidden and there was no exit wound; the bullet was still lodged somewhere in the dead man's brain. He looked oddly peaceful, eyes open as he stared up at eternity and the blue sky overhead.

'Mrs Pesek is going to be pissed,' said Holliday.

'I believe you're right,' said the nun.

14

Cornwall is the dangling foot of England, toes tentatively dipping into the English Channel at Land's End and the Lizard. It has always been a place apart, a place of lonely moors, strange sights and fog, the birthplace of mythic kings, druids and magicians. The language is secretive and musical and history is its stock in trade. Once it was a land of wrecking beaches on its cruel black coast and mines cutting deeply into the rock and peat, the miners looking for precious tin and silver.

It was Meg's turn at the wheel of the Peugeot rental. They'd left the airport hotel at Heathrow shortly after breakfast. It was noon now and they still had a hundred miles or so to reach their destination. They were roughly in the center of Dartmoor, just past the village of Two Bridges. In the distance the sky was a dark mass of roiling clouds the color of tarnished silver. The first few drops of rain were already spattering the windshield.

Holliday sat in the passenger seat beside the young woman, staring out the window at the dreary, almost sinister landscape. This was the Dartmoor of Her Majesty's Prison and Conan Doyle's infamous Hound of the Baskervilles. It was a long way from Venice.

Their escape had been utterly anticlimactic. They'd taken the homemade cabin cruiser across the muddy shallows at the airport end of the lagoon, finding a twisting path through the marsh, glad of the plywood's springy flat bottom. Eventually they ran the boat up on the beach and Holliday stuffed Pesek's body into the makeshift forward cabin. It was already a warm day and the little cabin was even hotter. The assassin's body would be a maggot-infested, bloated carcass within a day; if they were lucky nobody would find him until much later, at which point the body would be much more difficult to identify. As a precaution he'd taken the man's wallet, passport, and inscribed gold Patek Philippe watch and tossed them all overboard.

With the body hidden, Holliday and Sister Meg clambered off the boat and walked a quarter mile across a few farmers' fields to the village of Campalto on the main road to the airport.

There they bought toiletries and fresh clothes, putting their purchases in a pair of old Alitalia flight bags they found in a thrift store.

From there they continued down the Via Orlando, the village's main street, had some lunch in the hotel dining room, then caught a cab and went on to the airport, less than five minutes away. At three in the afternoon they were on a British Midlands flight to Heathrow, and an hour after that they were crossing the big glass-and-steel atrium of the Heathrow Hilton. Everything had gone without a hitch.

'What I don't understand is why,' Holliday said finally, looking out at the blurry countryside; the rain was coming down hard now, the wipers thumping back and forth rhythmically.

'Pardon?' Meg asked, concentrating on the narrow two-lane highway unwinding across the moor.

'We were nothing but tourists at Mont Saint-Michel, yet we get tailed across Europe by Cue Ball. In Prague Antonin Pesek, an expensive contract killer, picks up our scent and tries to take us out an hour after his wife skewers a junior clerk at the Venice Archives. The Peseks are pricey, and I'll bet Cue Ball wasn't cheap, either. And the big question is where are they getting their intelligence? Until I nailed Pesek on the boat they were always one step ahead of us. How are they managing that?'

'According to you, this so-called Vatican spy network has had it in for you for quite a while,' suggested Meg.

'Maybe it's you they're keeping an eye on,' answered Holliday, looking carefully at the young woman behind the wheel.

'Why would they be interested in me?' Meg asked. 'I'm an obscure nun doing some historical research into a religious who was only beatified in 1985; she's not even a saint yet.'

'Maybe it's this True Ark of yours,' replied Holliday. 'Could it have some real historical significance to anyone except the Catholic Church?'

'You said it yourself,' the nun said and shrugged. 'The True Ark is more myth than anything else. I'm sure the Blessed Juliana was trying to keep something entrusted to her safe, but there's no real indication of what it was. It could just have easily been love letters she wrote to her onetime fiancé, King Hedwig of Austria.'

'Well,' said Holliday, '*somebody*'s after *something*

and we'd better find out what it is before it gets us both killed.'

Joseph Patchin, Director of Operations for the Central Intelligence Agency, stood in the half-acre backyard of his enormous stone colonial on Upland Terrace in Chevy Chase, orchestrating the three hired chefs at work in front of his Beef-eater built-in barbeque and stainless steel outdoor kitchen. He had one hand in the pocket of his Gatsby-style cream-colored linen trousers and the other hand wrapped around a glass of vodka and tonic that was really just tonic. Had to keep your wits about you at parties like this, even if you were the one throwing it.

The half-acre corner lot of the Upland Ter-race house was surrounded by mature pines and cedars, as well as a six-foot cedar plank fence and an inner chain-link fence to comply with the neighborhood's strict codes about pool safety. The pool in question was a twenty-by-forty-foot concrete monster that had been installed when the house was built in the early 1950s and had been lovingly maintained by its various owners ever since. Pools in Chevy Chase were de rigueur because it meant you had the money to heat and maintain them and the time to make use of them. Patchin hadn't swum in the damn thing for a couple of years but he still enjoyed the happy asthmatic chugging of the automatic Kreepy Krauly pool cleaner blindly doing its job. The pool was just as much a status symbol as the car and driver that took him to and from the office every day. Conservatively, the house was worth about two million six.

Patchin's wife, Karin, was standing by the steps at the shallow end with a martini in her hand, talking to Ted Axeworthy, the senior partner at Axeworthy, Tate, Zwicker and Lyle, the firm she worked for. Axeworthy had been one of her first lovers outside of their marriage, back when Karin was a young associate.

When she was made partner three years later the relationship came to an end, the only codicil to the affair between them being Karin's promise not to sleep with anyone else at the firm. She'd faithfully kept to the agreement and had begun an endless marathon of sleeping with someone from just about every *other* firm in Washington, D.C.

The result was that she built up an enviable network of moles providing her with crucial intelligence concerning legal matters in the nation's capital, not to mention lots of gossip. Karin was a slut, but she was no fool; it was that gossip that had greased the rails of Patchin's career within the Agency and would, they both hoped, end with Patchin being nominated to replace the incumbent and ailing attorney general as soon as the pancreatic cancer forced him to step down.

There was very little chance that the nomination wouldn't be approved; thanks to Karin he had enough dirt on enough congressmen and senators to make him a shoo-in. He smiled; it was funny how things worked out. It was a nice symbiotic marriage: she got status and a chance to erase a scholarship past at an Idaho law school and he got what he'd craved since Harvard, raw power.

He watched one of the chefs flipping a pair of ten-ounce fois-gras-and-truffle-stuffed burgers on the grill. Fifty bucks a pop at Dean & Deluca, and he was serving them to a hundred or so Washington bigwigs on a Saturday afternoon. With the burgers flipped the chef turned his attention to the Kobe beef hot dogs. Buns made to order by Patisserie Poupon in Georgetown.

Patchin caught a glimpse of Mike Harris, his

deputy director. He was standing in his wife's glass conservatory-greenhouse attached to the side of the house. The lanky man was dressed in cargo shorts and a Tommy Bahama shirt over a white tee. There was a Toronto Blue Jays cap crammed down on to his head. He'd taken the 'casual dress' note on the invitation a little too seriously. Patchin's craggy-faced second in command was deep in conversation with an Agency 'gnome,' one of the faceless horde of CIA worker bees, whom Patchin vaguely recognized. He thought for a moment. Toby something or other from the Italian Desk down on Five.

A few seconds later the conversation ended, the gnome turned and headed back into the house, and Harris stepped out of the conservatory and on to the patio. He took enough time to light a cigarette then started walking toward his boss. Patchin turned his attention from the barbeque and met him halfway.

'I saw you with the gnome, what's up?' Patchin asked.

'Somebody lit the fuse on that Rex Deus thing you asked me to look into.'

'How's that?'

'Looks like the Pope's team brought in a heavy

hitter, Antonin Pesek, a contract killer. Ex–*Státní bezpec'nost* out of Prague.'

'The weird husband-and-wife team?'

'That's the one.'

'What about him?'

'It looks like he tried to whack Holliday and his new nun friend. Holliday whacked him first. They found him in an old cabin cruiser run up on the beach close to Marco Polo Airport. Venice.'

'I know where Marco Polo Airport is, Harris,' said Patchin.

Harris took a drag on his cigarette, knowing perfectly well that Patchin wouldn't have admitted *not* knowing it was Venice Airport even if you pulled out his fingernails with red-hot tongs. Patchin was the kind of man who had to know everything, whether he knew it or not.

'Yeah, well,' Harris went on. 'Holliday's bad luck. Couple of kids looking for a good fishing hole found Pesek while he was still warm. One in the throat from very close range. Looks as though they were duking it out and Holliday got the upper hand. According to his file Holliday was something of a whiz at unarmed combat. We logged Holliday and the nun getting on to a flight to London an hour later. We'd already had a passport advisory posted worldwide. We knew about it right away. It also looks like there's a connection to a murder at the Venice Archives. A clerk was killed and an old book was damaged.'

'Where is Holliday now?'

'He and the nun just stopped in a place called Marazion in Cornwall. It's on the coast, near Penzance.'

'And you know this how?' Patchin quizzed.

'They rented a car from Hertz. All the Hertz cars have Tracker units.'

'Tracker?'

'English version of LoJack.'

'Ah.' Patchin nodded. 'Any idea about where they're going? I mean, what's in this Marathon place?'

'Marazion,' corrected Harris.

'Whatever.'

'Mount St Michael is about half a mile off-shore. Presumably that's their destination.'

'I thought Mount St Michael was in France.'

'That's Mont Saint-Michel,' explained Harris. 'This is the English version, kind of like twin cities.'

Patchin took a thoughtful sip of his virgin

vodka tonic. 'I see,' he said, not seeing at all. Neither did Harris.

Harris took another drag off his cigarette. He could smell the hot dogs and the hamburgers grilling. He looked around at the crowd. Bureaucrats and lawyers, a lot of them from the AG's office. The rest were D.C. power players. He looked back at Patchin and wondered if Patchin knew who was screwing his wife these days, or if he cared.

Being one of Karin's little trophies was something he'd avoided. That kind of pillow talk was currency in Washington and you didn't want to become an ear in the blond woman's network of jungle drums. It was like a sexually transmitted disease: you had no idea who was going to be the ultimate recipient of your unfortunate whispers. This city was like that, and so were Chevy Chase parties like this one. Harris wouldn't be surprised to discover that the patio lanterns and the trees themselves were wired. Suddenly, out of nowhere he remembered a stanza from a book of poetry he'd found in a Princeton bookstore a long time ago. It was a chant, maybe the first rap song. The epitome of gossip:

Walk with care, walk with care,
Or Mumbo-Jumbo, God of the Congo,
Mumbo-Jumbo will hoo-doo you,
Beware, beware, walk with care,
Boomlay, boomlay, boomlay, boom.

'Pardon?' Patchin said, frowning.

Harris blinked, abruptly aware that he'd quoted the poem out loud. 'Sorry. A verse from my misspent youth.'

'What the hell does that have to do with Holliday and Rex Deus?'

'Nothing, I suppose.'

'You're sure it was the Vatican that sicced Pesek on Holliday?'

'I can't think who else it would be,' Harris said with a shrug. He looked around for somewhere to butt his cigarette but there was nothing nearby. He had an urge to put it out in Patchin's drink but thought better of it.

'What about the shadow we had on him?'

'Lost him and the nun in Prague. Our man said that it looked as though Holliday made him.'

'You'd think with all these unemployed commie spies around that we could hire better help,' Patchin sighed.

'It's the recession,' said Harris, managing to keep a straight face.

'Do we have anyone in the neighborhood? Someone a little more subtle than our fat ex-Stasi friend?'

'We used to have a couple of babysitters in that area,' answered Harris. 'Toby's checking into it right now.' A babysitter was exactly what it sounded like, a freelance or occasional Agency asset sent into an operation to covertly protect a warm body that the Agency was interested in.

'That's not the only problem,' said Harris. 'Holliday left fingerprints everywhere. The AISI goons in Rome already had a file on him.'

'What the hell is AISI?' Patchin said. 'It sounds like something you get from a toilet seat.'

'Agenzia Informazioni e Sicurezza Interna,' replied Harris. 'The Italian FBI. They'd like to talk to Holliday as a "person of interest." They've already called the Home Office in England. Holliday's going to have cops all over him before you know it.'

'Shit,' said Patchin succinctly.

'Exactly,' said Harris. There was a hoot of laughter from the pool. The first guest of the afternoon had tripped and fallen in. It was going to be that kind of party. Patchin felt a headache growing like a time-lapse tumor.

'Get someone on them as fast as you can,' he said. 'I don't want the Holy Father or anyone else to have their way with our Colonel Holliday until we find out just what the hell it is he's doing.'

15

St Michael's Mount lies four hundred yards off the southern end of Cornwall, connected to the mainland by a narrow granite causeway, geographically making the round, high-topped and craggy island a tombolo, or tied, landform.

St Michael himself was said to have liked such places for their strategic military value – their isolation and high ground made them easy to defend from the demons and dragons he specialized in smiting with the sword of the Lord. Originally, the island had been the center of the Cornish tin and copper trade and was known as the Grey Rock. St Michael's was founded as a religious sanctuary by an Irish cult of the vengeful 'Warrior Archangel' in the ninth century.

The island stronghold was first occupied by a simple chapel, then a monastery, and was eventually fortified. A small harbor was built at the foot of the cliffs surrounding the monastery and became a favorite watering place for ships from the

European continent on their way to the Irish ports of Cork, Galway and Dublin.

With the Norman Conquest of 1066 by King William of Normandy, the Benedictines from Mont Saint-Michel built a monastery there, eventually turned into a fortress by Henry VIII. In 1659 the entire island was purchased by Colonel Sir John St Aubyn, the eldest son of the High Sheriff of Cornwall and a staunch supporter of Charles II against the wily republican Oliver Cromwell. St Aubyn then began the process of transforming the old church, the abbey and the castle into a single enormous family house on the summit of the island. The island has been in the family ever since and is still occupied by them, although vested ownership of St Michael's Mount is in the hands of the National Trust.

By five in the afternoon Holliday and Sister Meg had parked the car on King's Road in Marazion, and with the causeway covered by high tide they'd taken a sightseeing launch over to the island.

It was still raining fitfully and a gusting wind had put up a healthy chop on the tarnished silver of the ocean. Only four old diehards had come with them, huddled in the bows of the old lifeboat in rented oilskins. It took them less than ten minutes to cross the little cove to the twin-armed harbor, but it was enough for the elderly couples to scuttle into the Sail Loft pub as soon as they arrived.

Holliday and Meg climbed the steep narrowing pathway up the hill alone, the forested crags and the castle looming over them like Dracula's fortress in the Carpathians. The brooding sky and the harsh, distant crash of the waves didn't make things any more attractive. Halfway up, Holliday was seriously thinking of beating a retreat to the pub himself, but the tough uphill march seemed to energize his red-haired companion. Meg's expression was set in a grim, determined smile.

The trees on either side of the rough cobbled path were a combination of familiar pines and cedars as well as an assortment of odd-looking succulents, semitropical palms and even something Holliday swore was a magnolia straight out of Truman Capote's South.

At long last they reached a mottled stone wall and an arched gate that led to a paved courtyard within. They crossed to another arched doorway leading to a short corridor. A bored-looking man with white hair wearing a military-style Corps of Commissionaire's uniform sat on a stool in front of a high lectern at the end of the little hallway, reading a copy of the *Cornishman*, the local paper from Penzance.

The old soldier seemed a little surprised and more than a little annoyed to see them. He took Holliday's Visa card, swiped six euros off for each of them and waited for confirmation before he handed them their tickets. He gestured toward a table full of colored brochures and went back to his newspaper. They edged past the lectern and continued down the corridor and then down a short set of stone stairs to a vestibule of sorts, short corridors going to the left and right with another set of stairs and a longer hallway straight ahead.

'Do you really think we're going to find anything after all this time?' Meg asked, looking through the brochure she'd picked up. Somewhere in the distance, muffled by the thick stone of the castle, Holliday could hear the thumping chatter of a helicopter. He was surprised; it was hardly flying weather. Probably some Sunday sailor in need of rescuing.

'You never know,' said Holliday. 'They came

here on the return trip; maybe they also stopped on the way to wherever they were going. The church was here at the time. The old records might tell us something if they still exist.'

'According to the brochure the entrance to the church is down the stairs, straight ahead. The St Aubyn Library is to the right past something called Sir John's Room and the Armoury.'

'Church first,' said Holliday.

The Priory Church formed the core of the sprawling castle, cloisters, kitchens and other chambers and halls leading off from it. The church itself was quite plain, quarried stone, two aisles of arches and a Rose window at either end, which was uncommon. There was a carved wooden altarpiece in the shape of an eagle with outstretched wings and rows of light wood chairs, spindly beside the heavy stone pillars of the arches stretching back from the choir.

The stonework was very old and undecorated in the old Benedictine way. Not so the triptych east window, all three panels showing an immense winged figure of the archangel Michael, massive sword in his right hand and a long narrow shield clenched in his left, the famous motto clearly visible: *Quis Ut Deus.*

'I am like God,' translated Meg, staring up at the enormous figure outlined in lead. St Michael's robes and armor had been done in glass squares and diamonds of deep yellow and blood red. The blue eyes were so dark they looked almost black.

'I could never understand if that meant he was God, or just the representative of God,' said Holliday, vaguely recalling a few bits and pieces from his parochial school past.

'He had been invested with the power of God so that he could smite the Devil in the desert,' answered Meg.

'That obviously didn't work out for him,' said Holliday. 'Because the Devil's still in business.'

Meg ignored the observation.

'He was also the first knight and the one who invented the concept of chivalry,' she said as though it was an answer.

Holliday didn't argue. 'More to the point, he was the archangel most often associated with the Masons and the Templars,' he responded.

Meg stared around the room, scanning everywhere in the gloomy wood-beamed hall for anything that would provide a clue to Jean de Saint-Clair and his voyage with the Blessed Juliana.

'There's nothing for us here,' she said finally.

Holliday nodded in agreement. 'Let's try the library,' he suggested.

They went back through the church, leaving through the south exit this time, directly across from where they'd entered. They went up a short flight of steps and into a complex of rooms that had originally been the residence of the prior of the church. All the rooms were arch-roofed within, the oak black with age. As they went down the short connecting passageway the small glass panes in the leaded windows began to rattle.

The helicopter Holliday had heard before now sounded as though it was directly overhead. It was a big one, and Holliday thought he could detect the telltale signature slow *thump* of a multi-rotored Sikorsky S-61, or its British counterpart, the Sea King. Maybe the capsized day sailor had gotten lucky after all, pulled out of the drink in the nick of time; the weather outside wasn't getting better as the day wore on, that was certain. Holliday could hear the rain pelting the window like hail. The walk back down to the harbor wasn't going to be any picnic, either. He was surprised the helicopter was flying at all. Holliday and Sister Meg continued down the hall as the chopper thundered overhead, the sound of the rotors fading.

The library was immense, lit by leaded clerestory windows that would have illuminated the rows and rows of leather-bound volumes in the bookcases that lined the room if there had been any sun. As it was, the gloomy weather outside turned the room into a dusty cavern. Riding above the bookcases on the interior side of the room was a huge medieval embroidery, unrolled, cased in wood and glass like the rare books below.

According to a discreet National Trust plaque beside the open doorway, the embroidery predated the Norman Conquest and was thought to have been created by the original Benedictines who had occupied the island.

Purportedly the two-hundred-and-seventy-foot banner had been stitched by a young monk, Morgan of Clare, who swore he'd seen a vision of St Michael in the ovens of the abbey while he was baking bread in the early morning hours one day. He dedicated the rest of his life to creating the long linen work of art. The embroidery, like the much more famous Bayeux Tapestry in France, was actually an illustrative timeline of the abbey and of St Michael's Mount.

Dismayed, Meg stared at the cases of books. She tried the handle on one of the multi-paned glass doors. Not surprisingly it was locked. She turned to Holliday and shrugged.

'Now what?' Meg asked. 'We can't look for clues in books we can't get at.'

'Maybe we won't have to,' said Holliday, squinting up at the long embroidered banner above the bookcases.

16

'The tapestry?' Meg asked. 'What about it?'

'I think our friend Brother Morgan of Clare was something of a historian,' explained Holliday, squinting up into the gloom. 'He certainly had access to whatever constituted a library or scriptorium in the old abbey.'

Meg followed his glance.

'What exactly are you looking at?'

'There, just to the left of where the middle window starts.'

'A knight in armor being attacked by another knight. A man being burned at the stake. Two men on a single horse. A battle?'

'It's a date. Friday, October 13, 1307. The Templars are being attacked, their leaders burned at the stake. The two knights on a single horse is the symbol of the Templars. The whole embroidery's been done that way. Not only was Brother Morgan a historian, he was also a canter.'

'A singer?' Meg asked.

'Canter with an *e*,' said Holliday. 'It's a term in heraldry where the designer of a coat of arms makes visual puns from a person's name. Elizabeth Bowes-Lyon, the old Queen Mother and the wife of George VI. The family crest is bows and arrows and lions, Bowes, Lyons. Princess Beatrice of York has three bees – bees thrice, over the royal arms of York. A canter invents the crests. Morgan was doing the same thing here. It's a rebus, an old-fashioned word puzzle.'

'You lost me back at bees thrice,' said Meg.

'It's simple. Look at the embroidery. Two knights on a horse. The Latin word *Iulia* and a woman wearing black robes, followed by a two-masted, lateen-sailed ship with a sail flying an engrailed cross, followed by an island with a castle on it, and the Greek word *ichthys* enclosed with the symbol of the fish.'

'The old symbol for the Christian Church,' said Meg. 'I get it now. Sort of.'

'The two knights on a horse means a Templar, *Iulia* and the woman in the robes is your Blessed Juliana, a boat with a lateen sail like that was a classic Venetian design, and an engrailed cross was the arms of the Saint-Clairs. *Ichthys* was an ancient puzzle on its own: iota, chi, theta, upsilon, sigma were all letters referring to Christ. Arranged in a five-character square it could be read in any direction. It's called a palindromic acrostic, or a magic square. On top of all that, Ichthys was also the original name for St Michael's Mount. Put it all together and you get: A Templar knight and the Blessed Juliana came to St Michael's Mount in a Venetian "nau" sometime after the fall of the Templars in 1307.'

Meg looked at the next set of symbols and letters.

'Some barrels, something that looks like meat being butchered, the ship with the cross on the sails again and then the word "Iona" with a ball and cross after it.'

Holliday translated the stitched, doodle-like images.

'The ship took on water and food then left for the island of Iona. I wrote a paper about Iona when I was at Georgetown. It's an ancient sacred island in the Scottish Inner Hebrides. Norwegian, Saxon and Scottish kings are buried there. There was an abbey on Iona a lot like this one. It's also just about the end of the world, or it was at the time. Go north and you might hit Iceland if you were lucky. Go west and there was nothing between you and North America.'

'That was remarkably simple,' said Meg.

'Sometimes things are exactly what they seem,' said Holliday with a grin. 'Like Freud said, sometimes a cigar is just a cigar.' He shrugged. 'You don't have to look for clues and secret symbols everywhere in history; Hitler wasn't in league with the Devil or the Illuminati, he was just your average everyday maniac. Stalin was another one.'

'And sometimes life is more complex than it looks,' warned Meg. 'Sometimes symbols are everything.'

They started out of the library, heading into a long passageway that the brochure indicated was the way to the exit.

'Are you talking about the Dan Brown character's idea of symbolism or the Catholic Church?' Holliday asked.

'I'm talking about the fact that symbols often mean a great deal to people. Christian relics are like that. The Shroud of Turin doesn't have to be genuine for people to take great peace and solace from it. If it leads them to prayer or contemplation that's enough sometimes. A relic doesn't have to perform miracles. The discovery of the True Ark would bring many doubters back to the faith. That's why it's so important to find it.'

'Like seeing the Virgin Mary cooked into a taco shell?' Holliday said.

'Whatever toots your horn,' said Meg as they headed down a narrow flight of stairs. Coming from a nun the line was so unexpected that Holliday burst out laughing.

He glanced out the streaming arched window on his right, the laughter fading. The view through the old leaded glass panes was of the forest pathway up to the castle and the harbor beyond. At the foot of the harbor Holliday could make out the fat, insectlike shape of a black Westland Sea King helicopter, its eight-bladed rotor still spinning lazily. The big side door of the sinister-looking machine was open and men in black riot gear were pouring out, one after the other. Not a rescue mission after all.

'Jesus,' whispered Holliday.

'Pardon?' Meg asked, startled.

'Trouble,' said Holliday. 'SO19. The Brit equivalent of a SWAT team.'

'Swat?' Meg said. Holliday's eyebrow rose.

'Special Weapons and Tactics,' Holliday explained.

He stared out the window and down to the base of the wooded hill. Twenty men had formed up in two lines in front of the big black chopper.

'We've got to find another way out of here,' said Holliday. 'And we've got to find it fast.'

'Maybe they're here for something else,' suggested Meg, staring out the window now. Holliday let out a short barking laugh. Could she really be that naïve?

'They're here for us, believe me.'

He tried to remember what he knew of the elite armed response police. He vaguely recalled that they carried Glock 17 automatic pistols, Heckler & Koch MP5 machine guns, HK G3 assault rifles and Benelli riot shotguns. They also carried stun grenades, Tasers, tear gas and pepper spray. Twenty of them were enough to start a small war. It was unbelievable overkill to capture two unarmed civilians. Someone had called in a fat favor, that was for sure. But who?

There was no time to think about that. Holliday tore the brochure out of Sister Meg's hand and scanned it, his brain working furiously. The SO19 team would have been briefed and prepared, most likely using aerial photographs. It wasn't hard these days; you could plan an operation like this using Google Earth.

The twenty men would have been divided into squads, two to flank and one up the center through the woods. There were three paths: the middle one through the woods, one to the left following the sloping terrain, and one to the right going down the steeper western side of the island stronghold, beginning at the old abbey ruins and the ornamental gardens. Ten men up the middle, through the woods, five each on the flanking paths. There was no way to escape.

'What do we do?' Meg asked.

Holliday's first commanding officer had a primary rule in critical situations – make a decision as fast as you can. It may be the wrong one, but even a wrong decision is better than no decision at all.

'What they don't expect,' said Holliday. He grabbed Meg by the hand and headed back the way they'd come, going back down the hallway, through the library and back into the chapel. They cut across the nave of the church, ran up the steps and out on to the south terrace, looking out to sea. It was still pouring with rain and they were soaked in seconds.

There was a single stone staircase in the old battlement tower. It had to lead somewhere. Holliday stepped up, looking out and down, trying to orient himself, praying that there was a pathway down the southern cliff that could take them down to sea level. The tide was just beginning to turn; maybe a strip of beach would be exposed, allowing them to circle around.

He peered through the curtain of rain, holding his hand above his eyes. There was no obvious path, but maybe they could pick their way down over the tumbled litter of boulders and through the briars and gorse clinging to the precipitous, slightly sloping wall of stone. The clifflike wall of the castle had been well placed, facing out to sea, huge thirty-two-pounder cannon mounted in every second slot of the crenellation. If the castle was true to type there would be a secondary 'postern gate' at the bottom of the battlement tower stairway. A postern gate that wasn't shown in the brochure and wouldn't be visible on any diagram or photograph used by the SO19 squad.

'This way,' urged Holliday. He took Meg by the hand again and led her to the battlement tower.

The stairway offered some protection from the rain and cold as they descended. At the bottom of the stairs, as Holliday had hoped, there was a hallway that followed the line of the castle wall. Fifty feet along the narrow tunnel was an iron-strapped arched doorway.

Holliday took a deep breath, then pushed down on the latch and pulled. The well-oiled door opened without a sound. The present occupant of the castle, Lord Levan, clearly took care of his property. They stepped out into the rain again.

'Hurry,' said Holliday; reflexively he looked back over his shoulder, expecting to see a figure in black Kevlar step out and mow them down with his MP5. So far there was nothing.

'It's slippery,' complained Meg as they threaded their way down the sloping field of boulders and loose, rain-slick stones.

'So is spilled blood,' answered Holliday. It took them almost fifteen minutes to climb down. Any minute now one of the armed response team would stick his head over the side of the castle wall and spot them.

At the base of the cliff the terrain flattened to a layered shingle of rock that ran down to another sandy shelf, which stood less than a foot above the present sea level and was obviously submerged at full high tide. The heavy rain had flattened out the sea and it was absolutely flat without any swell at all.

'Look!' Meg yelled, raising her voice over the

drumming chatter of the pounding rain. She pointed. Two hundred feet farther along the dark slick shingle and barely visible in the drifting sheets of rain, Holliday could make out a set of stone steps that led down to the narrow beach.

The steps were roughly cut and probably as old as the castle. A smugglers' beach, ensuring that his lordship in the castle had a ready supply of French brandy in both peace and war. A wreckers' beach as well; Cornwall was famous for its wreckers and their famous prayer:

> Oh please Lord, let us pray for all on the sea
> But if there's got to be wrecks, please send
>   them to we.

'Come on!' Holliday said. They ran down the plateau-like shingle, slipping and sliding on the rock until they reached the steps. They paused for a moment, getting their bearings, then started down. The visibility was getting worse by the minute. The only way Holliday knew they'd reached the bottom of the steps was when his foot crunched on the pea gravel of the beach. The rain slowed briefly, and out of the gloom, hanging between sea and sky, an apparition loomed.

A man in a classic old sou'wester and a sloping rubber rain hat stood in the center of an eighteen-foot lapstrake-planked lobster boat, hauling on a steel-bound wire jigging line with two canvas-gloved hands. An enormous gray-bellied conger eel of perhaps twenty pounds appeared on one of the triple barbed hooks.

Deftly the man doubled up the line around one elbow, taking the strain, freeing the other hand to pick up a three-foot gaff and catching the barbed hook in the snakelike creature's gill, just behind the small stiff pectoral fin. Barely pausing, the man twisted his wrist with one smooth motion and flipped the two-foot-long conger into the bottom of the boat. The fisherman was no more than fifty feet from shore.

Holliday turned and looked back the way they'd come. The cliff and the castle high above were barely visible, no more than shadows in the rain. He couldn't see them but he knew the armed response team was there, in the castle, going from room to room. There wasn't much time. He turned back to the man in the fishing boat, hailing him.

'Hey!' Holliday yelled, cupping his hand beside his mouth. The fisherman paid no attention.

'The rain is coming in from the south,' called Meg. 'He can't hear you.'

'Unless he looks this way in the next minute or two we're going to be screwed.'

In answer Meg extended her lower jaw a little, stuck her thumb and index fingers into the corners of her mouth and blew out a classic, three-note come-hither whistle. The fisherman looked up instantly, startled by the familiar school yard call, eyes scanning the shoreline. He had the dark-eyed, black-haired and faintly Basque good looks of what Holliday's uncle Henry used to call Black Irish.

Holliday raised his arm and gestured for the man to bring the boat to shore. The fisherman balked at first, but Holliday dug into his pocket, pulled out his wallet and took out a hundred-euro note, waving it over his head. The fisherman shrugged, brought in the rest of his jigging line and then pulled up a small aluminum Danforth anchor. It seemed to take forever.

'Come on, come on!' Holliday whispered.

He gave another anxious look toward the castle battlements; still nothing. He turned back toward the dark waters of the English Channel.

The fisherman sat down, fitted the pintles of

his oars into the locks and let the blades fall into the flat gray sea. He backwatered, turning the oars in opposite directions, and the boat turned smartly, bow toward the shore. The fisherman pulled strongly and the boat headed inshore, slicing through the water.

The man at the oars neared the beach, and after a single look back over his shoulder he backwatered the boat again, this time bringing it all the way around so the stern of the boat was facing Holliday and Meg, a tantalizing ten feet away. Holliday could see the neatly painted name on the transom: *Mary Deare*.

Even from a distance Holliday could see the twinkle in the man's black eyes and the smiling narrow face. The fisherman reminded Holliday of Otter in *The Wind in the Willows*. Charm was second nature to a man like this.

'What can I do for you two soggy castaways?' The accent was definitely Irish but not the Dublin lilt that Holliday was familiar with. 'Two' became 'tuh' and 'soggy' became 'saggy' in a sleepy, easy drawl.

'Get us off the island. Fast!' Holliday called out.

'And wha' whou' tha' be wirt to ya?' The fisherman grinned.

'Name your own price,' called back Holliday. 'Just get us the hell out of here.'

'That's the sort of price a poor fisherman wants to hear,' replied the man at the oars. 'What's the matter, the Devil himself on your tail?'

'Worse,' yelled back Holliday, hoping that the guy was as Irish as he sounded. 'British Specials with machine guns.'

'Bugger me, Jack,' said the fisherman, eyes widening. 'Is that for true?'

'In about two minutes they're going to start coming down that cliff behind us on ropes like something out of James Bond, and that is most definitely for true,' answered Holliday.

'Never did have much use for the feckin' limeys, 'specially the Bluebottles; climb aboard, friends, and step lively.' The fisherman gave three hard backstrokes with the oars and the stern of the boat ground its way on to the beach. Holliday and Meg stepped into the boat.

Half a dozen conger eels were writhing in an inch or so of rainwater in the bottom of the dinghy, mouths gasping for air, the long slimy bodies thrashing hard as they suffocated. Lying flaccidly between the footboards were small bulbous squid. The bait. Holliday and Meg sat down and Meg drew up her feet, looking at the giant, slug-shaped fish.

The fisherman pulled strongly on the oars and they moved off, the Irishman grimacing with exertion. Within two minutes the island had vanished behind the cloak of rain. A stubby rusted hulk began to take shape in front of them. It was no more than sixty feet long with a high wheelhouse amidships and a raised afterdeck behind. A short, dark funnel rose from the middle of the afterdeck. There was a mast crane and rig close to the bows; it was some kind of coastal trawler.

'What's that?' Meg asked.

The fisherman glanced over his shoulder then turned back to face his passengers, his features smiling proudly.

'That's me old girl the *Mary Deare*, last of the old Clyde puffers, and I'm her captain, Sean O'Keefe, yeah?'

17

'Aw and well, it's just a culchie from Cork City, County Cork, that I am and all, yeah?' O'Keefe said, pronouncing Cork as 'Caark' and adding the particularly Irish query at the end of his sentences. He was sitting comfortably in a padded swivel chair bolted to the steel deck of the wheelhouse as he piloted the *Mary Deare* southwest across Mount's Bay toward Land's End, running blind through the gray, dreary sheets of rain, one eye on the radar screen to his left, the other eye on the floating compass needle in front of the old-fashioned wooden wheel. Holliday stood at O'Keefe's side, dressed in borrowed clothes from the Irishman's wardrobe. They were close to the same size, although the arms on the redchecked flannel shirt were a little short.

'You run the ship alone?' Holliday asked. They'd been aboard for almost an hour and he'd seen no sign of any crew.

'*Mary*'s more a boat than a ship, yeah?' O'Keefe said. 'But yes, there is no crew, if that's what you're asking. We're quite alone.'

'Must be tough,' said Holliday.

'Not so much. *Mary*'s displacement is no more than an outsized cabin cruiser. It's not that I do much heavy lifting, yeah? If there's no harbor they send out a lighter and a crew to take off cargo, and if there is a harbor they send out a bum boat with a couple of mooring hands and there's stevedores on the quayside. That's the way of it, yeah? Puffer's been going up and down the coasts along the Irish Sea for a hundred and sixty years. Victualling boats they called them, yeah? Supply boats in the Aran Isles and the Hebrides, out-of-the-way places. Everyone has to eat, yeah? They had a shallow draft and were narrow across the beam, less than eighteen feet so they could travel in the canals.'

'Surely the *Mary Deare* isn't that old?' Holliday said.

'Nah, nah,' O'Keefe said and laughed. '*Mary*'s a young colleen. Built 1944 by J. Pimblott and Sons on the river Weaver in Cheshire. She was used as a water carrier at Rosyth during the war and then laid up by the Admiralty. For a while she was a cargo ferry from Ardrossan in North Ayrshire to the Isle of Man, which was where I bought her for a song, yeah?'

'What sort of cargo do you carry?' Holliday asked. Somehow he suspected that it wasn't always legal. A boat with the *Mary Deare*'s shallow draft could snuggle very close to shore on *Moonraker* nights.

'Whatever a person is willing to pay for,' answered O'Keefe, turning to Holliday, black eyes twinkling, his small mouth puckered in a smile.

'An itinerant tramp steamer captain then.' Holliday nodded.

O'Keefe lowered his voice into a rich baritone and recited: *'I have been a king, I have been a slave, nor is there anything, fool, rascal, knave, that I have not been, yet upon my breast a myriad heads have lain.'*

'William Butler Yeats,' answered Holliday promptly, and then proceeded to quote the entire text of 'The Second Coming.'

'Jesus, Mary and Joseph,' said O'Keefe, eyes wide and obviously impressed. 'You memorized the whole bloody thing and even better you pronounced his name good and proper.'

'I used to teach "The Second Coming" in my World War One classes. I still think it's one of the greatest pieces of poetry ever written. Easily as good as any Shakespeare.'

'What's a Yankee teacher doing running from the *Gardai* on St Michael's Mount?' O'Keefe asked, raising a dark eyebrow.

'I taught military history at West Point and it's a long story,' answered Holliday.

'It's a night and a day to Wicklow Town, which is where we're going, yeah?' said O'Keefe. 'All the time in the world and nothing I like better than a good yarn, boyo.'

Meg came through the narrow companionway door behind the two men, wearing an old blue cotton boiler suit of O'Keefe's that was ludicrously large. The cuffs were rolled up and so were the sleeves. The word 'cute' popped into Holliday's head. Better not go there, he thought.

'Have I missed anything?' she asked brightly.

'We were just getting down to it, my love,' said O'Keefe. 'Your friend Doc here was about to spin us a tale.'

They made their slow way along the Cornish coast while Holliday talked. The rain eased as they went around Land's End between the rocky coast and the Longship's Lighthouse. There they turned north for the long run up the Irish Sea.

Running at a respectable eight knots, it would take them a full twenty-four hours. As darkness fell the exhausted pair were bedded down, Meg in the captain's cabin just behind the wheelhouse and Holliday in the smaller engineer's berth farther aft.

As dawn broke O'Keefe awakened Holliday and gave him a short lesson in following a course, keeping the needle of the compass aligned to a single bearing along the Irish Coast, watching the radar screen for any errant blips, and if he did see anything in the fairly crowded sea lanes, always bearing to the right.

While O'Keefe catnapped in his dayroom, Holliday took the plodding *Mary Deare* past Tremore and Rosslare Harbour, Wexford and Enniscorthy and up to Courtown, where O'Keefe took the wheel again.

While the Irishman piloted the rust-streaked ship, Meg and Holliday cobbled together a meal in the little galley above the old boiler room, making fried egg sandwiches with rashers of streaky bacon and sliced tomatoes on thick slices of Irish soda bread, which O'Keefe had somehow managed to bake himself in the galley's tiny oven.

They made coffee and carried everything up to the wheelhouse, where they picnicked on the small chart table in the corner. An hour after the early afternoon meal the town of Arklow passed on their port side and an hour after that they rounded Wicklow Head and reached the enclosing breakwaters of the old harbor. O'Keefe eased the *Mary Deare* between the breakwater groynes, backing the engine and warping into the dock as though he was parallel parking a car.

'You make it look easy,' said Holliday as a couple of wiry-looking men in heavy sweaters and rubber boots caught the mooring hawsers and snugged the boat in.

'To me it is.' The Irishman shrugged and glanced at his wristwatch. It was plain with a black dial and white letters, obviously very old. Holliday immediately knew what he was looking at. It was a Granta World War Two – vintage German military timepiece.

'Interesting watch,' he said.

'My father's,' said O'Keefe. 'Took it off a German pilot down the road in Arklow.'

'What was a German pilot doing in Arklow?' Holliday asked.

'Bombing it,' said O'Keefe. 'He ran out of gas

204

and crashed into the estuary. My father rowed out and picked him up out of the water before the tide got him.'

'What happened to the pilot?'

'My father shot him with his old pigeon gun, then took his watch. The bugger killed his brother in the bombing, yeah?'

O'Keefe pushed the engine telegraph to All Stop, stood back from the wheel and stretched.

'How long will we be here?' Holliday asked.

'Long as you like,' the Irishman said and shrugged. 'I'm not on what you might call a strict schedule. Got a few things to pick up and drop off to the north, but nothing that can't wait a day or so.'

'I just thought it'd be nice to stretch our legs.'

'Be my guest. I'm doing an Irish stew and box-tys for tea, but that's not for a couple of hours.'

'We'll be back,' promised Holliday.

Instead of heading directly into town they turned past the lifeboat shed on the far side of the southern groyne and walked up a stony path to the bluffs above the harbor. There were the ruins of what might have been an old castle and a clear, brilliant view all the way across the Irish Sea to the distant smoky hills of Wales on the horizon. Holliday could imagine a Viking standing where he was now, looking out to sea and wondering what worlds there were left to conquer.

'You'd think there would be a plaque or something,' commented Meg, looking at the black stone ruins of the ancient fortress.

'The Irish aren't too good at that sort of thing,' said Holliday. 'I went to a conference once at University College in Cork. They were putting up a parking garage near the river, and during the excavations for the foundation they came upon the remains of an entire Viking settlement, perhaps the first settlement in Cork. Instead of calling in a team of archaeologists they simply put down a sheet of heavy plastic and built right on top of it. Pretty crude.'

They walked along the bluffs down to Wicklow Head. It was a cruel and bitter place, dark hills and jutting cliffs running down to the sea. In a storm it would be foul and in a fog it would be dangerous, both to ships and to anyone stupid enough to walk along the cliffs.

'*Wuthering Heights.*' Meg smiled, looking out over the sparkling water. 'Catherine calling for Heathcliff across the moor.'

'Makes you wonder why people live in places like this,' said Holliday.

'You could say the same thing about Minnesota in the wintertime. It depends on what you're used to.'

'I suppose,' grunted Holliday. They turned and walked back to the Dunbur Road and headed back into town. 'What do you think of O'Keefe?' he asked finally.

'It was lucky he was there at St Michael's Mount,' answered Meg.

'Luck's hardly the word,' said Holliday.

'What's that supposed to mean?'

'Think about it,' said Holliday. 'You don't organize a raid of SWAT cops like that on the fly. It has to be organized and that takes time. Someone knew we were going to be there.'

'Who?' Meg said. 'These mythical Vatican spies of yours?'

'Someone who could track us through my credit card,' said Holliday. 'It's the only way they could have known.'

'Who could do that?'

'The only people I can think of is the police in Venice,' said Holliday, 'but that's a stretch.'

'What about that bald man in Prague, or the

man you . . . killed on the boat. The one you said was an assassin?'

'I suppose, but that doesn't make much sense, either.'

'What does any of that have to do with Mr O'Keefe?'

'Don't you think it's a bit of a coincidence that the *Mary Deare* was anchored fifty feet offshore just when we needed it?'

'It happens,' said Meg.

'Only on reruns of *Columbo*,' snorted Holliday. 'O'Keefe was waiting for us just as sure as that SWAT team knew we were going to be there. We were *meant* to get on board. We were *meant* to escape.'

'Maybe you should get help for these paranoid delusions of yours,' said Meg skeptically.

'I don't think it's a delusion at all. I think it was meant to take us out of the loop, convince us that we were fugitives on the run. Someone is keeping track of us and what we're up to. Some-one who wants us to keep unraveling clues until we find what we're looking for.'

'That's just plain old-fashioned nuts,' said Meg. '*We* don't even know what we're looking for.'

'Just keep your wits about you when you're

talking to O'Keefe; he's not the happy-go-lucky leprechaun he pretends to be,' Holliday cautioned. 'He's just too good to be true.'

The actual town of Wicklow had the look of an old man or woman desperately trying to imitate youth. Every storefront was painted a different bright color but each slate roof was sagging and there wasn't a building on the High Street less than a hundred and fifty years old. Charles Dickens would have felt right at home. For a town of ten thousand it had an extraordinary number of restaurant-bars, seventeen by Holliday's count.

The sidewalks were narrow, the traffic was crushing and everything looked like it needed repairing. There were so many blobs of pressed old bubble gum on the sidewalks it looked like some sort of inlay. If for nothing else Holliday stood out for his size; it seemed that the average Wicklownian male was short and the average woman was both short and tending to fat. A pack of teenagers in magenta and gray forced Holliday and Meg off the sidewalk as they powered onward, three-quarters of them smoking, all of them talking and none of them paying any attention to anyone else.

They stopped at the local Cead Mille Failte – a

hundred thousand welcomes – Tourist Office and picked up a brochure.

'It says here the Gaelic name for Wicklow means Church of the Toothless One,' said Meg.

'Toothless one,' said Holliday, looking at the dreary collection of pastel buildings. 'That sounds about right.'

'Boxtys are potato pancakes.'

'Pardon?'

'What Sean's cooking for dinner,' answered Meg.

'I bet his name isn't Sean at all. It's probably John but the girls like Sean better.' Holliday shook his head. 'Toothless,' he muttered.

They reached what passed for a town square in Wicklow, a pocket-handkerchief-sized triangle of grass with a wrought iron two-foot-high fence around it and a statue in the middle. The statue was of a dour-faced bearded man in an old-fashioned ship captain's outfit. He looked constipated, but most Victorian men and women seemed to look that way. According to the brochure he was the captain of the *Great Eastern*, the ship that laid the first transatlantic cable. Someone had spray-painted *Pat Kenny is a git & a wanker!*

in fluorescent pink all over the base of the monument.

There was a miniature department store on the square and they managed to buy some clothes and backpacks to put them in, then continued their walk. They turned down Bridge Street and headed back down the hill to the port. They went into Bridge Books, a cottage-like building with apartments above the store, the whole place painted a horrible shade of robin's egg blue. They asked if there was anything in the store about the island of Iona.

Holliday wasn't expecting anything at all and he was surprised when they actually had two volumes: a history of Iona from its founding in the sixth century to the present, including a detailed map, and a book of prayers from Iona Abbey. Holliday bought the history and Sister Meg bought the prayers.

Having toured Wicklow they went back to the ship and helped O'Keefe with the dinner. They stayed the night in port and headed north the following morning at daybreak.

18

Iona, according to the Reverend James Walker, author of the book *The Wild Geese Fly: A History of the Sacred Isle of Iona from Ancient Times to the Present*, is an island five miles long and two miles wide lying a mile offshore of the Island of Mull, a much larger but equally windswept and lonely place in the Inner Hebrides of Scotland's western coast.

It is, to the Scots Presbyterian minister, 'a thin place,' so isolated and distant from the world that it exists in a very narrow space between reality and things spiritual, thus bringing it that much closer to God. Its first occupant after man's Stone Age forebears was a saint from Ireland, St Columba, an exiled priest-soldier kicked out of the country for leading the losing side during the Battle of Cul Dreimhne in A.D. 561.

Columba arrived on Iona two years later, bringing twelve men with him and establishing a monastery. Each monk was required to build a cairn of stones on the beach equivalent to the sins of his life, and the remains of those cairns can still be seen on the beach, now romantically known as the Bay at the Back of the Ocean.

After St Columba came the Vikings and after the Vikings a flock of Benedictine nuns, complete with a priest and a prior and then an abbey, built in 1202. The nuns built a nunnery to go along with the monastery, and a village, Baile Mòr, which ironically translates as Large Town. No crops grew on the stony, boggy ground, but sheep could be bred on the windblown gorse and stunted grass, and the resulting wool harvested and spun. A poor living was all the island offered, and a poor living was all that was needed.

As the decades and the centuries passed, Iona spread the word of God, first to the craven, pagan English, and then to France and the rest of Europe. By the time Jean de Saint-Clair and the Blessed Juliana arrived at Iona in 1307 on their Venetian ship the *Santa Maria Maggiore*, the island was already deemed holy and at least fifty-six kings of Scotland and Norway had been buried there, not to mention four Irish kings, one saint, and one former leader of the British Labour Party named John Smith who had enjoyed holidays on Iona several times.

The *Mary Deare* came upon the Holy Isle two hours after dawn on the following morning, the mist still lying along the narrow strait between Iona and Mull, the island itself no more than a thin green line rising only a little above the darker green of the sea. As they neared the island and the mist cleared, Holliday could see a scattering of houses at the foot of a low, twin-humped hill.

The houses looked like so many perching gulls spread out along the shore, their roofs dark slate and the walls a brilliant washed white that glowed in the rising sun. At the northern end of the island they could see a second hill, much smaller, but much higher than the one with the houses huddled below it. The second hill had to be the famous Dun I, Iona's Hill, called Mt Zion by St Columba and Temple Mount by the nuns and priests who came after him. According to Reverend Walker in his book, the summit of Dun I was St Columba's favorite place to meditate as he vainly looked back for a sight of his beloved Ireland. The next nearest landfall was actually seventeen hundred nautical miles away on Newfoundland's Avalon Peninsula, home to the first European settlement in the New World.

O'Keefe radioed the harbormaster and they

eased into the tiny bay, warping into the simple stone and concrete pier that jutted out from the rocky shore. On the other side of the pier the MV *Loch Buie*, a small passenger and car ferry, was loading up with walk-ons going back to Fionnphort on the Island of Mull, a mile away across the narrow strait to the east.

From the look of the steel gray clouds and the silvery curtain that lay over Mull, it was raining cats and dogs, but Iona was graced with a kind, warm sun with just enough breeze to puff out the sails of a Sea Scout squadron of Bug-class Lasers on a race round the small island.

'It's beautiful,' said Meg as they stepped off the boat, Holliday behind her. He looked back at the wheelhouse of the *Mary Deare* and saw O'Keefe was still standing at the wheel. He'd told them he had work to do in the engine room when he declined Meg's invitation to come with them, but there he was talking into the radio microphone.

Holliday didn't bother mentioning his growing suspicions to Meg; she was completely taken by the man's smooth and smiling charm. Yesterday, standing at the wheel, he'd crooned a succession of maudlin Irish ballads, like 'Four Green Fields' and 'The Rising of the Moon.'

Holliday had tried to bait O'Keefe into revealing his true colors by casually mentioning that in his opinion the Irish fought so much simply because they enjoyed it; after all, they were the only nation in the world who had a district of their capital city named after a style of drunken brawl: Donnybrook. O'Keefe had just smiled and said, 'Now isn't that the bloody truth then, yeah?'

Holliday turned again, following Sister Meg down the pier. O'Keefe was no Hollywood Irishman; there was something deeper and darker going on there. When they got back to the *Mary Deare* he was going to find out just what it was. The first step perhaps was a look in the old puffer's cargo hold.

They cut through the crowd of outgoing and incoming passengers and reached the end of the pier. Ahead of them a dozen or so men sporting marine haircuts and carrying identical enormous black sports bags were laughing and talking together.

Holliday kept well back and watched them carefully until he saw that they were wearing matching black windbreakers with '48th Fighter Wing Paintball Team, Lakenheath' emblazed on the back. Flyboys from the Statue of Liberty

Wing down in Suffolk. Holliday and Meg reached the end of the pier and asked a likely-looking local wearing gum boots and a tattered roll-neck sweater for directions. He pointed to a small white building close to the shore to the left of the pier.

'Tha's post office,' the local drawled. 'E'll tell ye were to go all right.' The man laughed at his small joke, hawked and spat into the water. They went to the post office. A grave-looking man named Mockitt gave them directions to the abbey where the Reverend Walker was working. Holliday bought a Mars Bar from a display on the counter and they left the post office.

They walked up a gravel pathway to the main north-south road. There wasn't a car to be seen; the road was full of walkers with a few wobbling, hired bicycles here and there. The wind picked up and Holliday looked back toward Mull. Then he broke the gooey Mars Bar in half and handed the larger piece to Meg.

'They deep-fry Mars Bars here,' commented Holliday. He took a bite of the tooth-achingly sweet candy bar.

'No way!' Meg responded.

'No word of a lie. Same oil as the chips.'

'That's disgusting!' Meg answered.

'When in Rome and all that,' Holliday said and grinned. He took another bite from his portion and smacked his lips. 'Yum-yum.'

'Now you're being disgusting.'

The Sea Scouts had disappeared behind the sheeting rain off the coast of the larger island. He grinned; they'd be soaking wet and enjoying every minute of it, safe from their mothers' anxieties about catching their death.

The cadets at West Point had been just the same, thriving on muddy maneuvers in the rain or on the obstacle course, their uniforms filthy, their faces even dirtier, their eyes bright.

He missed his kids and the teaching. He missed West Point, something he hadn't thought possible. Most of all he missed Amy, as he knew he would as she lay dying, more than ten years in the past. He turned to the road ahead, Meg a few steps ahead of him now, and thought about Amy all the way to the abbey.

Mockitt's directions had been correct; the abbey stood on the slightly sloping ground a mile or so from the town, a group of gray stone buildings huddled on the sparse land, a low stone fence running along beside the road for a hundred yards or so, enclosing an anonymous field of gorse.

As abbeys went there was nothing exceptional about it except for its isolated location. According to the Reverend Walker's guidebook it had been built on the site of St Columba's original parish church in 1203 and expanded over the years to include a refectory, a nearby nunnery and even a scriptorium, in which it was said the magnificent illuminated manuscript known as the *Book of Kells*, Ireland's most prized possession, was created, even though it had originated on the little Scottish island.

They found Walker in the refectory on the far side of the cloister. The big man was up on a ladder scrubbing what appeared to be a square of plastic wrap against something high on the wall between two narrow windows.

The reverend was large in every sense of the word, tall, big-bellied, ginger-haired with a full beard and a thick curling mustache. Sensing their presence, the big man twisted slightly on the ladder. Like many men his size he was quite graceful. He wore old-fashioned tortoiseshell spectacles, his eyebrows riding over the lenses like furry red caterpillars.

'Hi-ho,' he said, his face breaking into a wide smile. 'Come to see a man of the cloth fall from grace, have you?' He gave a snorting laugh. 'Wouldn't be the first time, that's certain enough!' The accent was Scots but the burr had been softened after years elsewhere. At a guess Holliday would have bet on Cambridge or perhaps Oxford.

'Reverend Walker?'

''Tis I,' said the big man. He came down the ladder and greeted them properly, hand extended. He shook Holliday's first and then Meg's. They introduced themselves.

'Just taking molds of a few more Mason's Marks. One finds them in the strangest places.' He held out his hand and showed them the small reverse impressions of the obscure glyphs: arrows, reversed number fours, circle letters, two Xs side by side.

The minister had made the impressions with some sort of plasticine. 'It's called flex-dough,' explained Reverend Walker. 'It's not dough at all, of course – it's some sort of plastic. It's usually used by stroke victims to exercise their hands with, but it makes a perfect matrix for taking mold impressions. I make plaster reproductions of all the marks with it.'

'What were they for?' Meg asked. 'The marks, I mean.'

'Every master mason had a different mark,' the minister explained. 'Each block they laid was given the mark for payment. Sometimes they were also used for decoration or to show later masons who had come before them. They were used a great deal in Freemasonry, as well. Follow me and I'll show you some I took yesterday. It's quite a lot of fun, actually.'

The minister trotted off to the front of the refectory, where a large crucifix stood against the wall. Below the crucifix a table had been constructed, a door laid across two sawhorses. They followed and he showed them at least a hundred more of the obscure marks, graffiti from almost a thousand years ago. Suddenly Holliday froze.

'That one,' he said, pointing. 'Where did it come from?'

'That? Yes, it is a little odd. The first time I've seen one like it, as a matter of a fact.'

'It's the only one in the church?' Holliday asked.

'As far as I know,' said Walker. 'What's the matter, young man? You look white as a sheet.'

Holliday almost laughed. It had been a long time since he'd been called young man.

'I've seen a ghost,' he said, smiling faintly. The little blob of bright red flex-dough bore the mark of Saint-Clair – an engrailed cross. It was unmistakable. 'The cross, where did you find it?'

'In the undercroft,' answered Reverend Walker.

'What's the undercroft?' Holliday asked.

'A crypt if it's beneath a church, a basement storage area anywhere else,' explained Meg.

'Quite right, my dear,' said Walker, impressed.

'And here?' Holliday asked.

'The refectory was once the abbey dining hall. Originally the undercroft was the kitchen. Eventually the undercroft was used as a crypt, as your friend said,' replied Walker. 'I took that impression from directly above one of the old burial slabs.'

'A knight?' Meg asked quickly.

'Good Lord!' Walker said. 'How on earth did you know that?'

Meg slipped off her backpack, dug into it and pulled out the little book of prayers she'd purchased in Wicklow. She flipped through the pages until she came to the prayer she wanted, then began to recite:

Lord God, in Jerusalem's temple crowned,
We your steadfast soldier and your handmaiden
    ask
Only for thy grace and favor found

If as thy servants we complete the task.
Save us from Satan's royal vengeance once more
And give us Mary's holy wings to fly
Us to the farther sable shore
Then we shall keep thy treasures safe
In Arcadia's pale enclosing arms once more.

'Astounding,' said Walker. 'The Knight's Prayer. Just about the oldest recorded prayer from the abbey.'

'From 1307, to be precise,' said Holliday.

'Curiouser and curiouser,' muttered Walker, staring closely at them. 'How could you possibly know when the prayer was written? Even I don't know that.'

'Because we know who the "steadfast soldier" and the "handmaiden" were and we know exactly when they came here and why,' said Holliday. 'Now, please show us where you found that particular Mason's Mark.'

19

The refectory undercroft was a long, low-ceilinged chamber supported by a series of four heavy stone pillars down the center. There were stairs at the east end and a small root cellar at the west end. In between the steps and the root cellar twenty stone burial slabs were laid against the north wall, their upper surfaces all but worn off. A brass rubbing in white against black hung on the wall above each slab.

Walker, Holliday and Sister Meg walked along the aisle formed between the slabs and the pillars, Holliday carefully checking the brass rubbings. At the ninth slab he stopped and stared at the rubbing.

'This is the one,' he said.

'How do you know?' Walker asked, fascinated by the story he'd been told.

'The shield is quartered,' said Holliday, pointing to the faint image on the rubbing. 'In the upper left you have Saint-Clair's engrailed cross, in the upper right you have the image of a Venetian ship with a lateen sail, and in the bottom quadrant you have two crescents, both facing inward. If it was in color the two crescents would probably be green – islands.'

'Fanciful, but how do you know they're islands? They could just as easily signify moons, or even Arabic crescents.'

'The poem,' said Meg, suddenly seeing it the way Holliday did. *'And give us Mary's holy wings to fly us to the farther sable shore,'* she quoted. 'The farther shore – the other side of the Atlantic.'

'And sable?' Walker asked.

'According to the book the poems were originally written in Gaelic – all except the Knight's Prayer. That was written in French,' said Holliday.

'That's right. French was the language of chivalry. Most of the aristocracy spoke it in medieval times,' said Walker, still looking a little bewildered.

'In French "sable" means sand, as in a beach,' added Meg.

'Well, that's all fine and good,' argued Walker. 'That makes your quest quite simple then, doesn't it. Just find a sandy beach somewhere on the east coast of North America, that's all.'

'The whole prayer was written as a code,' said Holliday. 'The answer's in there somewhere.'

'Oh, dear,' the rotund minister said and sighed. 'Must everything be in some sort of code? It's all a bit much, don't you think? Illuminati, the Masons, Opus Dei. Why is it that everybody sees religious conspiracies everywhere these days?' The minister shook his head. 'Nobody cares that much for religion anymore, believe me.'

'They did back in the fourteenth century,' said Holliday. 'You don't have to twist reality around to see the meaning of the prayer.' Holliday took the book from Meg. '*Satan's royal vengeance* is King Philip of France killing the Templars. *Mary's holy wings* are the sails of the *Santa Maria Maggiore*, their ship, and *Arcadia's pale enclosing arms* almost certainly refers to Nova Scotia – new Scotland – in the Canadian maritimes, a place that was originally known as Arcadia. To top things off the inscription on Jean de Saint-Clair's tomb in the old chapel at Mont Saint-Michel on the Normandy coast of France reads *In Arcadia Est.*'

'That's all very entertaining, but it still seems rather fanciful.'

'It *is* rather fanciful,' Holliday said. 'Imaginative as hell.'

'So you agree then, your coded message and a few old rubbings could amount to nothing.'

'Of course,' said Holliday, 'but so far we've been led from Mont Saint-Michel to Prague, to the Venetian Archives, then to St Michael's Mount, and finally to here by the same kind of fanciful clues. There's a pattern and a logic to it all.'

'Coincidence,' argued Walker.

'Maybe,' said Holliday. 'But I'm betting on Jean de Saint-Clair's imagination and the imagination of the Blessed Juliana. They were rescuing a treasure trove of relics, hiding them from a vengeful king and a power-hungry Pope. They wanted to get the relics as far away from both men as they possibly could, but they wanted to do it without starting a war.

'If King Philip had attacked St Michael's Mount it would have been the perfect excuse for Edward the Second of England to attack his old rival. To have attacked Iona would have inflamed Scotland and incurred the wrath of the Irish, supposedly allies of the French as well as the not inconsiderable Scandinavian kingdoms.

'On the other hand, neither Jean de Saint-Clair nor Juliana knew when, or even *if*, they would be back to retrieve the treasures. They had to leave some sort of clues behind; clues that would out-live them for a very long time, perhaps hundreds of years. What better place than the burial ground of kings?' Holliday smiled. 'The Knight's Prayer speaks for itself. It's survived for more than seven hundred years in much the same way as the Lord's Prayer has survived even longer.'

The burly minister laughed heartily and clapped his hands.

'Bravo, Mr Holliday. You've almost convinced me.'

'But not quite,' said Holliday.

'Enough for me to take another rubbing for you of your mysterious knight here,' replied the Reverend Walker. 'I can have it ready for you this evening. Perhaps you and the good sister would be my guests for dinner. I do a rather nice cabbie claw even if I do say so myself.'

'Well,' began Holliday, speaking tentatively.

'We'd like that very much,' said Meg. 'We have a friend, the Irishman who brought us here. Per-haps we could bring him along.'

'By all means.' The minister beamed. 'Shall we say six o'clock, then? I live halfway between here and town. On your left, the cottage with the blue door and ducks in the yard. You can't miss it. I've got quite a library of Iona lore; p'raps we can find out some more about this Jean de Saint-Clair of yours. I'm something of the island's unofficial historian; if the Templar knight of yours is part of Iona's past, then I should know about it.'

It took them a few minutes to say their good-byes to Walker, and then they headed back to town and the *Mary Deare*. As they reached the main road leading away from the abbey they fell in with a straggling group of tourists coming down from Dun I, at three hundred feet the highest point on the island and a favorite vantage point for pictures. It felt a little odd to be walking in the center of a road without a car to be seen, but on the other hand, it gave Holliday a real feeling of what it had been like in the time of the pilgrims.

They reached Reverend Walker's house with its blue door, no more than a whitewashed cottage with half its slates missing. The ducks were there as well, perhaps a dozen of them herded behind a low stone fence that kept the noisy, angry creatures from attacking people walking along the road.

Just beyond the house, on the right, Holliday could see a narrow path leading to the marshy area known as Lochan Mor, the 'Abbot's Fishpond,' once an artificial lake dammed to provide power to the old granite diggings and now nothing more than a swampy marsh, cut through by a granite causeway that led into the moorland beyond. The sky was steel gray. The rain had followed them across the narrow strait.

'Colonel Holliday?' asked a polite voice behind them. Holliday stopped and turned. A young man with a marine haircut and wearing a black windbreaker and black chinos was standing right behind them. One of the paintballers. There was a pair of binoculars in a case slung over his left shoulder. The kid looked about eighteen. Too young to be one of his old students. He kept his right hand in his pocket.

'Excuse me?' Holliday said. 'Do I know you?'

'You don't have to know me, sir. You just have to do exactly what I say.' He pushed his hand forward in the windbreaker pocket and used it to open the jacket so both Holliday and Meg could see the small black metal submachine gun hanging from its sling. There was a fat sausage-shaped suppressor screwed on to the stubby little barrel.

Holliday felt Meg grab his arm, clutching hard at the sight of the weapon.

'Doc?' Meg said.

Holliday kept his eyes on the young man. The gun was a US-made MAC 11, the subcompact version of the MAC 10, once the weapon of choice for the bad guys on *Miami Vice* and shows like it. The MAC 11 had never found much acceptance with the police, the Secret Service or Special Forces. It was an open-block weapon that was hard to control, and with a small sub-sonic .380-caliber load it didn't have much stopping power and was only useful in closed environments like airplanes. Holliday couldn't think of any group for whom it was standard issue. All of which meant that the young man standing in front of him probably wasn't any part of the U.S. military.

'Who are you, son?' Holliday asked, trying to engage the young man.

'It doesn't matter who the hell I am,' said the boy. 'Just turn around and keep walking. When we get to the path turn right. And I'm not your son.' There was heat in his voice and wire-taut moves. Holliday knew he was just as likely to squeeze the trigger of the MAC 11 out of fear as anything else. The kid was a firecracker and he was about to go off.

'Doc?' Meg asked.

'Do as he says,' answered Holliday. At the path they turned off and headed for the marshy area. As they left the road it began to rain, a light hard spit with promise of a harder downfall in the low dark clouds overhead.

'Where are you taking us?' Meg asked.

'Shut up!' snarled the boy with the MAC 11.

'Boro Bacheh Kooni,' said Holliday quietly. *'Khar Kos seh, maadar jendeh.'* There was no response from the young man behind them. Considering what he'd just said to the kid in Farsi, it was unlikely that he'd ever been in Afghanistan or Iraq. *'Madar-e-to Gayidam,'* he added, just to be sure. No reaction from the boy in the windbreaker. A hired gun. A mercenary, but one without much experience. It began to rain harder, gusting sheets rolling across the marshland. The visibility was only a few feet ahead, so presumably they were now invisible from the road as well.

'You haven't been doing this very long, have you?'

'Long enough,' the young man answered briefly, his voice tense.

'How old are you, seventeen, eighteen?'

'I'm twenty-one!'

'Sure you are,' snorted Holliday, his voice dripping with derision.

'I told you! Shut the hell up!'

Holliday slowed. It was time to play soldier. He took a deep breath; the young man with the submachine gun was way out of his depth. Holliday blinked the rain out of his eyes and spoke.

'One thing you should know if you want to live to see tomorrow, kid: the slide safety in front of the trigger on a MAC 11 should be in the rear position when you're so close behind your prisoner.'

Holliday heard the sudden indrawn breath and the faltering step as the young man hesitated. His eyes would have dropped and his right hand would be coming out of his pocket to check the safety. Perhaps a three-second advantage.

Holliday pivoted on his left foot and brought the right around in a side kick to the boy's thigh, pushing him off balance and making him stumble. He lashed out with his left hand, palm outward under the young man's chin, snapping his head back brutally, sending the kid backward. Without even thinking about it he bent his knee and dropped down with all his weight on the boy's chest.

The sound of breaking ribs was audible, bone splintering, as Holliday's knee forced the shattered end of the third rib into the pulmonary artery, rupturing it. The young man gagged, blood spurting from his mouth and nose. He was dead almost before he knew he was on the ground. The boy's bright blue eyes rolled back in his head and he went limp. Holliday stood up.

'Is he dead?' Meg asked in a dull voice.

'Yes,' answered Holliday.

'Couldn't you have just . . . disarmed him?'

'No,' said Holliday without any more explanation or justification. Kid or not the young man with the submachine gun had threatened their lives. The boy was supposedly some kind of soldier, and thus had automatically entered into the contract that had existed between enemies since Cain battled Abel: tit for tat, no quarter asked and none given. Kill or be killed.

'So now what?'

'Roll him over and get his jacket off,' instructed Holliday.

Meg did as he asked. Holliday looked around. They were well out of sight of the road and no shots had been fired. The only potential problem was someone rushing along the pathway from the other side of the island, anxious to get out of the cold, stinging rain.

Meg finished taking off the kid's jacket and stood up. Holliday squatted down beside the body and stripped off the King Arms Bungee sling and holster, then went through the dead boy's pockets. Keys, a few coins, English and American mixed, a fat Swiss Army knife with all the bells and whistles. A wallet identified him as Ian Andrew Mitchell, twenty-one years old and a resident of Wilmington, Delaware. He also had a Delaware concealed-carry permit, a Beretta .380-caliber mousegun in an in-the-pants holster against his spine. The permit was made out to Mitchell under the authority of Blackhawk Security Systems of Odessa, Delaware. The passport was made out to Andrew Mitchell and listed him as a security consultant.

There were three hundred euros in cash and several credit cards, all of which Holliday took. He stood up and threw the wallet and the rest of its contents as far into the marsh as he could. He put the mousegun and its holster against his own spine, slipped into the gun sling and reattached the MAC 11 to the straps. Finally he shrugged on the black windbreaker and slung the binoculars over his shoulder.

'Help me drag the body behind that patch of gorse,' said Holliday, pointing toward a mound of low shrubbery a few yards away to the right. Meg took one of the boy's wrists and Holliday took the other, and together they dragged the body facedown through the spongy mud and turf, then made their way back to the path. They were both soaking wet, but the steady downpour would hide any evidence of a struggle within a moment or two.

'You seem so calm,' said Meg, a note of bitterness in her voice. 'As though killing children comes naturally to you.'

Holliday gritted his teeth, her words unlocking a memory so vivid and fresh it could have been yesterday. 'I happened to be at the Assassin's Gate in Baghdad one morning when a nine-year-old girl came through the checkpoint. The Iraqi soldier with me said it was rare for kids that young to wear the full burqa, complete with a veil. The Iraqi soldier told the kid to stop where she was but the kid began to run right at us. The Iraqi soldier shouted at her again but the little girl kept on coming. I was carrying an old .45-caliber automatic as a sidearm. The Iraqi soldier was hesitating so I shot the kid in the chest.'

'Did it make you feel better?' Meg said coldly.

He could almost feel the talcum powder sand on his skin, the kind that had made him feel grimy ten minutes after he showered.

'The kid was maybe fifty feet away when I hit her. The suicide vest she was wearing under the burqa blew a crater in the road ten feet across and three feet deep. Bits and pieces of shrapnel from the vest killed the Iraqi soldier. Two women running a fruit stall outside the gate were killed by the explosion, as well. I was blown out of my combat boots by the blast. So don't tell me about killing children, sweetheart.'

For a second it looked as though the red-haired nun was going to say something in reply but then she thought better of it.

'So what do we do now?' Meg said finally, standing there in the rain, her long hair hanging in stringy tangles around her face.

'The kid wasn't a killer,' said Holliday. 'He was a delivery boy.'

'What's that supposed to mean?'

'He was taking us to someone,' answered Holliday. 'I intend to find out where and to whom.'

20

'I knew it,' said Holliday angrily. He was looking through the big Steiner military binoculars he had taken off the dead kid. He and Sister Meg were lying on the stony bluffs above the Bay at the Back of the Ocean, the rough, curving beach that ran along the western shore of Iona.

He handed the binoculars to Meg, pointing and keeping his head low just in case someone was watching. It was still raining and they'd both given up any thought of drying out a long time ago. Drawn up on the beach itself was an old red-painted dory, its bow turned toward the flat, featureless ocean, the stern pulled up on the sand, a big old Mercury outboard flipped up on the transom.

An unidentified man was huddled in the back of the boat, protected by a small tarpaulin that was probably meant for the motor. From their vantage point Holliday could see that the man in the dory was wearing a black windbreaker that was a mate to the one they'd taken off the body in the swamp. Presumably another employee of Blackhawk Security, which was something else to think about: Who the hell was Blackhawk Security and why were they trying to kill him?

'Sean,' said Meg, surprise in her voice as she looked through the binoculars. 'That's the *Mary Deare.*'

Holliday nodded, his jaw set in anger. 'If Sean is his real name,' he said, looking out to sea. Without the binoculars the little ship was nothing more than an indistinct blob on the rain-filled horizon. With the Steiners he could make out individual patches of rust and primer paint on the hull. The *Mary Deare* was lying about a mile from shore anchored fore and aft, waiting. For what? The only logical answer was that O'Keefe's old ship had left the little port on the east shore of Iona and come around to the west shore for a rendezvous with the red dory.

The red dory, on the other hand, was waiting in the pouring rain for Ian Andrew Mitchell to arrive with his freshly captured prisoners. Somebody had it all neatly planned out. But why go to all the trouble? Why not simply wait until they returned to the ship on their own? It wasn't as though they had anyplace else to go.

'I don't understand any of this,' said Meg, passing back the binoculars. Holliday took them from her and slipped them back into their case.

'Somebody's trying to stop us any way they can,' said Holliday. 'Your boyfriend O'Keefe is working for whoever's got us targeted. Odds are we were supposed to go back aboard the *Mary Deare* without anyone seeing us. Whoever was waiting on board would torture us to find out what we know and then drop us into the ocean.'

'Sean is not my boyfriend, and I find it hard to believe he'd do a thing like that,' said Meg.

'You can have whatever the hell kind of fantasy you want,' said Holliday. 'The harsh reality is sitting in that red dory wearing the same Blackhawk Security windbreaker as I am,' he added. 'And he already *has* done a thing like that.'

'All right,' answered Meg. 'What are we supposed to do about your so-called harsh reality?'

'Fake it,' said Holliday.

They argued back and forth for five minutes and then Holliday and Meg stood up in full view and walked slowly down the shallow-sided dune below the higher bluff, Meg in the lead, Holliday close behind her. Seeing movement on the bluff, the man in the red dory looked up and peered into the gray curtain of rain. He stood, the tarpaulin around his shoulders, one hand shielding his eyes. Holliday and Meg reached the bottom of the sloping dune and walked toward the boat drawn up on the shore. As they walked both Meg and Holliday kept their heads down.

'You promised you wouldn't hurt him,' reminded Meg, keeping her voice low as they stepped toward the boat, their feet digging into the wet, gritty sand.

'Not unless he tries to hurt me first,' said Holliday, wishing the nun would shut up and let him concentrate on the next few seconds.

'You really are some kind of bastard,' said Meg bitterly.

'Hey!' the man in the dory called out. 'There was supposed to be two of them! Where's the other one?!'

Holliday and Meg kept on walking toward the boat. All he needed was another ten feet or so.

'Hey!' the man in the dory yelled again. He swept back the tarpaulin and reached for the sling under his windbreaker. He was armed just like the first one.

Holliday used his left arm to sweep Meg out

of the way. She stumbled and fell to her knees. He fired the little Beretta .380 through the slit he'd made in the pocket of the windbreaker with the Swiss Army knife, trying for the left shoulder and arm, hoping to immobilize the shooter. The Beretta had an eight-round, single-stack magazine and one in the chamber, nine rounds in all. Holliday kept firing until the man fell down, dropping forward over the transom of the dory and flopping out of the boat and on to the beach. Any blood was invisible against the black of the windbreaker. The man was writhing on the sand, his left hand clutching his right elbow. He wouldn't be signing any contracts for a while but he'd live if they got him to a hospital within the next half hour. Holliday had fired seven rounds and hit the man with four, one in the elbow, one in the meat of the upper arm and two in the shoulder. Three out of the four were through and through; the fourth was still lodged in his biceps. His face was pale and his teeth were chattering. He was going into shock.

'What have you done?' Sister Meg groaned, stooping down over the wounded man. Holliday pushed her aside and removed the sling and the submachine gun. He laid the MAC 11 on the sand and rolled the man over, none too gently. The man screamed.

'You're hurting him!' Meg said furiously.

'Good,' said Holliday blandly. The man was carrying a Beretta identical to the one Holliday had shot him with. 'Push the boat into the water. I'm going to drag this one up beyond the tide line.' Holliday grabbed the man by his collar and started hauling him up the beach.

'We can't just leave him here!'

'We're sure as hell not taking him with us,' said Holliday. He reached the tide line, marked by a line of drying kelp and driftwood, and let the man drop. He walked back to the boat, ignoring Meg, and heaved on the transom. As the boat slipped into the water Holliday levered himself over the gunwale and dropped down on to the flat wooden bench. He eased the outboard over the transom and started looking for the starter.

'What are you doing?' Meg asked, staring at him, a little wild-eyed.

'Leaving before your friend Sean figures out what's going on and calls in the cavalry,' said Holliday. 'If you're coming, you'd better get in.'

Holliday found the electric starter and punched it, one hand on the throttle arm. Small waves were already moving the old clinker-built fishing boat into deeper water. Meg hesitated for a second longer, then waded out into the water and threw her backpack into the boat. She grabbed the gunwale and boosted herself up and in. The engine caught with a coughing roar. Holliday twisted the tiller arm and pointed the dory out to sea.

Katherine Franklin Sinclair, widow of the late Angus Pierce Sinclair, the onetime ambassador to the Court of St James in London, and mother to Senator Richard Pierce Sinclair, sat at a corner table in the Senate Dining Room having lunch with her son. Katherine was enjoying the bacon-wrapped scallops and her son was having a tuna sandwich, toasted on white with a side of fries.

The Senate majority leader was at a table behind them and the head of the Armed Services Committee was eating a cheeseburger one table over. Heady stuff, but if Kate Sinclair had her way it was going to get a lot better on 8 November next year, the date of the next federal election.

Katherine was adorned in a red Nancy Reagan dress, her white hair done in a sprayed and brittle-looking perm. She looked like a once-beautiful, dried-up Palm Beach matriarch, which was exactly what she was. Her son was dressed like a senator: dark chalk-stripe suit, dark Florsheims, white shirt with gold and cobalt blue presidential cuff-links given to him by G.W. himself to commemorate his Senate appointment, and a burgundy and silver Phillips Exeter Academy Alumni tie.

'There's nothing to discuss, Richard. The immigration bill is key to your election.'

'The Latino vote in California was one of the keys to Obama being elected; I'll lose it if I vote for a bill that requires all Mexicans to register with Homeland Security and carry a special photo ID card. It's like putting yellow stars on Jews.'

'It will play in every state in the union except California. It will win you back all the Bush states that McCain lost. It will also show that you can stand firm for the principles that made this country what it is.'

'Your principles, Mother.'

'Who cares whose principles they are? They've worked in the past and they'll work now. The country's a mess; you can clean it up and the first step is to throw out the trash.'

'It won't do too much for my status in the party,' said the handsome forty-something senator. He took a bite out of the oozing sandwich and put it down on his plate again. He chewed and sighed simultaneously. Kate Sinclair looked at her son and wished he had a little more spine. On the other hand, she knew where the soft side of his nature came from; growing up as Angus Sinclair's only son and in the ambassador's long shadow hadn't been easy. Most of Richard Sinclair's life had been ordained without him having any choice in the matter. Schools: Exeter and Yale. Discipline: law. Career: public service, followed by a strategic and well-thought-out jump to the Senate. Next logical step: a run at the White House. It had been Angus Sinclair's plan even before his son's birth, the banner eagerly taken up by Katherine upon her husband's death.

'To hell with the party,' the aging woman said at last. 'You have real power on your side.'

'You mean your so-called friends in high places?' Senator Sinclair said, his lip curling. He knew exactly what his mother was talking about.

'Your friends, too,' answered Katherine. 'They've helped you along the way, helped pave the road to your success.'

'You mean they paid for it,' said the senator. 'Which makes me beholden to them, right?'

'They only want what's best for the country,' said Katherine. She sliced a scallop in half with her knife, added a daub of creamed spinach and popped the morsel neatly between her thin lips. She chewed without appearing to move her jaw, a trick she'd learned at Miss Porter's School in Framingham many years before.

'That's what Hitler told the Poles just before he invaded,' her son answered sourly. He took another bite of his toasted tuna.

'Don't be irritating,' snapped his mother. 'You know exactly what I'm talking about and who. There's no choice in the matter. You are the next in line; simple history makes you heir if nothing else. You'll be the de facto head of the order and all its resources. Electing you president will be easy after that.'

'You really believe Rex Deus still has that kind of power?' Senator Sinclair scoffed, popping a French fry into his mouth. He chewed.

'I know they do,' his mother answered. 'And you know it, too.'

She was right, of course. The senator let out a long breath. Rex Deus and his place in it had been part of his life for as long as he could remember. Rex Deus, once also known as the

Desposyni, supposedly the bloodline of Jesus Christ through Mary, his mother, leading all the way to the Merovingian royal families of Europe, was historical fact, at least insofar as its historical existence was concerned.

At one time the Desposyni had been regarded as the aristocracy of the early Church, but over the centuries Rex Deus had become an underground secret society with money and power at its core. Like the Masons, Rex Deus was attractive to the early colonizers of America, especially during the prerevolutionary 1700s, and there were as many Rex Deus signers of the Declaration of Independence as there were Freemasons, including, among others, Benjamin Franklin, of whom Katherine Sinclair was a direct descendant, and Robert Payne, an ancestor of Angus Sinclair.

By 1776 the battle lines had been clearly drawn; American diplomacy with their colonial masters was at an impasse. It was clear that the British would eventually ban slavery, if for no other reason than stopping the growth of the American cotton industry. Added to this was the tax imposed on the colonists by the crown to pay for the French and Indian War, plus the increased prices for manufactured goods imported into the colonies.

The Masons and the members of Rex Deus were either wealthy landowners or equally wealthy merchants, and it was no coincidence that a third of the signers of the Declaration were slave owners. The Continental Congress and the Declaration of Independence were established to fuel an American financial revolution just as much as a political one. Then, as now, it had been all about wealth and power.

'There are other people who want to be elected head of the order,' said Senator Sinclair. 'It's not as though I'm the only one.'

'The Magdalene Conclave is in less than two weeks,' insisted Katherine, her voice low as she leaned across the table. 'We *will* win the election and you *will* become the new head of the order.'

Senator Sinclair sighed; he'd seen his mother in this mood before. He remembered an embarrassing incident at basketball tryouts that had made him the punch line of a hundred jokes at Exeter. He sighed again and fingered his alumni tie. It was remarkable how easy it was for his mother to get under his skin.

'Why in God's name is this so important to you, Mother? Don't you think I can become president on my own?'

'Not without the help of the order, dear. With the order at our backs we can get the best of everything; we can bring the whole world over to our way of thinking. The order has unlimited resources; with you at the head we would be unbeatable.'

'I'm not even sure I want to run, let alone win,' said the senator, feeling the tuna sandwich making its mayonnaise-heavy way through his digestive system.

'Of course you want to be president, Richard,' said his mother, looking up and staring around the lavishly decorated dining room. 'Everyone wants to become president of the United States. It's the fulfillment of a lifetime dream. It was your father's dream. And mine.'

Not my dream, thought Richard Sinclair.

'Yes, Mother,' he said.

'Good,' said Katherine. 'That's settled then. Let's have dessert, shall we? Perhaps the peach cobbler with a little ice cream?'

'Yes, Mother.'

21

They reached Mull shortly after one thirty in the afternoon, ditched the boat and managed to find a taxi in Fionnphort to take them to Tobermory and the little seaplane port on the bay. From there they took a Cessna Caravan to Glasgow and managed to catch a direct flight via Air Transat to Pearson International in Toronto.

By that evening, hungry and a little tired, they were half a world away from the sacred Isle of Iona and booking themselves into the Royal York, a twenty-eight-storey chateau-style edifice from the twenties with more than a thousand rooms and its own apiary capable of producing seven hundred pounds of honey a year, or so said the brochure.

Once upon a time it had been the largest hotel in the British Empire and came by its 'royal' name honestly, having hosted three generations of the Royal Family on a number of occasions, from the Duke of Windsor to Princess Diana, with a few proper kings and queens in between.

The hotel also had the advantage of being directly across the street from Toronto's old Union Station, a monstrous granite leftover from the Grand Central era that looked more like the British Museum than the British Museum did. There were trains departing for Montreal throughout the day and an evening overnight train to Halifax.

Despite the paranoid 'ultra-surveillance' movies loved by Hollywood, Holliday knew that in reality you didn't retask satellites to look for people like them in places like Toronto, and tracking credit cards wasn't as simple as it looked for Jason Bourne and his ilk. Holliday gave them at least a couple of days' grace before whoever was tracking them got their bureaucratic ducks in a row. Taking the train would confuse things even more, especially if they paid for their tickets in cash. Before that, however, Holliday had an old friend to see.

Steven Braintree, a professor of medieval history at the University of Toronto, had an office on the top floor of a neo-Corinthian building at the corner of Bloor Street and Avenue Road that looked more like an old-fashioned bank or insurance company than a university faculty building.

Appropriately enough, the Royal Ontario Museum was located directly across the street. The Center for Medieval Studies building was one block west of the exact center of the city at Yonge and Bloor, the division of east and west, uptown and down.

Braintree's office was a free-form collection of stacks of books, scatterings of files and snowstorms of paper littered over every flat surface in the twelve-by-twelve room, filling sagging bookcases, overflowing from filing cabinets and seeping out of cardboard boxes on the floor. There was a plastic model of a knight in armor on the windowsill beside a dying aspidistra on the radiator with a single drooping purple flower. The flower still had its tag from the nursery and the knight's shield had been replaced by a Quidi Vidi beer bottle cap from the Newfoundland microbrewery of the same name.

The office was under the eaves of the old stone building and without air-conditioning. At this time of the year Toronto was usually as hot as New York. The grimy windows were glued shut with a hundred-odd years' worth of paint and a solid Scots-Presbyterian regard for keeping heat in over the winter.

Braintree was just about as wilted as the aspidistra on his radiator. He was wearing jeans and a *Chaucer is my Homeboy* T-shirt. His long dark hair was lank and stringy from the heat, with a few more streaks of gray since Holliday had last seen the man. Sitting at his desk, the professor stared owlishly at Holliday from behind a fashionable pair of dark plastic-framed glasses, his hands tented under his frowning mouth as he listened to the tale of Jean de Saint-Clair and the Blessed Juliana.

'The poem is certainly interesting,' he murmured. 'As you know, medieval codes and cryptography are something of a specialty with me.'

'You think it's a code?' Meg asked.

'It's awkward enough to be one,' said Braintree, glancing at the red-haired nun. 'One of the ways you can tell an old-fashioned code is through the awkwardness of its construction. The key words *have* to be there even though they don't really fit.'

'Such as?' Holliday asked.

'It's mostly in the second verse,' replied the young professor. He repeated the second stanza of the prayer aloud, emphasizing what he felt were the key words:

'Save us from Satan's *royal* vengeance once

more / And give us Mary's holy wings to fly / Us to the farther *sable* shore / Then we shall keep thy treasures safe / In Arcadia's *pale enclosing arms* once more.' He shook his head. 'It's just not right.' He turned away and started rummaging through a toppling pile of books on the floor behind him.

'What do you mean?' Meg urged. 'It's just not right?'

'According to you this was written in the early thirteen hundreds. About the time of the Lay of Havelock the Dane.'

'Who?' Meg asked.

'What,' corrected Braintree. He pounced on a thin book bound in pale brown buckram. 'Aha!' he said. 'The Clarendon Press edition, 1910. Quite valuable. Thought I'd misplaced it.'

'What?' Holliday said.

'Exactly,' said Braintree. 'I thought I said that already. The Lay is a *what* not a *who*.'

'*What* does it have to do with our prayer?' Meg asked, frustrated.

'As I said, it's awkwardly constructed. Poetry, songs, prayers, verse of any kind was almost always written in eight-syllable rhymed couplets, like the Lay of Havelock the Dane, or Chaucer.' He grinned, sticking out his chest, and recited,

'*Bot I haf grete ferly that I fynd no man / Dat has written in story how Havelock his lond wan.*'

'Easy for you to say,' Holliday said and laughed. Middle English had never really been his thing.

'It's about a Danish prince who settles in the town of Grimsby in England – *his lond wan*, so to speak. Shakespeare's source for Hamlet.' Braintree cleared his throat. 'The point is your Jean de Saint-Clair and this Blessed Juliana either didn't write your prayer at all or wrote it for purposes other than prayer.'

'The original was in French,' said Holliday.

'Doesn't matter,' said Braintree. 'Conventions in French poetry at the time were identical – rhymed couplets were the only way to go. If they actually meant it to be a proper prayer, that's the way it would have been written.

'And as I said before, some of the word associations are strained – "Satan" and "royal" would never be used together unless there was some second meaning, as you suggested. Same with the farther *sable* shore. Sable is redundant; in French it means sand, all shores are sandy, at least in poetic terms.

'There had to be a reason for its use. The same goes for Arcadia's *pale enclosing arms*. Arcadia was a paradise, a place where anything grew. It was early propaganda to get people to uproot themselves and travel to the so-called *farther shore* to colonize the New World. *Pale enclosing arms* doesn't sound particularly inviting.'

'So what does the prayer refer to?' Meg asked.

'Nova Scotia,' said Holliday. 'Arcadia.'

'Check out a map. Nova Scotia looks like a lobster that's missing a claw. No pale enclosing arms.' Braintree paused, suddenly struck by a thought. 'But there *is* a place that fulfills all the criteria. In fact, it's perfect. If Jean de Saint-Clair and this Venetian ship of his were crossing the Atlantic to the farther shore, they'd be almost certain to at least go by it, if not actually run into it. It's got pale enclosing arms, that's for sure.'

'Where is it?' Meg asked.

Braintree pushed away a pile of papers on his desk, revealing a black-cased Hewlett-Packard laptop. He hit a few keys then peered myopically at the screen, pushing his glasses down low on to his nose and looking over them.

'Forty-three degrees ninety-five minutes north by fifty-nine degrees ninety-one minutes west,' he said. 'Often referred to as the Graveyard of the Atlantic. At least three hundred and fifty shipwrecks since 1583. That's a lot of firewood, kids. A thirty-mile-long sandbar shaped like a sickle moon right in the middle of nowhere. Sable Island.'

Located approximately a hundred miles off the coast of Nova Scotia, Sable Island was a long, curving, low-lying arc of sand shaped very much like a compound bow, its center thicker than the two flared ends. The enormous spit was perched within a mile or two of the edge of the continental shelf and was right in the middle of the whirling vortex of currents, tides and winds where the Labrador Current met the Gulf Stream head-on.

The island was on the exact track of the first trade routes to the Atlantic Coast and the Caribbean, on the edge of the Grand Banks, where Basque fishermen had come to fish five hundred years before. The island had probably been first discovered by Eric the Red in the early eleventh century.

It was also the first landfall of major storms, fog banks, hurricanes and rogue waves as they approached the North American continent, the furious winds, currents and tides altering its shape as the years went by.

In modern times it had become the focus of oil exploration, and one failed rig had been established on the island years before. Several other working rigs were located nearby. The island's only permanent residents were a team of four government workers who maintained the automatic lighthouses located at either end of the sandbar and also cared for the feral ponies that seemed to thrive there.

The only other occupant was a lone researcher who lived in a makeshift shack and studied the strange ecology of the island. Visitation was banned without a permit and the only way on or off the island was via a special soft-tired small plane that landed on the beach. Any unauthorized approach resulted in a fine.

The few people who did visit were usually ecotourists there to see the feral horses on tours organized by the Sable Island Trust. It didn't quite fit the description of a desert island since there were several brackish ponds and small lakes, the largest being Lake Wallace close to the center of the sandbar. Without the fresh water, the ponies, about four hundred of them, would have been unable to survive.

Although no one was quite sure of the horses'

origins, the best historical guess was that they were the result of the Great Expulsion of Acadians in the early seventeen hundreds. The horses were booty, their transportation to Sable Island organized by Thomas Hancock, uncle to the much more famous John Hancock, signer of the Declaration of Independence, a fact that seemed to interest Meg a great deal.

'We have to go,' said Meg urgently. 'As soon as possible. The ark is there, I know it.'

'Hold on for a minute. We're not running a race,' said Holliday.

'You'll have to sneak in,' warned Braintree. 'You could land in jail.'

'We're past that, I'm afraid,' said Holliday.

'It *is* intriguing,' mused Braintree, sitting back in his chair and putting his feet up on a rickety stack of books. 'The True Ark is one of those juicy medieval urban legends that probably has at least its big toe based in fact. Maybe more.'

'It's quite real,' said Meg firmly.

'So is the Shroud of Turin,' Braintree said and smiled, 'except it's a fake along with all those bits and pieces of the True Cross and miraculous vials of the True Blood you can find in cathedrals all over the world. If you put it all together the cross would have been as big as a skyscraper and Christ would have bled enough to fill a supertanker.'

'You're not a believer, are you?' Meg said.

'I'm a medieval scholar,' Braintree said with a shrug. 'I believe in history and what it can teach us.'

'You don't believe in God?'

'I didn't say that.'

'You don't believe that the word of God is true as it is written.'

'I've never seen anything God wrote,' Braintree said and smiled, obviously enjoying the argument. It was only irritating Holliday. Somehow tracking down an old Templar knight had taken him from the frying pan into some sort of murderous fire yet again, and now his companion was having a theological debate. On top of everything else, he wasn't sure he liked the slightly fanatical tone in Sister Meg's voice, or the true believer's gleam in her eye. He'd seen the same look coming from Taliban suicide bombers in Afghanistan and Hutu machete killers in Rwanda.

'You don't believe that the Gospels are the word of God?'

'They might be somebody's interpretation of

what that somebody thought was the word of God, but that's as far as I'd go.'

'And isn't history just "interpretation," as you call it?'

'Of course,' Braintree said and laughed. 'In real terms neither the past nor the future exists, only the single ever-changing instant of the immediate present, so everything is open to interpretation.'

'There's that word again,' said Sister Meg, as though she'd scored some sort of point. 'Interpretation.'

'Why are we having this discussion at all?' Holliday said finally, standing up.

'The True Ark is real,' said Meg firmly, almost as though she was trying to convince herself. 'It exists! The Grail, the Crown, the Shroud and the Ring.'

'There's only one way to find out for sure,' said Holliday. 'Let's go and look for the damn thing and leave poor Professor Braintree to his Chaucer.'

'Let me know how it all turns out,' said the long-haired man as they said their good-byes. 'Nothing I like better than being proven wrong.'

They took the old cage elevator down to the

main floor and went through the heavy oak doors and into the bright sunlight. They went down the wide granite steps to the sidewalk.

Holliday saw the setup in a split second and knew there was absolutely nothing they could do about it. Two men at the corner walking toward them, both dressed in dark suits, dark shoes and dark glasses. Two more just like the first pair coming from the other direction.

At the curb a dark blue Econoline blocked their way to the street, a man standing at the open sliding door with his hand tucked into the pocket of a windbreaker far too warm for the sunny summer weather. A man in jogger's clothes coming down the steps behind them, hand in a fanny pack in front of him and what looked like an iPod earbud in one ear but was most likely a radio. He came up behind them fast, blocking their way back.

'Into the truck, Colonel Holliday. You and the woman. Any arguments, any conversation at all and I'll Taser the hell out of you. Got it?'

'Got it,' said Holliday.

The man behind them herded Holliday and Meg toward the open door of the Econoline. The man standing beside the sliding door took a

step to the side. Six men and a truck, but no obvious show of official muscle. One of those quiet
hijackings nobody noticed until they saw it on
the news the next day.

Three more steps and it would be too late.
Who were they? Not cops. Cops were never this
quiet about their work. The Blackhawk people?
Maybe, but they were taking one hell of a risk.
Canada might be America's best friend, but it
was still a foreign country and it wouldn't take
kindly to paramilitaries operating on sovereign
soil.

'What do we do?' Meg whispered, obviously
frightened.

'We do what we're told,' said Holliday. 'We get
into the truck.'

Which was exactly what they did.

22

'Hello? Is anybody there?' Meg's voice came out of the darkness, croaking and dry from whatever drug they'd been given after getting into the van.

'I'm here,' answered Holliday. His voice was just as scratchy as hers. He had a splitting headache and his tongue was glued to the roof of his mouth. The room was pitch dark. He had no idea how much time had passed since they'd been picked up off the downtown Toronto street.

The back of the van had been dark and smelled of gasoline. Somebody had been waiting for them inside, and the man standing at the door had climbed in after them. They'd each been given a shot. Holliday had fought it off for long enough to hear voices speaking and somebody say, 'Four-oh-one to four hundred and then north.' Directions obviously, but he had no idea where to. Presumably somewhere north of the city.

'Doc?' Meg's froggy voice again.

'I'm here.'

'Where are we?' There was a rattling sound. Holliday tried to move his arms and heard the scrape of metal on metal. He was handcuffed to a bed. From the sound of her voice Meg was about ten feet away.

'Are you handcuffed to a bed?'

'Yes, I think so,' she responded, her voice clearing a little.

Holliday inhaled. Cedar, without a doubt, and lots of it. Overhead, forming vaguely out of the darkness, he could see roof beams. Outside there was a distant sound. Slapping water. A high-pitched whine. A boat? Water-skiing?

'I think we're on a lake or a river somewhere,' said Holliday. 'Maybe a cottage. I can hear a motorboat.'

There was a pause and then Meg's voice again. 'I can hear it, too.'

Holliday turned his head left and right. To the left there was a faint, square outline of light. A boarded-up window perhaps. To the right, almost out of his line of sight, was a bright red dot of light. He tried to move his arms. Nothing but the metal sound and the harsh pinch of his wrists against steel. These weren't joke-shop cuffs – they were the real thing; the only way out was going to be a key. Even so, somebody was being very careful – two sets of handcuffs per person. The same somebody who'd cuffed him knew his record. He could have done a lot of damage with even one free hand.

Holliday kept listening. The motorboat sounds faded. He could hear wind blowing in trees. The softer rustling note you got with evergreens. No traffic noises. They were definitely off the beaten track.

A door opened and the room was flooded with daylight. Ten by twelve up under the rafters, wood plank floors and two single iron beds with ticking covers on thin mattresses. A baby minder on a night table, the source of the red light in the darkness. A man stepped into the room, alerted by their voices – the one in the jogging clothes, except now he was wearing denim shorts and a T-shirt that read *Pizza in twenty minutes or a free lap dance. Now can I get into Canada?* on the front. Some sort of inside joke.

'Funny, I guess,' said Holliday, reading the shirt as the man took off one set of handcuffs.

'Listen up,' answered the man in the T-shirt. 'Get out of the other cuffs, get your friend out of hers and come downstairs. Breakfast in fifteen.

There's a bathroom at the top of the stairs if you have to go.' He tossed a small plastic key tag on to Holliday's chest. The man's accent was as flat and Midwestern as a Kansas cornfield.

Breakfast. So at least a day had passed. Holliday picked up the key tag and got to work on his other hand.

The main floor of the cottage was large and lavish. Holliday had seen places like it in Vermont and Connecticut; big family summer homes without families anymore, put on the weekly or monthly rental market to pay their way. The kitchen was immense, one wall of windows looking down on to a broad tree-lined lake. A set of steps from a large back deck led down to a dock. There was an old wooden Chris-Craft speedboat tied up, the kind that cost as much as a Bentley these days. The cottage appeared to be perched on a rocky outcropping surrounded by mature cedars.

A man was at work at a butcher block cutting table between the stove and a large maple kitchen table. The chairs were well polished and original pine arrowbacks. Pricey antiques popular in the sixties or thereabouts. The table was set for three, two on one side, the third directly across from the other two. There were tall glasses of freshly squeezed orange juice at each place setting. In the center of the table was a complete coffee service and a large sterling silver toast rack already filled with thick slices, half buttered, half dry. There was nobody else in the room but there was a man in a suit sitting on an Adirondack chair on the deck. He had a short-stocked MAG-7 shotgun in his lap. Still no clue to the nationality of their abductors; the MAG-7 was made in South Africa.

The man at the butcher block was chopping vegetables by hand. Green peppers, onions and celery. There was already a mound of diced ham and a pile of grated cheese off to one side. The man was wearing a blue-and-white-striped apron of the kind once seen on greengrocers in London's Covent Garden. The man was in his fifties, wearing horn-rimmed glasses and with a graying military haircut. Under the apron he was wearing a white shirt with the sleeves rolled up.

'The secret of a perfect breakfast is timing,' the man said. The voice was completely accentless, some kind of mid-Atlantic melding of English and American. The man had either been born in the States and educated in England or the reverse; it was impossible to tell which. Holliday found the voice oddly sinister, almost machine-like. 'You've got to have everything set to go in perfect order.'

As if to demonstrate his rule, the man scooped up ingredients from the butcher block on the end of a spatula and tipped them one by one into a large cast iron frying pan on the stove behind him. He seemed to have several other pans on the go. Even from the back his movements were quick and deft. He liked cooking and he was good at it.

'Do sit down, Colonel,' the man said, his back to Holliday. Meg came down the stairs and stepped into the kitchen, her face scrubbed but still bleary-eyed. She was rubbing a line of chafed skin on one wrist. The cuffs. A reminder; he might be dressed in an apron but the man at the stove was still their kidnapper and jailer. Holliday sat down, poured himself a cup of coffee and waited. Sister Meg followed suit. The cups holding the coffee were Kutani Crane pattern.

The man in the apron transferred food on to plates lined up on the counter beside the stove and carried them to the table, two on one arm, a third in his other hand. He laid them down as smoothly as an experienced waiter. Perfectly turned half moons of omelet, three rashers of bacon and a generous pile of pepper-and-onion-cooked home fries on the side. The man slipped the apron over his head, hung it over the back of his chair and sat down. He poured himself a cup of coffee, added cream and smiled at his guests, fork poised over his omelet.

'Eat up,' he said pleasantly in that strange, flat voice. 'Before it gets cold.' He carved off a precise piece of omelet and popped it delicately into his mouth. Holliday followed suit and so did Meg. The omelet was excellent, perfectly cooked. The coffee was dark and strong without being bitter. Pressed, not dripped.

'You know who we are, obviously,' said Holliday. 'Who are you?'

'Are you enjoying your breakfast?'

'It's fine. Who are you?'

'My name is Quince, like the jelly. Nathan Quince.' The man smiled. 'I'm sure my mother had a fantasy that I'd grow up to be a gay English professor at a little college in some place like Nebraska. Perhaps write a book of poetry or two. Something low-stress. Alas, her dream hasn't come true.'

'So what are you then?' Holliday went on, eating his omelet. 'If you're not a poet from Nebraska?'

'I'm a facilitator. I make things happen. I give history a nudge now and again, that's all. You're a historian. I'm sure you can see the value in that.'

'And we're in the way of a nudge, is that it?'

'Not necessarily,' said Quince. He plucked a slice of toast from the rack and tore it in half. He loaded a piece of omelet on to one of the toast halves and put it in his mouth. He chewed, looking across the table at Holliday. He swallowed and spoke again. 'We're just keeping an eye on you.'

'Is that why you kidnapped us?'

'It's a stormy world out there, Colonel Holliday. Sometimes it's best to come in out of the rain.'

'I didn't feel any rain.'

'You would have,' said Quince. 'There are a great many parties interested in your little quest.'

'Including you.'

'Including us,' Quince said and nodded. He took a sip of coffee. Outside on the lake the water-skiing boat was back.

'So who is us?'

'An interested party.'

'One of the three-letter boys, CIA, DEA, NSA, or one of the new crop that's sprung up over the past ten years?'

'Not federal at all,' said Quince. 'The world has changed. Think globally. Corporately.'

'You're private then, whoever you are.'

'Contract employees. As I said, facilitators. Problems arise; we solve them.'

'Thugs,' said Holliday, sipping his coffee.

'Certainly,' said Quince pleasantly. 'If thugs are necessary.'

'But why us?' Holliday asked.

'According to my information you and the good sister are looking for something called the True Ark. To some people this relic has certain symbolic value well in excess of its monetary worth. It is our task to ensure that this True Ark – if it exists at all – does not fall into the wrong hands.'

'What constitutes the wrong hands?' Holliday asked.

'Any hands other than my client's.'

'And who is your client?'

'I can't say. Security reasons.'

'Logjam,' Holliday said. He picked up a piece

of toast and started spreading it with preserves from a little pot beside the toast rack. The pot had a small paper label: *Moira's Plum Jam*. He bit into the toast. Moira was to be congratulated.

'Why kidnap us?' Meg said, speaking for the first time.

'To my sure knowledge you have five separate police agencies and the Vatican Intelligence Service looking for you. You've left a litter of bodies in your wake. We're just trying to differentiate ourselves from the crowd, so to speak. Our sources tell us that your friends from the Vatican were getting very close. We decided to remove you from the playing field for a while. For your own safety and for the safety of your undertaking.'

'So you're on our side?' Holliday asked.

'Until I'm told differently by my client.'

'So for you it's about the job. No loyalties to anyone. It's all about the money.'

'Don't be naïve, Colonel. It's *always* all about the money. Wars are fought for all sorts of reasons by all sorts of people, but inevitably it is the people who sell the warriors their bullets who get rich. Life, Colonel Holliday, is a retail event, just like Christmas.'

The water-skiing boat was visible now, no

more than fifty feet off the dock below them. The skis of the man being towed behind the boat slapped the water noisily and the roar of a pair of big twin engines was enough to drown out conversation at the kitchen table. Everyone looked toward the lake, including the guard on the deck. There were four people in the speeding towboat, all wearing black life jackets. Directly in front of the dock the man being towed suddenly let go of the towrope and the boat throttled back to almost nothing. The four men on the boat turned toward the shore.

Who the hell wore *black* life jackets?

23

Not life jackets. Bulletproof vests.

'Get down!' Holliday yelled. He grabbed Meg by the arm and dragged her off the chair and on to the floor. The big window looking out on to the lake shattered, and the kitchen erupted in a hail of silent lead. The man on the deck was torn to ribbons by automatic fire even before he had a chance to stand up.

More fire came from the trees around the cottage. The water-ski boat had just been a distraction. They were coming from all sides. Quince was on the floor, facedown, arms spread, his right forefinger still hooked into the delicate handle of the ornate china cup he'd been drinking his coffee from. Most of the back of his head was missing. Moira's plum jam was everywhere. The gunfire muffled by silencers continued in an unbroken stream.

'Who's shooting at us!?' Meg screamed.

'Quince's competition!' Holliday yelled back.

Still hanging on to Meg's arm, he crabbed across the floor, dragging Meg along. He huddled under the stairs. It was probably the safest place in the house. They found their knapsacks tossed into the little alcove, probably searched while they were knocked out then cast aside.

'What are we going to do?' Meg asked. Her voice was a frightened panting sound. Holliday was in the groove. This was combat. Familiar territory. The rule book said always attack from the higher ground, but going up on to the second floor of the cottage would be suicide. The rule book also said that with insurmountable odds the best option was to make an orderly withdrawal – army talk for retreat. But they were in George Armstrong Custer territory now, surrounded on all sides.

'Grab your pack and put it on,' instructed Holliday, more to keep her occupied than anything else. He needed to think and she was on the verge of losing it, which wouldn't do anyone any good.

Meg lifted her pack off the floor and slipped it on while Holliday peeked around the corner of the stairway. The guard outside was bleeding all over the Adirondack chair and the men in the black life jackets were coming up the steps. Six of them, armed with various brands of riot guns and automatic weapons. They had thirty seconds at the outside.

Holliday felt Meg tugging at his sleeve. He turned to her, irritated.

'Not now!'

'Look,' she insisted. She'd swept his knapsack aside. Outlined on the floor he could see a trap-door or a hatch. It made sense. A crawl space. The cottage was built on a slab of bedrock so all the plumbing would be under the floor. There'd have to be some way of getting at it for maintenance. Not that it mattered. It was the only option now.

Holliday shrugged on his own pack and pulled on the brass ring inset into the floor. The hatch pulled upward, revealing three roughly made steps. He smelled stone and cedar. Gunfire exploded around them, chewing into the wood of the stairs behind them. Windows exploded and fist-sized holes appeared in the walls. Even silenced, that much ordnance was making a racket outside. Eventually someone was going to call 911, but it would almost certainly be too little, too late; a myopic summertime cottage cop with *maybe* a .38 on his hip.

'I'll go first,' said Holliday.

Meg nodded, eyes like saucers, wincing and jerking as each bullet struck the walls around them. He went down the steps. There was barely enough room between the floor joists and the ground to duckwalk forward.

He looked around. It was impossible to move to the back of the cottage; the rock sloped away toward the deck and the crawl space narrowed to barely a foot-high crack. Most of the fire seemed to be coming from the steps leading down to the dock.

He looked back over his shoulder. Meg was right behind him. Under the floor the ground was covered in old rotting construction litter and decaying leaves. There were spiders above them and dark slithering things below. It occurred to Holliday that the best horror movies came out of basements and attics. Most people didn't have the slightest idea of what was going on within the walls of their own houses. Domestic nightmares.

Holliday reached the edge of the cottage and paused, peering out into the open. Sun dappled down. There was about a thirty-foot clearing between the side of the cottage and the wall of surrounding trees. As he knelt, looking outward, someone emerged from the tree line in full combat fatigues and a dark green balaclava. The man's hands were covered with Camtech camouflage makeup. He was carrying an Atchisson AA-12 assault shotgun with a twenty-round drum magazine and a Glock or something similar in a waist holster.

The Atchisson had been developed for close-quarters combat. It fired a Magnum shell that could kill a Kodiak bear or an elephant. It could blow a man in half from thirty yards away and drill a through-and-through hole in the cottage from one side to the other.

The man with the shotgun paused for a split second at the edge of the trees and then raced forward. Ten points off in a tactical exercise exam at West Point, Holliday thought. He should have approached his target in a crouch. If he had, he might have seen Holliday lurking in the shadowed crawl space. The man in the camo gear ran forward, then paused next to the house. From the position of his feet Holliday guessed he was going to sidestep along the wall to a window. The feet were encased in sand-colored standard-issue two-pound Belleville combat boots.

Barely thinking about what he was doing, Holliday reached out with both hands, grabbed the man's ankles and pulled as hard as he could. Caught completely off guard, the soldier toppled backward, his head smacking into the rock and the shotgun flying out of his hands. Holliday heaved on the man's feet hard and dragged him under the cottage. The dazed man struggled but Holliday jammed his elbow hard into the man's windpipe and leaned on it with his full weight. Something in the soldier's throat cracked. He made a choking, gurgling sound and then stopped moving, blood streaming from his mouth.

Holliday hauled the body even farther under the cottage and stripped the soldier of his sidearm and an ammo pocket full of 9mm magazines. Two more drums for the Atchisson in a canvas pouch over his shoulder. Holliday slipped the pouch off and put the strap over his own head.

There was also a sheathed Ek Commando knife, like the one Holliday had used in the Rangers. Holliday took the weapon and slipped it under the gun belt. Easing the body to one side, he edged forward and peered out into the sunlight.

Somebody blew a whistle. A split second later there were explosions from inside the cottage: flash-bang stun grenades of the type used in hostage situations. Suddenly the air was filled with yelling voices and smashing wood. There was more gunfire, this time from above. Quince's people making a last stand on the upper floor. This was the push.

Holliday heard booted feet tramping hard as the assault team pounded across the deck at the side of the cottage facing the lake. This was the moment – all the attention was going to be inward; no one would be watching the perimeter. Holliday grabbed Meg by the wrist and dragged her forward as he scuttled out from under the cottage.

'Keep your head down and follow me.' He rushed across the thirty-foot opening between the cottage and the trees. A two-second count to the shotgun, which he scooped up, and another three seconds to the woods. He dropped to the ground, turning back the way he'd come. Meg dropped down beside him. He peered toward the cottage.

Smoke was billowing out of the windows on both floors, or maybe it was tear gas. There was intermittent gunfire and then silence. Holliday could hear the sounds of the assault team clearing each room. He edged backward, keeping his eyes on the cottage while moving deeper into the trees, Sister Meg following suit. Finally he stood. They were in full cover now, safe for the moment. He pulled the slide bolt on the top side of the shotgun. A shell popped out on to the ground. Bright green. A fragmentation round, a room cleaner.

'Come on,' he whispered harshly, easing backward, deeper into the shadows.

'Where are we going?' Meg asked.

'Away,' said Holliday.

They made a long arc through the trees, moving steadily downward, picking their way through the cedars and the big slabs of granite, moving downward toward the rocky shore below. A minute or two later they reached the edge of the trees at the shoreline and Holliday realized just how big the lake really was. He could just see the other side, a vague sense of a hazy farther shore. Sailboats skittered in the distance, sails bright in the hot sun. There were the faint sounds of voices calling across the water and the mosquito buzz of invisible motorboats.

He looked to the left. He was standing on a shallow cliff edge about twenty feet above the actual water. The cottage was clearly quite isolated – there was no other dock in sight. No wonder the cavalry hadn't arrived. He looked right. The Quince cottage dock was fifty yards away jutting out into the crystal-clear lake. He could see the water-ski towboat tied up and the old runabout on the other side.

The towboat looked like an old Bayliner, a little battered but perfect for what these guys had needed: room to cram at least half a dozen men in the forward cabin and another half dozen on deck with the twin outboards to provide the power. There was only one person visible – a man in a black wet suit – the decoy water skier. Holliday glanced out over the water. Where were they? He tried to remember his high school geography. They'd had at least one lecture on the Great Lakes.

Toronto was on Lake Ontario, and his uncle's place in upstate New York was on Lake Erie. So what was north of Toronto that you could see across? Some vague bell rang in his head – the abolition of slavery even before the British Empire. Then he had it, Lake Simcoe, one of the biggest freshwater lakes in the world. It didn't matter. What mattered was getting the guy in the wet suit off the boat before his friends came back.

'Stay here,' he whispered to Meg. She nodded

silently, shrinking back into the trees. 'When you hear shots, come running. No hesitation. You either make it snappy or I leave you here.'

Holliday slipped forward toward the dock, keeping within the band of shadows at the tree line, choosing his steps, careful to keep from treading on a noisy branch or a clattering patch of gravel. He reached a spot perhaps ten feet above the moored towboat and paused.

The water skier was alert, focused on the steps leading up to the cottage. He was seated at the controls of the boat, the door to the forward cabin low and to his left. One hand was on the wheel and the other held a blocky handgun. Another Glock.

The cottage at the head of the steps was silent. He didn't have a lot of time. He crouched down, put the AA-12 on to the soft ground, then opened the holster on the Glock he'd taken from the dead soldier under the cottage. He chambered a round and stepped into the light.

Seeing the movement, the man on the boat looked up. No time for fair play. Holliday fired a three-shot tap into the man's chest, toppling him out of the boat and into the water. He stabbed the Glock back into the holster, picked up the shotgun, then skittered down the steep slab of granite to the dock.

He flipped the selector on the shotgun to single shot and put half an earsplitting magazine into the hull of the old Chris-Craft. The fragmentation rounds bit into the varnished stringers, chewing the bottom of the fine old speedboat to splinters. The boat began to sink instantly.

Holliday turned away and undid the lines holding the Bayliner to the dock, dropped down into the towboat and made his way forward to the blood-spattered controls. He twisted the ignition key and the big outboards rumbled to life.

Seeing something out of the corner of his eye, Holliday turned. Sister Meg, pack slapping against her back, came sliding down the granite rock face and half fell, half jumped directly down into the boat, crashing into Holliday and almost knocking him over. There was another flicker of darker movement to the left. Regaining his balance, Holliday lifted the shotgun and fired a blind spray of the lethal rounds toward the stairs, empty shells flinging out of the ejection port in a steady stream, the weapon barking with a sound like the hounds of hell.

Without waiting to see the effect of the fire,

Holliday turned and rammed the twin throttles full forward. The Bayliner leapt away from the dock with a huge rooster tail of spray rising behind. A hundred yards out he risked a look back over his shoulder. The cottage on the rocky rise above the dock was wreathed in smoke and he could see a few dark figures milling around on the dock.

Holliday took a deep breath and let it out slowly, his hand gripping the wheel of the boat, his other hand easing back slightly on the throttles. Another few seconds back there and it would have been too late; they'd made it out just in the nick of time. His stomach was churning as the adrenaline drained out of his system.

He glanced at Meg. She looked remarkably calm as she stood beside him, her green eyes focused on the huge lake's far horizon, as though the hell they'd just left behind them was nothing more than a bad dream, her concentration fixed only on what lay ahead. For the first time since meeting the enigmatic nun it occurred to Holliday that the so-called True Ark she was looking for must have some basis in fact – enough for men to kill. Enough for men to die.

24

Halifax, Nova Scotia, is known for two things: During World War One it was the largest convoy center in North America, and on December 6, 1917, the whole city blew up when the *Mont Blanc*, a French munitions ship, exploded in the harbor, killing two thousand people outright, causing a tidal wave, obliterating buildings for miles around, starting a hundred fires and basically destroying the city. The Halifax Explosion is still rated as the largest non-nuclear explosion ever.

Halifax is also known as the birthplace of English Canada, which is ironic since it was originally called Louisburg and was colonized by the French. At the time Nova Scotia itself was referred to as L'Acadie, or Arcadia, the name eventually becoming simply Acadia. The British, being who they were, decided they wanted what the French had, specifically a deepwater harbor in the New World even better than New York.

They attacked the French colony in an effort

to gain hegemony over all of Canada and kicked out the 'Acadians'; most of the Acadians settled in the coastal states of Maine and New Hampshire, while others returned to France and a hardy few, about three hundred, migrated to the French-speaking areas of Louisiana, becoming the people now known simply as Cajuns.

For Holliday and Meg it had been remarkably easy to get to. After arriving without further incident on the shores of Lake Simcoe at a place called Jackson's Point, they caught a bus back to Toronto, arriving just before noon. Maxing out his credit and debit cards, Holliday gathered enough money for two train tickets to Montreal and ongoing accommodation on the *Ocean Limited*, the through train to the Maritimes.

Nobody seemed to raise an eyebrow at Holliday's use of cash, and no ID display was required. Apparently Homeland Security hadn't arrived in Canada yet and there were no obvious armed security personnel prowling around the echoing old Union Station. The high-speed train out of Toronto was modern and fast, complete with meal and bar cars. They arrived in Montreal with enough time for a little shopping in the underground malls connected to the train station and then boarded the *Ocean* just before it left at six thirty that evening.

The train was surprisingly sophisticated, made up of old Budd Streamliners like the old 20th Century Limited. The dining cars had real table-cloths and linen napkins, and there was even a domed observation car. If he hadn't been a fugitive wanted on two continents the trip might have been a pleasant little adventure. As it was he spent all his time alone in his private roomette trying to figure out just what was really going on. He barely saw Meg except for meals, and they both avoided talking about Quince and the events surrounding their kidnapping.

There was almost no doubt that the men who'd attacked the cottage were more of the mysterious Blackhawk Security bunch, but according to Quince he was just a hired gun as well. But groups like Blackhawk were usually hired by governments, or at the very least by giant multinational corporations. In fact, they were usually *owned* by multinational corporations.

So what multinational was interested in a piece of Middle Ages mythology to the extent that they'd send in people like Quince and his heavies or the Blackhawk people? It just didn't make any sense.

Someone had been on their tail since the bald guy who'd followed them all the way from Mont Saint-Michel to Prague. It was almost as if they knew more about the so-called True Ark than he and Meg did.

He wrestled with the problem all the way across the Canadian provinces of Quebec, New Brunswick and into Nova Scotia, but couldn't figure out a reasonable solution. By the time they arrived in Halifax at three thirty the following afternoon, the only conclusion Holliday had reached was that somewhere along the line he'd overlooked something, the missing puzzle piece that solved the problem.

Halifax itself had left behind much of its maritime past and now concentrated on being a government center and a modern, well-heeled tourist trap complete with menus without prices, obsequious waiters who gave you their first name before they took your order, a variety of city tours in assorted double-decker buses, and even a fleet of Vietnam War Lark amphibians that lumbered across the city and into the waters of the harbor, their aluminum hulls painted with bright green and yellow frogs.

Unfortunately, real frogs would never survive

in the harbor. Eighty-two million gallons of raw sewage was pumped into the water each day due to a malfunctioning water treatment plant, and giant deodorant pucks were now being used to control the rank odor that regularly swept across the revitalized waterfront, complete with its hotels and casinos.

Eventually Holliday and Meg found what they were looking for on the other side of the wide harbor channel in the town of Dartmouth, Halifax's industrial heart and the Atlantic home of the Canadian navy. Dartmouth had always been the rough edge of Halifax, far from maritime society, such as it was. There were no tourist attractions or tony restaurants in Dartmouth, but there were plenty of seafaring men who worked the docks and the navy yards and more than a few waterfront bars to slake their thirst after a long day of work.

The Admiral Benbow was located on a side street halfway up a steep hill that led up from the waterfront at Tuft's Cove, one of a dozen forgotten commercial byways on the Dartmouth waterfront. Once upon a time Tuft's Cove had been a thriving harbor for local lobstermen, but the big companies had long since made small-scale lobstering a marginal profession at best, and with the economy the way it was, it was easier to go on welfare than it was to waste gas and risk your life roaming around on the Atlantic.

Oddly, the Benbow, named after Jim Hawkins's pub in *Treasure Island*, had adopted a cowboy theme, complete with waitresses in spurs, bright yellow hot pants and ten-gallon hats, something called the Gal Corral for line dancing and a bull ride named Old Tex, which was restricted to young ladies with bust sizes exceeding thirty-six inches. Even the food on the bar menu had been westernized. Chili dogs were 'snake bites,' jalapeño fries were 'critter fritters,' and chicken wings were 'wang dang thangs.' According to a prominent sign over the bar, wang dang thangs were complimentary with a pitcher of draft between seven and midnight on Wednesdays. The big, high-ceilinged, onetime net warehouse had been redecorated within an inch of its life to look like the inside of a barn, but the lingering smell of fish was still there. It was early evening and the place was jammed. Big-breasted waitresses in cowboy boots hauled foaming pitchers of beer, Old Tex was going full steam ahead and the Gal Corral was full of lonely, generally plain women line dancing like rows of cowgirl penguins trying to attract a mate. It wasn't a pretty sight.

'I'm not sure I'm comfortable with this,' said Meg as they sat down at the bar. She was dressed in reasonably fashionable jeans and a man's white shirt with the tails out, but the look of disapproval on her face said it all: this was not a woman who spent a lot of time in bars.

'You don't *look* very comfortable with it, either,' said Holliday. 'You'd better lighten up or this isn't going to work.'

'Why do we have to come to a place like this to find a boat?' Meg asked.

A bartender wearing a *Cross the Line Your Ass is Mine* T-shirt with a picture of a mean-looking bull behind a barbed-wire fence on it took their orders; a virgin Caesar for Meg, which seemed to be a uniquely Canadian version of a Bloody Mary that used clam juice instead of tomato juice, and a local Glen Breton straight up for Holliday. Holliday waited for their drinks to arrive before answering the question. Giant speakers suddenly started belting out a bawling rendition of Stompin' Tom Connors's 'Bud the Spud,' a song about a potato trucker.

'We went over it on the train,' said Holliday.

'This Sable Island place is protected. You can't legally make landfall there, so a legitimate hired boat wouldn't take you; you'd get your boat confiscated. But it's almost impossible to land a boat there anyway because of the currents and the tides; that's why anyone who does go to the island flies in.'

'Then we rent a plane.'

'I can't fly. Can you?'

'As a matter of fact, I can,' she said primly. 'Light planes anyway. I got my license when I was a kid. Single engines. My dad owned a Piper Cherokee.'

'When was the last time you flew?'

'A while ago.'

'How long is a while?'

Meg shrugged. 'High school.'

'No, thanks. The planes they use have special soft wheels for landing on the beach. You up for landing on sand?'

'I guess not.'

'So it's a boat.'

'But why here?'

'Because that guy I was talking to at the last place suggested we come here.'

The last place was a hole-in-the-wall called

Buddy's Bar and Grill back in Bedford Basin at the extreme end of the harbor. The owner had been surprisingly specific; after giving Holliday and Meg a once-over he told them that if you ever wanted things moved between point A and point B without government interference, go to the Benbow and wait for Arnie Gallant.

Arnie's nickname was Super Mario, and for good reason; he was squat, dark, broad-shouldered and had a heavy Groucho Marx mustache, just like the character in the video game, and to make the comparison even closer he wore brown workman's coveralls most of the time. Apparently Arnie Gallant loved wang dang thangs more than life itself, and this being Wednesday evening he was almost sure to make an appearance.

Holliday had taken the time to find a book about Sable Island at a bookstore near their hotel in Toronto and he'd read it on board the train to Halifax. The book was called *A Dune Adrift* and chronicled the life and times of the deadly sandbar from its glacial origins to the present.

It was a fascinating story, but it certainly wasn't a pleasant one. The shifting crescent of sand, once a hundred miles long, was located at the center of every dangerous current and wind system in the Atlantic, perched on the edge of the continental shelf, its hidden shallows directly in the path of burgeoning hurricanes and perfect storms blowing in off the Grand Banks and Bermuda, a lurking trap for all sorts of shipping since man first crossed the Atlantic Ocean. A lot of lives and dreams had ended on Sable Island.

The place sounded decidedly unpleasant, and the more Holliday read the less he wanted to go there. If their quest for the True Ark hadn't stirred up such a deadly maelstrom of interest ensnaring him, Holliday would have opted out of the chase long ago. Now it was too late; he'd gone too far and was in too deep to give up. He still wasn't sure he believed in the existence of the ark, but other people – powerful ones – sure as hell did.

'Keith's IPA, my love, and a bucket of thangs.' A man in his late forties or early fifties plopped himself down on the bar stool next to Holliday. He looked like a scaled-down version of a defensive tackle: all shoulders and chest. He had dark curly hair, graying at the temples, a bull neck, big hands and a bushy mustache that was almost a joke. He wore bright red half-glass bifocals and his black eyes twinkled as though he'd just told a particularly dirty joke. His Keith's arrived in a stubby bottle without an accompanying glass and he took a long draw. He put down the bottle with a contented sigh and sucked the foam out of his mustache with his lower lip. He glanced at Holliday.

'You'd be Buddy's Doc,' he said, peering over the funny little glasses.

'How'd you know that?' Holliday smiled.

'The *Pirates of the Caribbean* eye patch is a dead giveaway,' said the man. He took another swig of Keith's. A red plastic basket lined with wax paper and filled with glistening, sauce-covered chicken wings was set down before him. He stripped the meat off one with practiced ease, wiped his mouth with a napkin and washed the chicken wing down with some more beer. He tossed the stripped bones back in the basket. 'You want to rent me and my boat for some illicit purpose, as I understand it,' he said. The strange twanging accent wasn't far off from Stompin' Tom and 'Bud the Spud.'

'Who said anything about illicit?' answered Holliday.

Arnie laughed. By the sound of it he was at least a pack a day man.

'You want a lesson in how not to catch the lobsters that are no longer there and that no one can afford these days, is that it?' Gallant picked up another wing, sucked off the meat and took another slug of beer.

'Maybe we want to go sightseeing,' Holliday said and shrugged. He took a small sip of the single malt. It was good, with a strange butterscotch aftertaste. 'Bud the Spud' came to an end, but Stompin' Tom went on; something that rhymed 'glory' and 'dory.'

'Look. I'm not a cop, you're not a cop, so why don't we cut the bull and get down to business?' Gallant went through his wing routine again.

Holliday stared at Gallant for a moment. The squat little man looked like something out of a Grimm brothers fairy tale. He had to be the real thing.

'We want you to take us to Sable Island.'

'That's against the law,' said Gallant, eyes twinkling merrily. He ate another wing. As far as Holliday could tell the glory-dory song was a fisherman's version of 'Swing Low, Sweet Chariot.'

'Like you said, illicit.'

'Illicit's expensive,' said Gallant.

'I can pay.'

'Why do you want to go to Sable?'

'Is that any of your business?'

'My boat, my business,' Gallant said with a shrug. 'My price.'

'We're looking for something,' broke in Meg. 'Something lost on Sable Island.'

'Buried treasure on Sable Island? Now, that's original. Any particular boat you're looking for? There's about five hundred of them.' He ate another wing. 'They even had one in the 1920s where a ship struck a submerged wreck and was wrecked itself.' He tossed the bones in the basket and took another hit of the honey-colored beer. 'You're crazy. The whole island moves, nothing stays in one place – that's why it's so dangerous.'

'We know where to look,' said Meg.

Holliday glanced at her curiously; this was the first he'd heard of a location. Now what was going on?

'What is it that you're looking for?' Gallant asked.

'A religious relic. Not a treasure really.'

'Not gold doubloons or Blackbeard's pearls or the like, then,' said Gallant, grinning.

'No,' said Meg, her voice serious.

Gallant ate another chicken wing and then

another, thinking, staring at the rows and tiers of bottles behind the bar. Finally he turned to Holliday.

'There's nothing like that on Sable Island,' he said. 'There's a hell of a lot of sand and a few ponies left over from God knows when, but there's no religious relics there. If there had been they'd have been found long ago. There's nothing even faintly religious about Sable. You're talking fairy tales.' He paused. 'But that's your business, not mine. You're playing some sort of game or fulfilling some fantasy or following some treasure map some idgit sold you off the Internet — well, that's fine too, but know this, whoever you are, Sable Island is no joke and it's no fantasy either. It's a serious, dangerous place surrounded by serious, dangerous waters. Go there and you go there at your peril.'

'When can we leave?' Meg said.

25

Joseph Patchin sat at the elegant table in the Domingo Room at the Café Milano in Georgetown, happily working his way through his grilled lobster and heart of palm salad, knowing that it was Kate Sinclair's treat, since she was the one who'd called the meeting. He and Kate were the only ones in the secluded room off the main restaurant, discretion guaranteed by a row of descending wooden shutters that ensured their privacy. He took a sip of his very expensive glass of Gaja Alteni di Brassica Sauvignon Blanc and patted herbed butter off his lips with his starched linen napkin.

'We've been here for the better part of an hour, Kate. That's enough time for every CNN reporter and *Washington Post* writer inside the Beltway to know that the director of operations for the Central Intelligence Agency is having dinner with the last best hope of the Republican

Party and to wonder loudly about it. Why don't we get down to business.'

The brittle, hatchet-faced woman ignored the sumptuous-looking veal cutlet on the plate in front of her and reached into the Lana Marks one-of-a-kind clutch purse on her lap. She took out a plain gold Van Cleef & Arpels cigarette case that had belonged to her mother and the matching lighter. She removed a cigarette and lit it.

'I thought that was illegal in Washington restaurants,' said Patchin.

'For the price I'm paying for this meal and this room, Franco can eat the fine,' said Sinclair sharply. She took a healthy drag on the cigarette and sat back in her chair. 'Tell me about this fiasco of yours in Canada,' she said.

'*My* fiasco? We didn't have anything to do with it,' answered Patchin, genuinely surprised.

'You're trying to tell me that Quince wasn't a Company man?'

'The operative word is "was,"' responded Patchin. 'As in twenty years ago. He went out when Clinton came in; part of George Tenet's new broom. He's been private ever since.'

'If Quince wasn't yours, who was he?'

'I have no idea. You know as well as I do that we've adopted a wait-and-see attitude about this matter.' It was the CIA man's standard come-back and the senator's mother wasn't buying it.

'Don't play games with me, Joseph, you'll lose every time. If my son doesn't become senior *adelphoi* of Rex Deus he won't have the clout to get the nomination next year. That in turn means he won't become president and you'll lose your shot as secretary of state. It's like playing domi-noes, Joseph – if one falls so do all the rest.'

'We have a contingency for that,' said Patchin quietly.

'Ironstone?' Sinclair asked. 'That's the next best thing to treason.'

'Nevertheless,' said Patchin, pushing his plate away, his appetite suddenly gone. 'If the senator doesn't get the nomination Ironstone may be our only chance. Another four years of that starry-eyed socialist in the White House and you'll be able to use the Constitution for toilet paper. He's already flushed the country down the crapper.'

'Could you guarantee Ironstone's success?' Sinclair asked. She doused her cigarette in a sixty-dollar glass of wine.

'With help from your friends? Yes.' He

shrugged. 'However, it would be considerably better if he could become head of your ... organization. Ironstone would fundamentally change the United States forever.'

'Some would say for the better,' said Sinclair.

'And some would call it the last gasp of a failing empire,' answered Patchin. 'Ironstone is not an alternative; it is something to be avoided at all costs.'

'Then help me,' said Kate Sinclair. 'If the ark is discovered, help me to ensure that it doesn't fall into the wrong hands.'

'Speaking of the wrong hands,' said Patchin, 'just who are we talking about here?'

'There are seven families of the Blood within Rex Deus, all descended from the Desposyni, the blood relatives of Christ, all families of royal blood.'

'I don't really care about all the religious gobbledygook and the secret handshakes. I just want to know what we're dealing with. Do all seven of these families have an equal shot at taking over?'

'No,' said the old Sinclair woman. 'All of them are descended from the children of Mary – Christ's brothers and sisters – but ever since the dissolution of the Templars, Rex Deus only accepts members of those families who survived and came to America. Of the fifty-six signatories of the Declaration of Independence, eight were members of Rex Deus and knew of each other. It was those eight who formed Rex Deus as it now exists.'

'I don't recall anyone named Sinclair having signed the Declaration,' said Patchin.

'Rex Deus and the Desposyni follow a matriarchal line, just like the Jews, which of course Christ was by birth. They are less the children of Jesus than they are the descendants of Mary Magdalene.'

'People still believe this stuff?' Patchin said. 'It sounds like it's straight out of *a novel*.'

'Are the Freemasons out of *a novel*, or the Bilderberg Group or the Roman Catholic Church, or Skull and Bones of Yale University out of *a novel*, Joseph? As I recall, you're a Bonesman. Class of eighty-four, wasn't it?'

'Eighty-two,' responded Patchin. He took a long swallow of the expensive wine, barely tasting it.

'Rex Deus is like all of those institutions, Joseph; trappings aside, they are about money. A great deal of money and almost infinite power.'

'Yet it's trappings we're talking about,' argued Patchin.

Kate Sinclair lit another cigarette. 'It's the one thing that Mr Brown got right in his book, and probably accounts for its success – the power of symbols on people's lives, even when those people have no idea of the symbols' origins.

'The lucky horseshoe is actually the gilt remains from paintings of saints' halos when all the other paint had faded. The cross has been used since the Stone Age and has nothing to do with Christianity. The color white is used for funerals in Japan, not weddings. The swastika was in use in Iceland as far back as the eighth century and was known as Thor's Hammer – it was in use in India long before that. But show a swastika to an Israeli and watch their reaction. An advertising person said it years ago – perception is everything.' The older woman paused and tapped ashes into the remains of her veal.

'The perception in Rex Deus is that the True Ark and its contents are the most sacred icons and symbols of an ancient and holy order. You can't crown the British king or queen without the Sceptre, the Orb and the Crown. Philosophically it is Rex Deus's job, its holy goal, to save America until Armageddon and the Last Judgment. The United States itself is the vessel through which humanity will survive and the True Ark is the symbol of that survival.'

'You believe all that?' Patchin said, dumbfounded.

'It doesn't matter what I believe, Joseph. What matters is that the person who returns the True Ark to its rightful place is guaranteed to be made *adelphoi* or chief elder of Rex Deus, with all the commensurate power such a position entails.'

'And his competition?'

'Of the eight families there are only three in real contention.'

'Who are they?'

Kate Sinclair opened up the expensive little clutch and took out a folded piece of paper. She handed it to Patchin. He unfolded the note and read the short list of names. His eyes widened.

'My God,' he whispered, staring at the little slip of paper.

'Precisely.' Sinclair smiled coldly.

'But the one at the top, that's . . .'

Kate Sinclair lifted a bony finger to her bright red lips, silencing him.

'Can you still help me?' Sinclair asked.

Joseph Patchin stared at her, wondering what kind of terrible snake pit he had stumbled into. He tried to shrug it off. In for a penny, in for a pound; the kind of thinking that got Bernie Madoff a hundred and fifty years in the slammer. He swallowed hard.

'I'll see what I can do.'

The sea was black glass. The only motion of the dark water was a slow, rolling swell that gave the thirty-two-foot lobster boat a faintly nauseating corkscrew twist that was turning Meg a faint shade of green. The *Deryldene D* was making a steady twelve knots and had been doing so ever since leaving Halifax at dawn, almost seven hours ago. Above them the sky was a featureless gray slab.

'I was expecting worse weather than this,' said Holliday, standing beside Gallant at the wheel and looking out over the slowly undulating sea. Laid out on the windscreen shelf in front of the wheel was a group of high-tech instruments, including a depth finder, a side-scanning sonar array, a fish finder, a color radar screen, and a marine radio.

'You know the expression "the calm before the storm"?' said the maritimer.

'Sure,' said Holliday.

'This is it,' Gallant answered flatly.

'There's a storm coming?' Meg asked anxiously, perched on the bait box close to the transom.

'We're in a high-pressure system that's moving with the swell. We meet a low-pressure system and you get what's called a cyclonic effect. Down south they'd call it a tropical storm. It's how you get hurricanes.'

'Please tell me we're not heading into a hurricane,' pleaded Meg.

'Maybe not a hurricane yet, but odds are it'll become one before long. They've already evacuated the island and the offshore rigs nearby; they don't do that for an ordinary storm. The only question is when she hits,' answered Gallant.

'Best guess?' Holliday asked.

Gallant shrugged and stroked his mustache. 'Trying to guess what the sea's going to do is a fool's game,' said the lobsterman. 'But from my experience and the Doppler radar I'd say we've got a few hours yet.'

'You're saying that Sable Island is deserted now?' Meg asked.

'For what it's worth,' answered Gallant. 'I've never seen one, but the captain of the *QE2* ocean liner reported a ninety-two-foot wave nearby. That's the height of a ten-story building. Sable's barely thirteen feet above sea level. I sure as hell wouldn't want to be anywhere on the island when a wave like that hits.'

'We should check all that equipment you bought,' said Holliday pointedly. Meg nodded. Holliday led the way through the small hatchway-like door to the left of the wheel down three narrow steps.

There was a galley with a propane stove and burners on the left and a fold-up Formica table on the right with a vinyl-covered banquette against the starboard bulkhead. Everything in the little space seemed coated with a light sheen of old cooking oil and there was the distinct odor of boiled fish in the air. Holliday edged his way through the galley, ducking low, and stepped into the forward cabin.

The equipment was made up of two collapsible camping shovels, a pair of bright yellow, handheld Lowrance Safari GPS units and two very-high-end Garrett metal finders, smaller mine-detector-style versions of the big Garrett metal detector gates used in airports and secure facilities. They were lightweight and computerized.

Holliday sat down on the neatly made bunk against the port-side bulkhead and waited for Meg to join him. They were sitting in the bow now and the sliding, mild roller-coaster movement of the *Deryldene D* on the light swell was more pronounced. Meg's color deepened and she put a hand on her stomach.

'What do you want to check?' she said, obviously irritated. 'The batteries are fully charged and the salesman calibrated the detectors for copper, bronze and iron as well as gold and silver. Those are the most likely metals the ark would have been sheathed in.'

'I wanted to talk with you privately,' answered Holliday.

'About what?' Meg swallowed. 'And make it quick. I need some fresh air as soon as possible.'

'All right. One quick question. When we were in that bar where we met Gallant you said you knew where the ark was buried. How is that possible since you didn't know about Sable Island until a few days ago?'

'My, my, aren't you the suspicious one,' said Meg. She swallowed again and closed her eyes briefly as a wave of nausea hit her.

'Call it professional curiosity,' said Holliday.

'Okay,' she said and nodded. 'To satisfy your curiosity.' She took a deep shuddering breath to control her seasickness. 'Hopefully it won't bruise that delicate male ego of yours, but I'm a historian as well, and sometimes I can figure out puzzles too.'

'What puzzle?' Holliday asked.

'The painting in Prague. The one by Cranach. You couldn't figure out the six monks around the well, remember?'

'I'm with you so far.'

'You told me there's a freshwater lake on Sable Island, right?'

'Lake Wallace. There's a spring somewhere but it's mostly rainwater runoff, which is why the water level rises and falls so dramatically, at least according to that book I read.'

'But would it have been there in the time of the Blessed Juliana and Saint-Clair?'

'Presumably.'

'Don't you see? Lake Wallace is the well,' said Meg, managing a faint smile of triumph.

'And the six monks?'

'Sext,' answered Meg.

'Pardon?'

'It's the most important of the canonical hours,'

explained Meg. 'It's even sacred to the Jews. Sext is the sixth hour of the day. Originally sext was seen as dawn, but by the Blessed Juliana's day and the advent of clocks, prime, the first hour of the day, was arbitrarily set at six a.m. and sext officially became noon, the time Christ was crucified. Sext was also St Benedict's most sacred time for prayer, and St Benedict was the patron saint of the Templars. That's where Jean de Saint-Clair and the Blessed Juliana hid their holy treasure. The six o'clock position on the face of a sundial or a clock. We'll find the True Ark at the six o'clock position on the shore of Lake Wallace.'

'Well, I'll be damned,' whispered Holliday.

26

Dr Rafi Wanounou, a professor of medieval archaeology at the Hebrew University of Jerusalem, sat under the fly tent that served as his office, sweating profusely and doing paperwork, most of which was scattered over the rough plywood table in front of him.

Through the open end of the tent he could see the entire archaeological site of the 4000 B.C. cult temple that had served the nomadic tribes passing through the desert. Beyond the ruins of the old temple where his students were laboring like busy little ants under the broiling sun, Rafi could see the white salt rime on the beaches and the blue-green expanse of the Dead Sea.

If he squinted he could faintly see Jordan ten miles away on the other side, and with a pair of good binoculars he could even make out the five-hundred-foot block of halite that was usually referred to as Mount Sodom.

It was well over a hundred degrees Fahrenheit

and it was almost time to call in the kids for lunch and a hydrating break and maybe even a trip to one of the springs surrounding the nearby Ein Gedi Oasis for a swim. Rafi sighed. The Chalcolithic period of Hebrew history was hardly his area of expertise, but like the rest of his colleagues in the department he had to lead his fair share of field trips to give the students experience doing site work.

Rafi sighed again; he was also worried about Peggy. She was only in her first trimester but he was already fretting over her. He had even been considering making the arduous hundred-kilometer journey back to Jerusalem later in the afternoon, even though Ein Gedi was hardly within commuting distance. Fifty miles on secondary desert roads in Israel wasn't like the same distance on a freeway in the United States. On the other hand, Peggy was worth it; in fact, meeting and falling in love with Peggy Blackstock had been the best thing that had ever happened to him; even his mother thought so, even though he'd married a *shiksa* who hadn't changed her name when they got married. He smiled; convincing Reyna Wanounou of *anything* was a small miracle, even his father said so.

Rafi reached down to the cooler underneath his table and pulled out a plastic bottle of Neviot spring water and twisted off the cap. He took a long swallow and then another. Peggy wasn't used to the extreme heat of an Israeli summer and that was worrying him, too. He grinned. It was a fundamental part of the Jewish psyche to worry about one thing or another. Presumably Peggy hadn't reached that part of the conversion process yet.

He heard the sound of a vehicle coming down the approach road to the temple site. There was a heavy note to the engine, more like the sound of a truck. Rafi slipped on his old Serengeti Driver sunglasses and stood up. He went to the open end of the tent and stood in the blinding sunlight. He watched as the vehicle came down the winding approach road. It was a Humvee in mottled desert camouflage. The Humvee was Israeli Defense Force.

The squat, boxy, armored all-purpose vehicle pulled up beside the fly tent. It was an M1145 model, the one the US Army was using to replace the original version. Whatever branch of the service it came from they had pull in the motor pool. As far as Rafi knew there weren't more than a handful in the country. During his mandatory stint in the military they were still using Jeeps.

An officer climbed out of the passenger seat and two grunts got out of the back. They were all wearing identical tan uniforms but the officer had three olive branch pips on his green shoulder tabs; a full colonel. The grunts had the triple stripes of staff sergeants on their sleeves. All three were wearing the dark green berets of Military Intelligence Command.

The colonel had a holstered Desert Eagle pistol on his belt; the sergeants both carried futuristic-looking Tavor assault rifles. The colonel approached Rafi. The man looked to be in his late fifties, his square face seamed and lined, the hair at his close-cropped temples grizzled salt and pepper. The two grunts took up positions on either side of him and slightly behind. Their eyes shifted like wolves', always in motion. They were the colonel's bodyguard; whoever he was, the colonel was high on the food chain.

'My name is Abraham Ben-El'azar. I am with IDF Intelligence,' said the colonel. 'I am looking for Professor Rafi Wanounou.'

'That would be me,' answered Rafi. 'What can I do for you?' he asked, curious.

'It's your wife, Dr Wanounou. I'm afraid she has been kidnapped.'

Peggy Blackstock walked slowly along Mahane Yehuda Street in central Jerusalem, alternately taking photographs and shopping for dinner and anything else that looked good in the *shuk* Machaneh Yehuda, the city's famous open-air market. She'd already picked up some fresh dates, pistachios and a bag of meat-and-potato-filled 'cigars,' the Moroccan version of pierogies and one of Rafi's favorites.

Peggy smiled, thinking of her sometimes too serious husband. He'd be out of his mind with worry out there by the Dead Sea if he knew she was shopping alone.

In Rafi's mind she'd changed from the adventurous girl photographer who'd spent two months in the Amazon rain forest with the Matis Indians learning how to use a blowgun and going through the *Kampo* frog poison ritual – *Kampo* being the oily sweat of the Amazon monkey frog and a drug that was a combination of methamphetamine and the world's most powerful laxative – all to get her photo story.

Somehow the act of getting pregnant had stripped her of all her toughness and turned her into a delicate flower of womanhood who would wither away if exposed to direct sunlight. On the one hand, it was sweet and romantic; on the other hand, it was a little bit overprotective and claustrophobic, not to mention just plain silly.

Even more worrying to her professorial husband would be the fact that she was shopping alone in the *shuk*. The *shuk* Machaneh Yehuda had been the site of three terrorist suicide bombings in two attacks between 1995 and 2002 and still had barrier checkpoints with armed guards at both the Agrippas Street entrance and the entrance at the Jaffa Road end of the market. It was a ridiculous precaution, of course, and basically just for show. The *shuk* was a rabbit warren of alleys and side streets and anyone who wanted to get into the market unnoticed wouldn't have the slightest trouble.

Peggy wandered through the noisy throng, looking at the tiny shops standing cheek by jowl with each other. A store selling nothing but halvah in different flavors next to a dealer in Judaica, a barbershop beside a backgammon club so crowded that its tables spilled out on to the already crowded street. A discount CD store next to a fancy jewelry boutique. She glanced upward to the second and third floors of the old buildings. She knew from her research that a lot of the apartments and lofts above the shops were now occupied by artists, writers and musicians. The *shuk* was in transition, going from simply popular to trendy. Greenwich Village in the desert. It was a little sad.

There were two policemen approaching, threading their way easily through the crowd. They were wearing their short-sleeved light blue summer uniforms, at odds with the variety of colorful exotic costumes all around them. One was a plain-faced, middle-aged man, the other a younger woman.

Peggy brought up the Nikon and took a few quick shots. The two cops came to a stop directly in front of her, blocking her path. The crowd broke around them like the current of a river giving way to a boulder in midstream. Shopkeepers paused in the middle of their noisy sales pitches, sensing a bit of drama. Peggy was a little confused; as far as she knew there was no law in

Israel against taking pictures of cops. It wasn't as though they were Mossad or anything.

'Peggy Blackstock?' the male cop asked. Peggy noticed that the female had her hand on the holstered butt of the Jericho 915 on her hip. She also noted that neither one of them had any rank insignia.

How the hell do they know my name? Peggy thought.

'Yes,' she said.

'I am Pakad Yakov Ben-Haim of the Israeli Police, Headquarters Division.'

A pakad – what was such a high-ranking officer as a chief inspector doing wearing a patrolman's uniform?

'What can I do for you, Chief Inspector? I hope you don't mind me taking your picture.' The cop ignored the question.

'Please come with us,' said Ben-Haim quietly. 'It's about your husband. I'm afraid there has been an accident.'

Their first sighting of the lonely island was nothing more than a distant smudge on the eastern horizon, balanced on the curving edge of the world, a frighteningly dark mass of clouds in the background, so dark at the spreading base that it was almost black.

'Once we make landfall you're not going to have much time,' cautioned Gallant. 'A couple of hours at most.' The burly lobsterman with the Groucho mustache shook his head. 'Any longer than that, you're on your own and I'm gone.'

Holliday glanced at Meg, expecting some kind of plea or argument, but she said nothing, simply looking blankly and without expression through the windscreen of the *Deryldene D*'s cabin, staring at the slowly forming smudge on the horizon. Holliday found himself hypnotized by the cold, black, roiling clouds that formed a background to the image of the island. It was like staring at a vision of the future, and the future wasn't good.

They continued east for another hour and a half, the island growing steadily more visible as they approached. Meg had gone below, overcome by her seasickness. At first Sable looked much bigger than it actually was, an illusory desert island shaped in a long crescent, its narrowing arms pointing toward the New World, Arcadia.

Slowly but surely the illusion faded; this was no island of palm trees and beautiful native girls; it was a windswept desolate sandbar, its back to the open sea, its center a spine of wandering dunes barely held together by the tough grasses and bushes that somehow clung to life through the seasons.

A steady wind was blowing from the east, and nearing the shore Holliday could see the blowing wisps of sand rising from the crests of the dunes like wind-borne snow in the middle of a blizzard.

The *Deryldene D* suddenly seemed to lurch in its onward course, the bow swinging abruptly to the south. Gallant cursed under his breath and turned the wheel hard back to port.

'What was that?' Holliday asked.

'That's the reason so many ships went down on Sable,' said Gallant, grunting with effort as he dragged on the wheel, one eye looking ahead, the other focused on the digital depth finder. 'It's called a gyre. Out west they call it a skookum-chuck.'

'What on earth is a skookumchuck?'

'A vortex,' said Gallant, fighting the wheel.

There are four main currents that flow around Sable Island. The Labrador Current, the St Lawrence Outfall and the Nova Scotia Current running south along the island's southeastern shore, and the much more powerful and deeper Gulf Stream flowing north along the outer shore.

As huge volumes of water race past the island they set up a whirling Coriolis effect, creating spinning currents of water just below the surface. Sailing ships of the past riding the Gulf Stream up from the Caribbean on their way home to Europe would suddenly find themselves torn off course and thrown up on the ocean-facing banks and bars, while ships heading along the Atlantic Coast to New York and points south would find themselves cast up on the inner beaches.

A map of Sable Island shows hundreds of known wrecks almost evenly divided between the two shores with a slight advantage held by the Gulf Stream coast, probably caused by ships running before the storms. Gallant nodded toward the instruments in front of him as he struggled with the wheel.

'Keep an eye on the echo sounder,' he instructed. 'Read me the depths every ten seconds. If you see a yellow-white patch ahead of us, call it out. Same for port and starboard, got that?'

'Got it,' Holliday said and nodded.

With Holliday calling out the numbers they moved steadily toward the island, Gallant guiding them toward the starboard end of the crescent-shaped strip of sand. At some point Meg came up from the cabin, but Holliday barely noticed. She looked toward the shore, then went back down into the cabin and retrieved the two metal detectors and their backpacks. Holliday kept reading off the numbers.

The hidden sandbars threatening to ground them were all at right angles to the shore, which Holliday found strange, but this was no time to ask questions; Gallant was concentrating hard on the approaching coast. The water beneath them became shallower and shallower. Two hundred yards from shore it was barely eight feet. At a hundred yards it was six feet, and at twenty-five yards it was barely four.

'What's the draft on this thing?' Holliday asked.

'Three feet three inches,' said Gallant. 'We'll ground in a few seconds.'

'Aren't you afraid of getting stuck?' Meg asked cautiously.

'This time of day the tide's coming in, not going out,' said Gallant, grinning.

There was a rough grating sound as the *Deryl-dene D* pushed up on the sand. Gallant pushed the throttle forward, beaching them even more firmly, then switched off the engine.

They had arrived.

27

Cardinal Antonio Niccolo Spada, Vatican secretary of state, sat beside the large pool at his villa just beyond the north end of the Rome Ring Road. He was wrapped in a thick white terry-cloth robe with the crossed keys and double-headed phoenix of his family coat of arms. It was one of the odd twists of fate that fascinated Spada.

The present Pope was the son of a Bavarian village policeman, while Spada was descended directly from the Borgias. Yet the policeman's son and onetime member of the Hitler Youth was the Pope, and Spada was only the Pontiff's second in command. Oh, well; true power often rested behind the throne, even if it was the Cathedra Petri, the Chair of St Peter.

Spada wrapped the robe more tightly around his shrunken chest. He still loved to swim each day, but even though the afternoon was warm he felt a chill. Another sign that he was getting on in years, the first being that his oldest friends were beginning to die around him.

He wondered if he would go to hell for his transgressions when he died. Established Catholic doctrine said that if he made a final confession and was given extreme unction he would go to heaven but he wasn't sure he believed in either heaven or hell. Sometimes the old man hoped that death would be more straightforward, a simple end to consciousness and then the everlasting dark.

For Cardinal Spada, Catholicism was far more political than it was spiritual. A true Catholic of the Holy Cross should, almost by definition, have no more personal ambition than to be a humble parish priest. Spada smiled at that.

As a trained lawyer his first appointment to the Holy See had been as an assistant to Cardinal Pietro Ciriaci, head of the Pontifical Council for Legislative Texts, the interpretive body for canon law. That had been the beginning, and he'd never looked back and never once regretted his long, sometimes vicious rise to the Red Hat and a seat in the College of Cardinals.

Father Thomas Brennan, head of Sodalitium Pianum, the Vatican Secret Service, came out through the open French doors of the villa and walked across the patio to where Spada was resting after his brief swim. It was early afternoon and the bright sun had turned the breeze-ruffled surface of the azure pool into a field of sparkling diamonds.

The pool area was absolutely secure, swept for electronic devices every day by Brennan's people and surrounded by a tall hedge on three sides; the villa itself was protected by a high, spiked stone wall, security cameras, and armed members of the Corpo della Gendarmeria, the Vatican police.

As usual the pallbearer figure of the Irish priest was slightly hunched, as though the burdens of the world rested on his sloping shoulders like some cosmic coffin, and as usual he was smoking, a trail of cigarette ash sprinkled over the lapels of his cheap black suit. He sat down at Spada's glass-topped, wrought iron patio table.

A servant appeared with a tray, a heavy ceramic ashtray and two tall glasses. One was a raspberry-colored negroni and the other was a rusty-looking Long Island iced tea. The servant placed the Long Island iced tea and the ashtray in front of Brennan and the negroni in front of the cardinal. The servant bowed slightly to the cardinal and then withdrew. The two men at the table sat silently for a moment, watching the chips of light dancing randomly across the swimming pool. Finally, with a certain regret in his voice, the cardinal spoke.

'Have you discovered anything new?'

'After escaping from the lake property they took a train to Halifax, Nova Scotia.'

'A train?' Spada asked, surprised.

'Quite smart, really,' replied Brennan. The priest took a long swallow of his drink. 'No airport security, no identification required to purchase tickets, no railway police to speak of, not on the trains at any rate.'

'Are they still there?'

'They met with a man named Gallant.'

'Who is he?' Spada asked.

'A fisherman. A lobster catcher, to be specific.'

'A fisherman?'

'This man Gallant has a somewhat dubious reputation,' said Brennan. He butted his cigarette in the ashtray and lit another. 'He is rumored to smuggle things between Maine and Nova Scotia: cigarettes, cheap Canadian pharmaceuticals and the like. Now he's vanished along with his boat. So have Holliday and the woman.'

'Could he be smuggling them into the United States?'

'It's a possibility. The normal crossings have become much more difficult to breach with everyone needing passports on both sides of the border.'

'But why now?' Spada asked. 'To give up their quest at this stage doesn't seem logical.'

'Perhaps they were frightened off by the attack at the lake property,' suggested Brennan.

Spada sipped his mouth-puckering drink and shook his head. 'There is the fundamental problem of why they went to Canada in the first place,' said the cardinal. 'And why this Braintree?'

'Braintree was a colleague of Holliday's uncle. He's helped Holliday before.'

'Ah, yes,' Spada said and nodded. 'The infamous Henry Granger, spy, Nazi killer, academician and the last of the Templars all in one.'

Brennan's thin lips twisted into a grimace. He spoke darkly. 'Not the last Templar, we know that much at least, thanks to the efforts of his nephew, Lieutenant Colonel Holliday.'

The expression on Brennan's face was enough to draw a smile from Cardinal Spada, something that rarely occurred these days.

'*Stare calme, Tomasso, stare calme.* Holliday bested

you, so accept it. You'll have your chance at retribution, I assure you.' The cardinal thought for a moment, then spoke again. 'Do you think Holliday has the slightest idea of what he's involved with, its scope?'

'I doubt it,' replied Brennan. 'He may well believe that he's dragged the woman into his troubles rather than the other way around.'

'They have come under fire on six separate occasions since joining forces. The man who followed them in Prague, the Peseks in Venice, St Michael's Mount in Cornwall, the attempted kidnapping on Iona, and finally the attack in Canada. Surely he's not so naïve that he'd think we were responsible for all of that?'

'He's run into the Peseks before, that unfortunate series of events in Libya last year, if you'll recall.'

'Vividly.'

Brennan lit another cigarette. 'So he puts the Peseks at our doorstep and perhaps that CIA hireling in Prague. He'd almost certainly assume that the police intervention in Cornwall was concocted by the Company as well; they're the only people who could orchestrate a thing like that so quickly.'

'And the rest?'

'He knows the failed kidnapping was by the Blackhawk people. Like an idiot the man he disposed of was carrying identification. The police questioned the man he wounded, so undoubtedly MI-5 and hence the CIA know of their involvement.'

'Would he know about Rex Deus's involvement with them?'

Brennan shook his head. 'Blackhawk is small, nothing near the size and profile of groups like Halliburton or Blackwater.'

'Sadly, of course, we *do* know of them,' murmured the cardinal. 'All too well, in fact.'

'You shouldn't have allowed the bank to do it,' said Brennan. 'If you'll recall, I advised you of that at the time, Your Eminence.'

'There was nothing that I could do about it,' explained Spada. 'RhineHydraulik and Aquadyn were both European companies and heavily invested in us. There was no way that the IOR could know that there would be a hostile takeover and consolidation of both of them by Sinclair's company.'

'The Vatican Bank *should* know,' replied Brennan harshly.

'Did you?' Spada snapped. 'The Istituto relies on you for such intelligence.'

'No,' said Brennan. 'But I knew that RhineHydraulik was weak and Aquadyn was vulnerable. Again, I told you that at the time, just as I told Bertone at the bank.' The Irishman shook his head sadly.

'Now a fundamentalist Christian organization that has a private army of its own is a business partner of the Holy See. If we withdrew our interest in Rhine-Aqua in this market we'd lose billions. If Rex Deus sold their interest there would be a run on the stock and we'd lose billions again. If they want to, Rex Deus can put the entire Catholic Church into a vice.'

'I am aware of all of this,' answered Spada. 'Which is precisely why we need some leverage with them. They must be controlled or dealt with some other way.'

Brennan looked mildly amused at the cardinal using such strong language.

'You'll have to be clearer than that,' said the priest. 'It's not as though I've got too many Antonin Peseks out there. I can't order up assassinations like a meal in a restaurant.'

'Forget that for the moment,' said the cardinal,

abruptly changing the subject. 'We were talking about Holliday. What about the Canadian incident?'

Brennan shrugged. 'At this point it is still unclear. The group that abducted Holliday and the woman has not been identified, although it is likely that their attackers at the lakefront property were Blackhawk.' Brennan drained the last of his drink and began crunching ice cubes between his teeth.

'We're missing something,' said the cardinal. 'This is too great a concentration of force from too many directions to be about a semi-mythical religious relic.' The old man frowned, his thin lips drawn down, his eyes cold and thoughtful.

A sudden gust of wind shook the branches of the hedge around the pool. As a child Spada was sure that sound was the voices of the dead whispering and heralding disaster. He shivered, shrinking into the heavy robe. Maybe he still believed it. 'Go to now, ye rich men, weep and howl for your miseries that shall come upon you. Your riches are corrupted, and your garments are moth-eaten.'

'Begging your pardon, Eminence?' Brennan said, confused.

'A verse from the Holy Scripture, Father Brennan. James, chapter five to be precise.'

'I'm not sure I take your meaning.'

'This whole thing is about money. I can smell it.' The cardinal thought for a moment, his head bowed, almost as though he was at prayer, something he hadn't done in a very long time. 'A year or so ago you heard a rumor making the rounds in Washington about something called Ironstone. Sinclair's name was involved. Did you ever discover anything else about it?'

'A little, and it wasn't about money. As far as I know it was the code name for some kind of military response to the threat of a major act of terrorism on American soil.'

'Nothing that would affect us, though.'

'Not directly, no,' said Brennan.

A young priest appeared in the doorway into the villa. He stood hesitantly for a moment and then came forward to where Spada and Brennan were sitting. One of Brennan's boys, certainly, if his dark good looks were anything to go by. He stopped and bowed to Spada and then turned to Brennan.

'*Is ea anois, an bhféadaim cúnamh leat*, Michael?' Brennan asked. Spada smiled for the second time since Brennan had arrived. The Irishman was speaking Gaelic, a requirement for all his couriers. A nice touch for keeping secrets, even from a cardinal, like the Navaho Windtalkers used by the US Marines during World War Two. The young man responded, speaking rapidly. Spada couldn't understand a word. The message was brief. When the young man was done he bowed respectfully to Spada and then departed.

'What was that all about?' Cardinal Spada said as the young man disappeared into the darkness of the villa beyond the French doors. 'Or am I not allowed to ask?'

'The situation regarding Holliday has changed direction. His cousin Peggy and her husband have vanished into thin air.'

28

Holliday turned the elapsed time bezel on his old Luminox wristwatch for two hours and then he and Sister Meg inputted their position into the two GPS handhelds, using the larger unit on the *Deryldene D* as a base guide. According to the big unit, Lake Wallace was located a mile and a half down the beach and six hundred yards inland across the low scruffy dunes.

The weather station, which employed five of the six permanent residents of Sable Island, was a mile farther down the curving arm of the crescent. There were a small handful of offshore oil rigs in the ocean several miles away from the island, but with the sandbar already evacuated in the face of the coming hurricane it was unlikely they would be interrupted.

It took them almost half an hour to reach the turn point indicated by the GPS. The fine dark sand was more difficult to walk in than either one of them had expected. It would take another ten minutes to reach the lake. That in turn meant it would take the same amount of time, if not longer, to make the return journey, and they still hadn't reached the lake.

That left them with an hour at most to discover an artifact that probably didn't exist and maybe wasn't even there – and even if it *was* there, it had been buried in the sand for seven hundred years. The odds of finding it were infinitesimal. They found a narrow windswept pathway leading up between the dunes. Finally they reached the summit and paused to take a breath.

Ahead of them now the sky on the horizon was a roiling vision of chaos, as though the sky itself was being torn and bruised. On the island they could now see the narrow oblong lake and the broad stretch of the southern beach, ten times as wide as the northern beach where the *Deryldene D* had grounded.

The sea between the beach and the horizon was a frothing horror, huge waves rising on the outer banks then roaring like freight trains across the inner sandbars to finally crash and break along the sand.

No wonder there had been so many wrecks here over the centuries; any ship foundering on the outer banks would be pounded into kindling, and anyone who survived the wreck itself would almost certainly be drowned before he reached the shore.

'This is madness,' said Holliday. 'We'll never find the damned thing. We should go back to Halifax and wait out the storm, then come back.'

'There's no time for that,' answered Meg grimly. 'The hurricane will flood into the lake and the True Ark will be under the water again.' She trudged forward, hitching her backpack higher on her shoulders, her feet sinking into the soft, fine sand. On the crest of a dune covered with some kind of thistle and rough eelgrass a trio of shaggy Sable Island ponies watched them, their long unkempt manes flying raggedly in the rising wind.

How many hurricanes and for how many generations had the wild horses' bloodlines survived? And how could Sister Meg be so sure that the treasure her precious Blessed Juliana had brought here would be submerged? According to the book he'd read on the train, Lake Wallace had steadily been getting smaller over the passing centuries. The original high-water mark could be very high by now in relation to the modern lake.

He knew exactly why, of course, and it wasn't the first time he'd seen the incredible streak of stubbornness coming from the red-haired nun. The iron faith of the True Believer. Darwin couldn't be right because the Bible never mentioned evolution, dinosaurs or cave men and strongly suggested that the sun revolved around the earth. Holliday checked his watch again. He estimated that it would be another five minutes of slogging before they reached the midpoint of the lake. He made the simple calculation.

In the final analysis the trek from the *Deryldene D* would take a total of forty minutes. That would leave them with barely the same amount of time for their search if they wanted to get back to the boat within the two-hour limit. Somehow he doubted that Gallant was a great fan of grace periods.

Holliday looked out over the rolling, deep green monstrosity of the open Atlantic and the hurricane hurtling inexorably down on them. It was close enough now that he could easily see the blinding, jagged spikes of lightning flashing across the jet black base of the clouds like a Goya vision of Apocalypse.

Holliday felt something curl and curdle in his

guts. Fear or warning? Maybe both. The fight-or-flight instinct the Neanderthal hunter felt when confronted by his first charging mammoth or saber-toothed Tiger. They slid down the pathway leading to the floodplain of the lake. The wind was rising in gusts, dragging up brief clouds of gritty sand into their faces. He checked his watch one more time. Another few minutes gone. He cursed under his breath. Meg half turned.

'Did you say something?'

'No, nothing,' he responded. She continued the slide down to the bottom of the dune and Holliday dutifully followed.

The hell brewing on the horizon was almost enough for him to force Meg's hand and abandon her, but he knew he couldn't bring himself to do it. They reached the floodplain and walked across the salt-encrusted hardpan toward the edge of the water. It was summer and the lake's edge was fringed with grasses and other low plants.

The wind was beginning to blow hard now, building wavelets on the dark water. Meg looked left and right and then behind her. The winter high-water mark was clearly visible. There was a shallow lip and perhaps twenty feet or so of slightly darker sand between the lip and the lakeshore. Meg paced back until she had reached the high-water lip in the sand, then went back twenty feet more. She looked left and right again, judging the rough midpoint of the lake. She paced off fifty feet to the left and stopped.

'This is the midpoint,' she said firmly. She dropped her pack on to the ground, unstrapped the folding shovel and took the headphones for the metal detector out of her pack and plugged them into the device's console. Holliday followed her across the sand and did the same thing. Finally they were ready. Holliday looked at his watch.

'We've got thirty-seven minutes to locate this thing and dig it up. If we haven't hit pay dirt in half an hour we're leaving. Agreed?'

'Whatever you say.' Meg nodded absently, her attention focused on adjusting the metal detector's arm brace.

'I mean it,' warned Holliday. 'One minute more than that and I'll leave you here.' He nodded toward the massive storm front rapidly descending on them. 'I don't want to be here when that thing hits.'

'I heard you the first time,' answered Meg. She scooped up her pack with her free hand and hung it over one shoulder. 'I'll go right, you go left.'

'All right,' answered Holliday, but she was already moving, the headphones clamped around her ears. He shook his head, watching her go, then fitted on his own arm brace and put on his headphones. He turned and began walking, moving slowly and methodically, swinging the disc of the detector back and forth in a sweeping motion a few inches above the sand.

The Sable Island book he'd read on the train had gone into minute detail about the geology of the place. Sable Island was a product of the last ice age. As the glaciers withdrew, sand was deposited in front of the retreating ice. In Sable's case the formation was referred to as a sand dump, and a very large one, deposited over a thick layer of Tertiary Period sediment, which eventually produced pockets of oil, hence the offshore drilling platforms.

The point being that there was no bedrock or any other kind of rock on Sable Island and hence no minerals. If the metal detector pinged and the LED gauge on the console gave him a reading, it was either the remains of an old shipwreck or Meg's True Ark.

He lifted his wrist and glanced at his watch yet again. He felt his jaw tighten. Ten minutes eaten up and the hurricane ten minutes closer; this had gone from insane to dangerous. A woman in the clutches of some sort of religious rapture was going to kill them all. There was no True Ark. He heard a sharp cry, dulled by the wind and the muffling headphones. He turned. Meg was standing three hundred yards away in the distance, waving her arms and yelling. He tore off the headphones as she yelled again. He barely made out the words.

'I found something!'

Holliday stared at the small, frantically waving figure in the distance.

'You've go to be kidding,' he whispered. He saw her drop to her knees and begin to scrabble at the sand, digging it out with the little folding shovel. Holliday heaved the metal detector over his shoulder and ran. A minute later he reached her position, chest heaving. The sand was blowing in the freshening wind and stinging his eyes. He stared into the foot-deep hole in the sand.

'It was like a miracle!' Meg said raggedly as she dug. 'The meter went off the scale and the headphones went from a steady ping to a long tone in an instant and I knew it was here! I knew it!'

'What metals?' Holliday asked.

'All of them! That's what is so incredible! Bronze, gold, silver! Even tin. It was reading some kind of heavy metals as well, probably copper or nickel or lead.'

'Most likely lead; they used it for drainpipes back then, or tin maybe.'

'Help me dig,' ordered Meg.

Holliday stripped off his backpack and unlimbered his own shovel. He checked his watch. Twenty minutes left. He dropped down on his knees across from Meg and began to work at the caked, dark sand, widening and broadening the hole. At two feet Meg's shovel hit something with a hollow thump.

Holliday flopped forward on to his stomach. He reached down into the cavity and started sweeping the sand off whatever it was with his outstretched fingers. A few seconds later a carved design appeared, deeply carved into a dark gray metal slab. An engrailed cross, the ancient mark of the Saint-Clairs. Below it was an almost rune-like series of letters. Some sort of motto: εν τού τω νι κα.

'That's not Latin, or French,' said Meg, a confused look on her face.

'It's ancient Greek,' said Holliday, who'd seen the phrase before. 'In Latin it's usually rendered as *In hoc signo vinces* – By this you shall conquer – meaning the cross. The Emperor Constantine saw the phrase in a dream the night before the Battle of Milivian Bridge in A.D. 312. He won the battle and the phrase became his motto thereafter. It was also the motto of the Knights Templar.'

'It's the True Ark,' whispered Meg, her voice reverent. 'We actually found it.'

'My, my,' said Holliday. 'Imagine that.' Sister Meg gave him a sharp look.

'Help me dig,' she said.

They swept away more sand, then dug carefully around the slab. It took ten minutes, half the remaining time, to reveal that the slab was actually a rectangular box roughly three feet long, eighteen inches wide and a foot high, about the size of an ossuary coffin used for relic bones in the medieval era and apparently made with sheet lead, the inset lid tightly soldered. They managed to lift the surprisingly lightweight container out of the hole and set it down. Both Holliday and Meg examined it closely. The box was perfectly sealed.

'A simple carpenter's cup,' whispered Meg, eyes wide.

'Sorry?' Holliday said.

'The Grail,' said Meg. 'It was a simple carpenter's cup, not some fine jewel. The True Ark is like that.'

'I thought you were quoting from an Indiana Jones movie, the one that had Sean Connery in it.' Holliday looked at his watch. Five minutes left. Good timing. He stood up and brushed sand off his jeans. He'd been an utter fool.

'How can you be so blasphemous at a time like this?' Meg asked, scowling, still kneeling in front of the box.

'Because I don't believe any of it,' said Holliday, his voice bitter. 'The whole damned thing has been impossibly convenient. The bald guy in Prague to give it all a sense of urgency, the Irishman O'Keefe and the *Mary Deare* just where they needed to be, the rubbing in Iona, the hymn, and then you find exactly what you've been searching for after looking for ten or fifteen minutes and only buried a couple of feet deep. There's a saying for it: if it's too good to be true, it probably isn't.' Holliday shook his head wearily. 'Let's cut the crap, sweetheart. This whole thing has been a crock right from the start and I fell for it hook, line and holy sinker.' He reached down, picked up his pack and slung it over one shoulder. He looked down at Meg. She was rummaging for something in her pack. 'It was all window dressing, and pretty expensive window dressing at that,' he said. 'I don't know quite what you're up to, but I hope it was worth it.'

He began to turn away as Meg stood up and then he froze. She had a heavy Stechkin APS 9mm pistol in a two-handed grip, rock solid and pointing in the general vicinity of his heart. It was the pistol of choice for Russian Special Forces in Afghanistan. He'd seen plenty of them in the hands of Taliban insurgents himself. Trophies from a lost war.

'Mother warned me that it wouldn't work,' said Meg, the gun never wavering. 'But I thought it was worth a try.'

29

'Pick up the ark,' ordered Meg. Holliday did as she instructed, grabbing the lead box and lifting it with both hands. It weighed about forty pounds, too light to be lead sheet unless it was very thin or just a protective veneer over something else, probably wood. Not the heaviest load he'd ever carried but it was going to slow them down.

'We won't make it back to the boat with me carrying this,' said Holliday, looking at Meg. Her red hair was flying wildly in the rising wind, her eyes squinting against the whirling sand. She picked up her pack and shrugged it over one arm. The pistol never wavered and she never looked away. She barely blinked.

The religious fervor was gone, replaced by something cold and hard. It was an entirely different creature than the pretty, defensive, red-haired nun he'd met at Mont Saint-Michel. This Sister Meg was capable of putting a bullet between his eyes without a second thought.

He was no shrink, but crazy seemed like a good enough diagnosis. Behind them the ocean roared and crashed as the gigantic rolling waves battered themselves to death on the broad beach, each one clawing itself a little higher up the sand.

'To hell with Gallant and his stupid boat,' Meg answered. 'We're setting our own timetable. Get moving.' They began to walk back along the hardpan, then veered left at exactly the place where they first walked down to the edge of the lake. He could tell because he could see their boot prints in the broken crust of the sand. They followed their own footsteps to the base of the low, hill-like dunes and found the deep cut trail that had led them here. They began heading up the path.

The sense of the Stechkin aimed between Holliday's shoulder blades was almost physical, like a sudden flash of sunburn or an itch. If he remembered correctly the tough little automatic had a twenty-round magazine and a rate of fire that was somewhere around six hundred rounds a minute. That meant she could empty the pistol into his back in two seconds.

'Smart,' said Holliday, speaking to the empty air in front of him. 'Using lead. There's no real way of dating it and I'm sure whatever little things you've got tucked away are nice and authentic.'

'Shut your mouth,' snapped Meg.

'You're not going to shoot me,' said Holliday, who wasn't quite sure he believed it. 'If you were going to kill me you would have done it by now. For whatever reason you still need me.' He paused. 'By the way, who *is* your mother?'

'You never thought to ask me what my last name was, did you?' Meg said behind him.

'I didn't think nuns had last names,' said Holliday.

'Nuns were ordinary people before they took their vows, and anyway, who said I was a nun?'

'Are you?'

'I was once, not anymore.'

'So what's your last name?' asked Holliday.

'Sinclair. My mother's name is Katherine, if that makes things any clearer.'

Holliday remembered a piece he'd read in *Time* magazine a few months ago, something about there being only a dozen female CEOs of Fortune 500 companies. Kate Sinclair had been number four in a list headed by Angela Braly at WellPoint, Indra Nooyi at PepsiCo and Irene Rosenfeld at Kraft Foods. Kate Sinclair ran an amorphous multinational that had something to do with water.

'The water lady?'

'I doubt she'd take too kindly to that description,' said Meg Sinclair. 'Mother is the CEO and majority shareholder in the American Fluid Dynamics Corporation. A utilities provider. Her son, my brother, is Richard Pierce Sinclair.'

'The senator?'

'That's him,' said Meg. 'The next president of the United States.'

'In your dreams,' said Holliday. 'He's the junior senator from some backwoods state like Tennessee.'

'Kentucky,' she corrected. 'But you'd be surprised what three years and a billion dollars can do for your image. Stop here.'

Holliday stopped. They were at the summit of the dune. He looked down on to the narrower north beach and the sea beyond. The *Deryldene D* was invisible, more than a mile away up the beach. Behind him he heard movement. It sounded as though Meg was looking through her knapsack, maybe distracted. Somehow he doubted it, and it wasn't worth the risk of trying to find out.

He heard something vaguely familiar and then

he remembered where he'd heard it before – it was the sound of someone breaking open the cylinder of a revolver, then snapping it back into place again. What was she doing? The Stechkin was basically a machine pistol; what did she need a revolver for?

There was a loud, explosive blast behind his back and then a white-hot hissing that sounded reminiscent of a roman candle going off on the Fourth of July.

Holliday looked up as a trail of white smoke arced up into the dark sky overhead, drifting and smudging in the wind. At the top of the arc it exploded into a bright red ball of light. Of course, thought Holliday, a signal flare. He wondered about Gallant. He'd see the flare, of course, and wonder what it was all about, but he doubted that the lobsterman would do anything about it.

'Move,' ordered Meg. Once again Holliday did as he was told and began moving down the sloping face of the dune.

'What was that all about?'

'You'll see,' said Meg.

Holliday's arms were beginning to ache from the weight of the ark. He glanced down at the lead veneer of the box and its inscription. *By this you shall conquer.* Maybe he could fake a fall, go head over heels and drop the box on his way down and make a run for it. Suddenly, from overhead he heard a faint droning sound, the familiar whine of a prop plane, and a fairly large one at that.

'That your ride?' Holliday asked without turning around. He gripped the box more tightly. If there was going to be a chance of getting out of this it would be now. He tensed, trying to judge the exact moment.

'Shut up,' Meg said, her voice flat and unemotional. Overhead the buzzing grew louder and suddenly he could see the plane. It was some kind of high-winged utility aircraft like the Defender, the one used by the British military. It was obviously about to use the beach as a runway. 'And don't think about making a break for it,' continued Meg. 'Your body English is betraying you. All that tension in the shoulders and turtleing your neck down like you are.'

'I don't think you've got it in you,' said Holliday, knowing that his moment had gone. 'Maybe you think you're some kind of hard case, but I don't think you're a cold-blooded killer.'

'Who knows?' Meg Sinclair answered. 'Try me and see.'

Off to the left the aircraft was in its final approach, its tail wagging back and forth with the force of the gusting wind. Holliday and Meg reached the bottom of the dune and stepped out on to the beach. Meg Sinclair stayed behind Holliday, giving him no chance to move on her. Carrying the lead-covered box was almost as good as being handcuffed.

The first fat drops of rain were hitting the sand. The drops were large enough to dig their own little craters when they hit. Gallant was going to have a hell of a time, his only advantage being that he would be running before the wind.

'How did the plane know when to pick you up?' Holliday asked.

'Satellite phone, an Ericsson R-290,' answered Meg. 'They've been flying in circles for an hour, waiting for my signal.'

'A satellite phone? Where on earth did you pick up one of those?'

'Think about it,' said Meg. Holliday could tell that she was grinning from ear to ear. 'It'll come to you.'

Holliday thought and then he had it. It was the only answer.

'Quince,' he said finally. 'He was one of yours.'

He cursed silently. He should have put it together long ago.

'Got it in one, Professor,' Meg said and laughed, obviously greatly pleased with herself. 'The whole abduction was just to make sure you were still off balance and not questioning things too much. Besides, I had to update Mother and her friends. Quince gave me the weapon and the phone while you were still knocked out.' There was a pause. 'We weren't prepared for an assault at the lake, however. That wasn't part of the plan at all.' The twin-engined turboprop touched down, its sticklike three-wheeled undercarriage and fat tires barely making an impression in the sand. The livery was stark black and white and the name on the side was Skybus Air Express.

'One of Mommy's companies?' Holliday guessed.

'Move,' said the young Sinclair woman.

'Why don't I just put the ark down and walk away?' Holliday suggested. 'No harm, no foul. You've got what you want.'

'Not yet,' answered Meg. 'We need you to authenticate the find.'

'What makes you think I'll do that for you?'

'You have an incentive,' said Meg Sinclair.

'What incentive would that be?' Holliday asked.

'Your so-called niece Peggy Blackstock and her archaeologist husband.'

'What about them?' Holliday asked, his heart beginning to race. He turned around to face Meg Sinclair, sour bile rising in his throat. Sinclair's face was blank and the gun was still unwavering in her hand. 'Tell me what you've done,' said Holliday.

'How touching, such family concern.' She paused. 'Oh, of course! Peggy's pregnant, isn't she?'

'Tell me!'

'At noon today, local Israeli time, Peggy and her husband were kidnapped. For the moment they are safe and unharmed. How long that condition lasts is entirely in your hands.'

Holliday froze. 'So help me God . . .'

'God can't help you,' said Meg Sinclair. 'But I can. Cooperate and they'll stay alive. One wrong move and they'll be dead. All three of them. Now move.'

Holliday stared at her. Never in his entire life had he experienced the utter fury and rage rising in his soul, not even in the heat of battle, not even when he'd felt the meaty slip-slide of his knife sliding across the exposed throat of a picket guard on the edge of an opium plantation outside of Garmsir in Helmand Province, Afghanistan.

'If you harm them in any way, when this is over I will hunt you down wherever you are and I'll see you dead and in the ground, you psychotic bitch.'

'You'd kill a woman?' Meg Sinclair asked, batting her eyes and smiling. 'I wouldn't have thought your chivalrous code would allow it.'

'In your case I'll make an exception.'

'Fine,' said Meg Sinclair. 'You've had your moment of heroic male posturing, but right now I want you to walk down the beach and get on that plane.' The rain began to fall harder. Holliday gave himself another second to burn her face into his mind and then turned away and did as he was told.

Five minutes later, turning into the wind, the plane rose into the air in a hard climb, then banked and headed south. As they turned, Holliday caught a glimpse of the *Deryldene D* putting out to sea, wake churning hard behind her as she backed away from the beach. He glanced at his watch. The time on the bezel had run out and true to his word Gallant had waited to the last minute. Holliday silently wished him Godspeed, watching the little lobster boat for as long as he could before it vanished into the sheeting rain.

30

The modern Rex Deus came to America before the United States even existed in the figure of a man named Jonathan Edwards, a Puritan pastor, theologian and missionary to the Indians – and anyone else who would listen to him.

Edwards was proud of his past and almost obsessed with his own genealogy. Like most members of Rex Deus he could clearly trace his ancestry back to the twelve original Merovingian kings, rulers of the twelve kingdoms of the Franks, which covered all of what is now France, Germany and most of Italy, including Rome.

Through the Merovingian kings, Edwards traced his past history to the Desposyni and the *adelphoi*, the younger brothers and sisters of Christ himself and the carriers of his bloodline into the future. Edwards firmly believed that it was his life's work to discover other descendants of the Desposyni in America and bring them together to forge a nation.

By the time of his death in 1758 he had discovered seven other Desposyni families in the New World, and with their coalition Rex Deus was born again. The eventual objective of the secret group of interconnected families was to infiltrate every aspect of society, politics and industry as quietly and efficiently as possible, eventually to hold benevolent and truly Christian hegemony over America and perhaps, at last, in the name and family of God, they would rule the entire world.

They were believers in a literal and strict interpretation of the Bible and almost all were slave owners – Joshua's 'Hewers of wood and drawers of water.' They also believed in a strict aristocratic system of government as far as the right to vote was concerned, and were classifiably revolutionaries since they swore allegiance only to Christ and no other king, including the king of England. Most of all, they valued secrecy and absolute obedience. The Sicilian Mafia's laws of *omerta* were no more than a casual oath to the members of Rex Deus.

By 1776, Rex Deus had grown considerably in wealth and power. There were eight Rex Deus signers of the Declaration of Independence and a dozen more within the Continental Congress. By the outbreak of the Civil War, there were scores of Rex Deus members, associates and acolytes on both sides and in every state and territory in the nation.

When it was clear that America's trading partners in the outside world were going to back the already industrialized North, the Southern members of Rex Deus did their best to ensure the failure of the Confederacy. Just after the war, strongly opposed to Lincoln's freeing of the slaves, Rex Deus saw to it that there would be no more such radical policies enacted during his term. It was the first political assassination Rex Deus had been involved in, but it wouldn't be the last.

By the beginning of the twentieth century, Rex Deus had elected mayors, governors, senators and congressmen and were a behind-the-scenes force backing everything from isolationism in the face of World War One to supporting ongoing trade with Germany until 1917, even though the United States was supposedly neutral until that time.

Between the wars they were strong proponents of Prohibition, but saw nothing wrong with investing enormously in Canadian distilleries, the major source of illicit booze in the United States for the better part of fifteen years. In 1929, warned well before the stock market's imminent collapse, Rex Deus removed almost all its interests in the New York and Chicago markets, saving billions of dollars for the members of the secretive group.

With the rise of Hitler in 1933, elements of Rex Deus in Europe either began allying themselves with the Nazi Party or began quietly liquidating their assets and reinvesting in the war industries of the United Kingdom and the United States.

Although philosophically against Hitler on a number of levels, his methods and administration were sound, taking a small group of men and turning them into a ruthless political, economic and military force almost overnight. An impressive man with much about his organization to be admired, but clearly insane, not to be trusted, and without a shred of tactical or strategic sense or knowledge when it came to waging war.

Through their political members within the Roosevelt administration and with the full cooperation of their friends and colleagues in Big Oil,

Rex Deus was also largely responsible for the foreign policy decisions that led to the choking off of all oil supplies to the 'Heathen Jap.' Not too surprising when you knew that Rose Francis Whitney Hull, the wife of Secretary of State Cordell Hull, came from a long line of Rex Deus members.

With their preferred policy in place, Rex Deus started investing heavily in war industries like small arms, rubber, steel and aluminum, well aware that the United States was being drawn inexorably to war. When Pearl Harbor came they were ready, all in the name of God, and particularly in the big-dollar, American God of Rex Deus.

After the war some members of Rex Deus, the Sinclairs in particular, began buying up utilities, both in the United States and abroad. Others continued investing in oil and others in real estate and banking. As America grew richer and stronger so too did Rex Deus.

The members of Rex Deus were not cracker evangelists who preached that prayer could bring you wealth and fame and took every credit card under the sun, even the Discover Card, just so long as you called their toll-free number *right now* with your faith offerings. The members of Rex Deus were True Believers, as devout and fanatical as the most ardent jihadist.

By the beginning of the new millennium, the senior members of the Rex Deus order were collectively the greatest single economic force in the United States as well as being the largest religious organization, and still, after more than two hundred years of remaining completely secret and off the radar, the existence of Rex Deus was barely rumored, and when those rumors did circulate they were invariably dismissed out of hand as nothing more than the paranoid delusions of the left liberal media and addle-brained, pot-smoking conspiracy theorists.

By 2008 the only thing Rex Deus hadn't done was to elect a president, and by the end of that year, with the abomination of a black man installed in the White House, it was clear to the Rex Deus elite that something had to be done before the country was irrevocably wounded, the very core of the nation's soul riddled with the cancerous tentacles of godlessness and unholy corruption. To fight this terrible scourge, Rex Deus would need a new leader and a new plan for the country if it was to survive. Drastic measures had to be taken and taken soon. A secret conclave of the Desposyni was called.

The Skybus Air Express turboprop resumed the normal flight path corresponding to the flight plan they'd filed earlier in the day and arrived in Bangor, Maine, an hour and a half after leaving Sable Island and well ahead of the newly christened Hurricane Otto that was now sweeping over the little outpost island in the Atlantic.

By the time they arrived at Bangor International Airport the ark had been transferred to a wooden crate already Customs-sealed and listed on the cargo manifest as medical isotopes. Holliday was provided with what appeared to be a genuine United States passport with his name on it and his occupation listed as copilot.

They were waved through the Customs and Immigration checkpoint as crew, and Holliday was immediately led to a private lounge. The two watchdogs who had been on the Skybus flight accompanied them, then turned them over to a new set of caretakers in the lounge. From their attitude and their demeanor Holliday assumed they were ex-military, and he also assumed they were armed.

Half an hour later they transferred to a Gulfstream G550 business jet in the black and red livery of American Fluid Dynamics Corporation. Slightly less than two hours later they arrived in Lexington, Kentucky. They were met on the tarmac by three hard-faced black men in white shirts and dark suits and three black Cadillac Escalade vans with darkly tinted windows.

Even in the brief moment that he saw their faces Holliday knew they'd seen war in one place or another, either Iraq or Afghanistan. They had the look in their eyes of soldiers who still saw things that haunted them in their dreams. Everyone climbed into the three vehicles and then, like a downsized version of a presidential motorcade, they swept out of the airport and on to Interstate 64.

From the interstate they made the brief thirty-minute commute to the state capital of Frankfort and finally, bypassing the small town of barely twenty-seven thousand, they arrived at Poplar Hill, home of the Sinclair family for almost two hundred years.

Originally Poplar Hill had been called Stoneacre Farm, named after the boulders that had been pulled from the soil by the earliest Sinclairs, and

the farmhouse had been more like the impover-
ished cabin mentioned in the state song, 'My Old
Kentucky Home.'

As the Sinclairs had prospered in the company
of Rex Deus the old cabin on the hill overlooking the Kentucky River and the growing town of
Frankfort had been replaced by larger and larger
farmhouses, eventually becoming the gigantic
combination neo-Norman, Gothic and Scots-
Baronial style castle-mansion that sprawled over
the summit of the hill today, a stone extrava-
ganza that came complete with a granite porte
cochere at the main entrance, several Disneyland
turrets, a conservatory as big as a bowling alley,
two secret passages – one on either side of the
massive fireplace in the study – the Sinclair coat
of arms inlaid in marble on the floor of the Main
Hall and a tunnel leading from the basement
kitchens to the stone stables and the coach house
behind the main building. Half of the original
stables were still used for their original purpose
and held the Sinclair thoroughbreds, and the
other half was used as a garage.

The building had been erected at obscene
cost by Richard Oswald Sinclair, the present
Richard Sinclair's great-great-grandfather. The

chateauesque mansion had been built between 1888 and 1895 in direct competition with his art-collecting colleague, George Washington Vanderbilt, who built the famous Biltmore Mansion during the same period. The two men had wagered on who would build the largest mansion in the country. Vanderbilt won, with Biltmore coming in at 175,000 square feet to Poplar Hill's 165,000 square feet. Sinclair argued that if you included the stables, directly connected by the tunnel to the main house, he should have won. The two men never spoke again.

Holliday stayed in his seat for what seemed a long time and then one of the babysitters who had accompanied them on the jet escorted Holliday into the building and across the Main Hall. The elaborate entranceway with its marble floor and soaring ceiling with the inlaid coat of arms made Holliday acutely aware that he was still dressed in the jeans, rough shirt and work boots he'd been wearing on Sable Island. Looking at his watch, he realized that it had barely been four hours since he'd been staring down the throat of a hurricane.

He wondered if Gallant had made it through the storm and silently vowed to find out about the lobsterman's fate if he got out of his present situation alive, something he was beginning to doubt. If he authenticated the bogus ark for the Sinclairs his continued existence would only be a liability. While driving into the estate he'd seen hundreds of acres of field and forest, all far from any public road; plenty of places to discreetly dispose of a body.

They turned left off the entrance hall and went down a passage that looked like something out of Buckingham Palace, complete with dusty Persian carpets on the teak wood floor and heavily framed and individually lit oil paintings on the green, moiré silk walls. The paintings were all European, mostly of horses in battle, their nostrils flared with the scent of fresh blood, their eyes crazed as their riders sliced each other to ribbons with their curved sabers.

They passed what appeared to be the doors of an elevator and a little farther on turned into a relatively small and comfortable-looking sitting room fitted out with couches and easy chairs centered around a reasonably scaled fireplace. Above the mantel was a simply framed painting of a small terrier-like dog in full flight.

'It's a Galla Creek Feist,' said an elderly, elegant

woman seated in one of the armchairs and noticing Holliday's interest. She had the rasping voice of a heavy smoker. 'It's the kind of dog that Daniel Boone used when he was hunting squirrel. His name was Langford's Rowdy. He was my favorite.'

Holliday noticed that the ark, uncrated, stood on the coffee table in front of her.

'You must be the mother,' he said.

'My name is Katherine Pierce Sinclair.' She lifted a hand and gestured toward the armchair facing her across the table. 'Sit down, Colonel Holliday, you must be very tired after your journey.' She gave the babysitter a look and he withdrew, closing the door behind him. Holliday had the feeling that he wasn't going far.

'You told Meg your little ruse with the box wouldn't fool me.'

'It never really had to. We had people watching Miss Blackstock from the beginning. I'm a great believer in leverage, Colonel.'

'I told Meg what I'd do if either Peggy or Rafi were harmed in any way.'

'There's no need for threats, Colonel Holliday,' said the elderly woman. She lit a cigarette and blew a curling stream of smoke into the air.

She held the cigarette like a man, between the lowest knuckles of the first two fingers. 'No harm will come to them as long as you authenticate the True Ark.'

'When did you plant it there?'

'More than a year ago. Among other things, Margaret is a trained archaeologist. She was quite capable of following the clues to the whereabouts of the ark herself. Sadly, those clues ran out on Iona. From there they could have traveled anywhere. There were a number of possible answers, including Sable Island, so we manufactured evidence to lead you there. Sable was the most attractive of the possibilities because it would prove the viability of Rex Deus's assertion that the ark came to the New World. We had the box created using authentic medieval tools and techniques and placed it in the ground on the edge of Lake Wallace. Margaret had the exact GPS coordinates so she knew exactly where to dig.'

'The inscription in Greek was a nice touch.'

'We thought so. Margaret studied ancient languages at Columbia.'

'A real Renaissance woman.'

'A daughter a mother can be proud of.'

'Handy with a gun, too,' said Holliday dryly.

'She's been hunting at Poplar Hill since she was a child. She's a better shot than her big brother.'

'The next president of the United States?'

'Quite so,' she replied.

'Why me?' Holliday asked. 'There are plenty of better-known medievalists around.'

'I've been interested in you ever since your trip to the Azores a while back,' she said. Her thin smile reminded Holliday of a snake swallowing a small animal. 'As much as we need you to authenticate your little find on the table, I'd very much like to leaf through that little notebook that Brother Rodrigues gave to you with his dying breath on Corvo. I presume you have it safely hidden away.'

In a safe-deposit box in a bank in Geneva, but he wasn't going to tell her that. 'You presume correctly.'

'Excellent. You can fetch it for us after the authentication at the conclave tomorrow. We'll take the G5 and make it a little celebration.'

'What makes you think I'll do that?' Holliday said, even though he already knew. Katherine Sinclair smiled and took a heavy drag on her cigarette, taking it deeply into her lungs. When she spoke smoke burst out of her mouth like a dragon exhaling. An emaciated dragon at the end of its withered, leathery life.

'You'll do it because your life depends on it and the lives of Miss Blackstock and her new husband.'

31

After Holliday's brief conversation with Katherine Sinclair he was escorted to one of the third- and top-floor tower rooms that overlooked the porte cochere and the lavish, formal terraced gardens at the front of the castle. The view was as grandiose as the castle itself. From the love seat beneath the curved glass windows Holliday was able to see the entire town of Frankfort nestled in the valley below the estate, surrounded on all sides by low hills, their flanks covered by lush green forests. From the high round room he could see the dome on the state capitol and the winding course of the Kentucky River, making its slow way north to join the broader reaches of the Ohio.

The tower room was lavishly decorated with scattered Persian carpets on the floor, a huge four-poster canopy bed at the far end of the room, a delicately scrolled marble mantel over a sizable fireplace hearth and a gigantic flat-screen television on one wall with a soft, comfortable couch in front of it. An en suite bathroom was next to the enormous bed and there was an antique circular breakfast table with two matching chairs next to the couch. There was even a bar fridge stocked with airline bottles of booze, mixers, cans of soda and a big jar of macadamia nuts. All the comforts of home if home happened to be a Hilton hotel.

After checking to see if the big oak door was locked, which of course it was, Holliday spent a long time pacing out the perimeters of the room and mentally going over his options. He knew he could almost certainly jimmy the old skeleton key lock on the door, but where would that get him? There could easily be a guard posted at his door, and even if there wasn't there were almost certainly lots of armed guards all over the estate.

The top floor of mansions like this was usually given over as the servants' quarters, but it could just as easily be a barracks for the security people. And barracks was the word; the security people he'd seen so far were all ex-military, Holliday was sure of it; none of the ragtag mercenary wannabes from that Blackhawk bunch; these guys were the real McCoy.

He tired of pacing the floor eventually and flopped down on the couch. He picked the remote up off the coffee table in front of him and clicked on the flat screen, scrolling through rock-star reality shows, Maury Povich dealing with an endless supply of pregnant trailer-trash women wanting DNA tests and reruns of *CSI* and *Law and Order*.

He watched ten minutes of Claudette Colbert in the title role and Henry Wilcoxon as Mark Antony in the original, 1934 version of *Cleopatra* on Turner Classic Movies and finally settled on CNN. There was no mention made of any abductions in Israel, but that didn't really mean anything; CNN seemed to think that the only international news worth reporting was plagues, floods, earthquakes and wars. Outside dusk was falling, the air itself glowing with the strange, ozone-heavy yellow light that usually precedes a storm.

At six p.m. on the dot he heard the sound of his door being unlocked. A few seconds later two of Kate Sinclair's goons appeared, the one in the lead carrying a large silver tray. Behind the two men Meg Sinclair appeared. She was wearing formal riding clothes, including tall black boots and jodhpurs. Her hair was tied back with a black velvet ribbon. The man with the tray set it down on the round table beside the couch and began setting the table for two and unloading the food, including a vacuum carafe of coffee.

'Come to gloat?' Holliday asked.

'I'm not the gloating type,' said Meg. 'I just thought you might like some company for dinner.'

'Very hospitable of you.'

'We don't have to be adversarial about this, Doc.'

'Yes, we do,' he answered. 'Your mother had Peggy and her husband kidnapped. You're holding me against my will. You can't get much more adversarial than that.'

'They won't come to any harm and neither will you.' She sat down at the table.

'As long as I do precisely what you and your mother want.'

'Come and eat your dinner, you must be starved.'

'You didn't answer my question,' said Holliday, sitting down. The dinner was four-star-restaurant grade: porcini-stuffed and balsamic-glazed filet mignon with a baked potato and grilled mushrooms. The soup was lobster bisque, some kind of ironic little joke from Meg, no doubt. Dessert looked like crème caramel.

He ate a spoonful of the bisque; it was perfect right down to the slight brandy aftertaste and the dollop of crème fraiche and flat-leaf parsley stalks floating on the pale pink surface of the white ceramic bowl.

'Why would it be so difficult to do what we ask?'

'Because it's a lie. A setup, a fake.'

'In aid of a good cause, though.'

'Who says?' Holliday asked, slicing into the filet mignon, the rich stuffing oozing out.

'I say,' answered Meg, beginning to work on her own meal.

'From what I gather you're going to use the counterfeit contents of the box as leverage to have your brother made head of your little cult.'

'The little cult, as you call it, has combined net assets of half a trillion dollars, and that's becoming a problem. Power tends to corrupt,' said Meg.

'And absolute power tends to corrupt absolutely,' said Holliday, finishing the quote. 'The first Baron Acton. It's the only noteworthy thing he ever said. It was in response to Pius IX's Bull about papal infallibility back in the 1860s.'

'Well, that's what's happening within Rex Deus. The order has so much power concentrated in such a small group of people that it has been corrupted. There are some people within the order who see it as a means to an end, that end being personal gain. They've lost sight of the principles that made this country great. They've lost their way, just like the rest of America.'

'And your brother's going to get the country back on track?'

'Yes.'

'What makes you think he'd be any better able to do that than anyone else in the Senate or anywhere else?'

'Doc, if the president is elected to a second term it will be too late. The country will become a socialist hellhole with the government sticking its nose everywhere, in business, health care, industry, Wall Street. Another Kremlin.'

'You really believe that?' Holliday said.

'I not only believe it, I *know* it,' answered Meg, fire in her eyes. 'Some of the members of Rex Deus know it too, and they're planning to take advantage of it.'

'How?'

'The cadre involved, if they can convince the

other members of the order, want to manipulate another market crash, among other things. When the smoke clears they'll be even richer and the entire country will be in extremis. It might never recover; we'd turn into a third-rate power overnight. We can't let that happen, Doc. *You* can't let it happen.' Holliday nodded thoughtfully. She'd used his nickname three times since entering the room, something she'd never done once that he could remember when they were together.

'So you want me to lie for you.'

'Not about anything real, about a myth, something that probably never was. Is that so hard?'

'Who's to say I want to put your family at the helm of the ship of state?' said Holliday.

'It's better than sinking it,' answered Meg Sinclair.

'This thing has been a lie from the beginning. You lied to me and now you want me to lie for you?'

'I'd lie if it was my family's lives at stake,' said Meg.

'All right,' said Holliday. 'If you promise to release Peggy and Rafi as soon as I've done what you want.'

'Of course,' said Meg. 'You have my word.'

Holliday didn't believe it for a minute, but he said nothing. Better to live and fight another day.

'Okay,' he said. He put down his fork, his appetite gone.

'What will you need to open up the box when the time comes?'

Holliday thought for a long moment then spoke. 'A pencil butane torch and a utility knife or a heavy-duty box cutter.'

'Why the box cutter?' she asked, her tone lightly suspicious.

'I'm going to hijack your mother and fly her to Cuba, of course.'

'Please,' said Meg. 'I need you to be serious.'

'The butane torch is to soften the lead seal; the box cutter is to slice through the softened lead.'

'I see,' said Meg. She stared at Holliday across the table, a strange expression on her face. 'It could have been different between us, you know, Doc,' she continued.

'No, it couldn't,' he answered, and that was the end of dinner. Without another word the red-haired woman got to her feet and went to the door. She tapped out a three-two knock code and the door was instantly opened by one of the goons who'd brought in the tray of food. She left without turning around or saying good night and the door was closed again.

Thinking about what Meg Sinclair had said, Holliday finished his dinner. The first axiom of a soldier: eat when you've got the chance; it may not come again for a while. He ate both desserts and drank almost the entire carafe of coffee. Even so he had no trouble falling asleep, fully dressed, in the big bed as the first raindrops tapped against the room's tall windows like a faint memory of the approaching hurricane on Sable Island.

It was just past seven when he awoke from a deep, dreamless sleep. It was still raining, a constant downpour spilling out of a sky the color of slate. It rippled down the tower room windows in long erratic tear streaks and dripped from the eaves. The view was gone and Holliday could see no farther than the bright splashes of color in the formal gardens. Beyond that everything was a universal gray.

Holliday turned away from the windows, stripped off his clothes and padded across the room to the bathroom. Everything was there just like a good hotel: shampoo, soap, towels, shaving equipment, deodorant, a toothbrush and toothpaste and even a big fluffy white bathrobe.

He ran the shower hot, shampooed the sand from his hair and then did it again.

He lathered his entire body, rinsed, then did it again. Squeaky clean at last, he got into the robe and spent another fifteen minutes carefully shaving. He wondered if the Sinclairs were going to provide him with new clothes. Presumably they didn't want him showing up at their so-called conclave looking like a bum. He also found himself feeling hungry again and wondered if the condemned man would get a last meal.

He finished up in the bathroom feeling refreshed and wide-awake. Stepping back into the tower room he saw that the Sinclairs were one step ahead of him. While he'd been in the shower the dinner things had been removed and a single place setting laid out. The bed had been neatly made and across the fluffy duvet there was a suit, shirt, tie, shoes, socks and even underwear laid out.

The white shirt was silk, the suit was a conservative dark pinstripe with a Zegna label and the shoes were black Crockett & Jones oxfords. The tie was handmade dark blue silk with a pattern of tiny Saint-Clair engrailed crosses in muted gold. The socks were black and silk as well.

Staying in the bathrobe, he sat down at the table and lifted the silver top of one of the salvers. Scrambled eggs, not too wet and not too dry. He opened up the rest of the covered dishes. Crisp bacon, sausages, home fries, fried green tomatoes and hush puppies instead of toast. He loaded up his plate, poured himself some coffee and dug in.

Breakfast turned out to be an anticlimax. He dressed carefully, enjoying the feel of the new clothes and even the slight pinch of the expensive British shoes. Everything fitted perfectly. Nine o'clock came and went and still no one had come to fetch him. At nine thirty the first of a dozen vehicles came out of the misting rain and pulled up under the porte cochere below the tower window. The first car was a black, six-passenger Lincoln limousine.

The vehicles that followed over the next two hours were a lavish assortment of Town Cars, Escalades, Mercedes and Jaguar sedans. There was even a Bentley and a Rolls-Royce. The color of choice appeared to be a discreet black. Watching them appear from his vantage point in the tower room, Holliday wondered if that many high-end cars would draw unwanted attention and then dismissed the thought.

This was the Kentucky of multimillion-dollar stud fees and Triple Crown winners. There were probably more Saudi oil princes driving around in cars like the ones he'd just seen than Americans. The world had changed over the last decades. Was Meg Sinclair right? Had the United States lost its way, or was it just adapting to new realities? Was there really anyplace left for the concept of a world power? It didn't matter; he was going to give her what she wanted if there was the faintest possibility that it would keep Peggy and Rafi from coming to any harm. He'd lasted this long and somehow he always seemed to survive. Go figure.

32

They fed him a Cobb salad lunch at noon and came for him at five to one. A pair of Katherine Sinclair's goons escorted him down to the Dining Hall on the main floor, an immense, high-ceilinged and narrow room that looked more like the nave of a cathedral than a place to enjoy a meal.

There were three tall, arched stained-glass windows at the curving far end of the chamber and a long refectory table capable of seating at least twenty but only set for sixteen.

The triptych of stained-glass windows had a sword-bearing St Michael in the center flanked on either side with knights in thirteenth-century armor, their shields emblazoned with the engrailed Saint-Clair cross. Today the Dining Hall was being used as a conference room, place settings replaced with glasses and water carafes and pads for taking notes.

Holliday was led into the churchlike room, the

sudden focus of everyone's attention. Katherine Sinclair was seated in the exact center of the table on the right, flanked by Meg Sinclair on one side and a handsome auburn-haired man on the other. The resemblance to both Katherine and Meg was obvious, so presumably he was Meg's brother, Richard Pierce Sinclair, the presidential hopeful.

He had a suitably somber expression for the job and temples shot with gray, so at least he looked right for the part. To Meg Sinclair's right was an empty chair, the only one at the table. The two goons led him to the vacant seat and then withdrew. Holliday sat and looked around.

Of the twelve other people at the table Holliday recognized some but not all. There was a four-star general he recognized from his years at the Pentagon, now a member of the Joint Chiefs, several congressmen and congresswomen, Miles Bainbridge with Ronald Reagan shoe polish hair and his hatchet-faced Shirley Jones clone wife, Beth, owners of the Gifts from God Prosperity Church and dispensers of its franchises.

GGPC was a billion-dollar business with churches in twenty-seven countries and with seven hundred and fifty thousand 'partners' following the church's simple credo: The best way to get God to give you money is to give some money to the Bainbridges first. Among other things the message had got them half a dozen houses spread across the nation and a Cessna Citation XLS to get to them in.

Beside the Bainbridges was a well-known real estate tycoon who, among other things, owned the biggest casino in Las Vegas, and beside him was the lady CEO of the biggest combined tobacco, agribusiness and soft drink company in the world. There were others at the table whom Holliday didn't recognize, but recognizable or not they all exuded self-confidence, utter assurance of their own worth and immutable power.

And there wasn't a Timex in the room. Every wrist was decorated with Rolex, Omega, Patek Philippe or at the very least Cartier. Miles Bainbridge and his wife took the prize wearing his-and-hers matching Jules Audemars-Piguet Grande Complication platinum-cased watches at seven hundred thousand dollars a pop. If nothing else, God had answered their prayers at least.

With Holliday finally seated, Katherine Sinclair stilled the muted chatter by rapping her knuckles on the old scarred walnut table.

'Before we start I'd like to express my condolences to all the members of the family of our late leader and brother in the order, William Henry Adams. He will be greatly missed.

'In light of his passing, by the rules and Constitution of the Order, we are required to immediately call for conclave to elect a new leader, which is the reason we have all been called together as heads of all the surviving Rex Deus families.

'However, before we begin the voting procedures, I would like to introduce my daughter, Margaret Sinclair, who, as you all know, is a biblical archaeologist of some note. For the last two years and recently with the help of Lieutenant Colonel Dr John Holliday, well-known medieval historian, Margaret has been on a quest for nothing less than the True Ark, which all of us here are aware of, I'm sure. I'll let Margaret make her announcement.'

Meg stood up. She was dressed in a dark, expensive-looking pantsuit, her bright red hair up in a businesslike French twist. She was wearing cat's-eye librarian glasses around her neck on a velvet cord, an added touch that gave her a serious, no-nonsense look even though Holliday was fairly sure she didn't need them.

'As all of you know,' she began, 'the True Ark is a central component of the Rex Deus mythology, a reliquary or box containing the Holy Grail, the Crown of Thorns, the Holy Shroud, and the Ring of Christ. Some of you I'm sure think the ark really is just a myth; others follow the theory that the ark is contained within the much larger golden Reliquary of the Three Kings, now on the high altar of the Cathedral in Cologne in Germany, also thought to contain the bones of the three magi who brought the infant Christ their holy offerings of gold, frankincense and myrrh.

'The more cynical among you may well believe that the True Ark and its journey to the New World is no more than a story, a hoax invented by Jonathan Edwards, the founder of our organization, represented at this very table by our sister in the order Jane Campbell Edwards, his descendant.' She nodded toward the Big Tobacco CEO seated beside the florid-faced real estate tycoon with the extravagant hairpiece.

'The short answer is that all of you are wrong. I know this to be a certainty because after a long and sometimes dangerous journey, I and my good friend and colleague Dr John Holliday, lately a professor of military history at the National Military Academy at West Point, both located the True Ark and excavated it from its hiding place on Sable Island, buried almost seven hundred years ago by Sir Jean de Saint-Clair and the Blessed Juliana of Navarre, Abbess of the St Agnes of Bohemia Convent and the Chapel of St Mary Magdalene in Prague. We did this in the face of an oncoming hurricane, I might add, but that's a story for another day.' Here Meg paused for the appropriate chuckles and laughter.

Somewhere in the middle distance, muffled by the incessant driving rain, Holliday thought he heard the thrumming chug of a helicopter's rotors . . . a serious enough accident in Frankfort to require a medevac? Not really surprising considering the weather. He turned his attention back to Meg's suitably edited set piece about their adventures, combining her research into the Blessed Juliana and Holliday's interest in Jean de Saint-Clair.

At the end of her speech she raised her voice slightly and in a breathless tone announced: 'Ladies and gentlemen, I give you the True Ark, at last returned to its rightful heirs and owners, the gathered Brothers and Sisters of Rex

Deus, last remaining members of the Desposyni in America.'

Someone must have had their ear to the door, or more likely the room was bugged, because at almost that instant two of Katherine Sinclair's dark-suited thugs brought in the ark, wrapped in a pale blue moving blanket, followed by a third man carrying the mini-torch and box cutter that Holliday had requested.

The three men set the box down in front of both Meg Sinclair and Holliday, then silently withdrew. Meg Sinclair pulled the quilted blanket off the box and tilted the entire lead-sheathed artifact toward the assembled people at the table.

Meg put on her scholarly eyeglasses. 'As you can see,' she said, 'the ark is still sealed. The lid bears the ancient engrailed cross crest of the Saint-Clairs and the inscription in Greek that translates as *In hoc signo vinces* – By this you shall conquer – the motto of the Knights Templar.'

She looked around the table. 'We kept the lid sealed so all of you here could see the opening firsthand.' She nodded in Holliday's direction and he dutifully stood up. With Meg Sinclair still standing at his side he picked up the mini-torch. It was a little BernzOmatic with a burner that looked like a miniature nozzle from a service station gas pump.

There was an automatic spark ignition in the little handle that he fitted between the thumb and forefinger of his right hand. With his left hand he turned the tiny valve release knob to start the gas and squeezed the ignition trigger. He was rewarded by a hissing sound and an instant burst of bright blue flame.

He picked up the box cutter and got down to work, melting a section of the lead solder around the lid and running the box cutter through the softened metal. It took him ten minutes to work his way around the entire lid. When he was done he put down the torch and the box cutter and silently turned to Meg.

'You open it,' she said with a smile that didn't go with the hard, almost dangerous look in her eyes. 'You were just as responsible for finding it as I was.'

Holliday nodded. The group around the table watched carefully. There was a muffled cough from somewhere. The Edwards woman looked coolly skeptical and Miles Bainbridge had one eyebrow lifted in mild, patronizing disbelief. His wife just smiled with her best Dale Evans-Partridge family sidekick look. The sixty-something blonde in the red dress and the Botox face looked suspiciously like her husband had prayed for a lobotomy and got his wish.

Holliday caught a shadowy hint of movement beyond the windows. He ignored it and carefully pulled off the lid and put it aside. The room was utterly silent. There was another muted cough. Holliday peered into the box and almost burst out laughing at what he saw.

The contents were a stroke of genius and a marvel of misdirection. He stepped aside and let Meg Sinclair do the honors since she had obviously masterminded the brilliant deception. There was another cough and this time Holliday realized it came from outside the door, but all eyes were on Meg.

She removed the contents of the True Ark one by one and laid them out on the soft surface of the moving blanket. The Holy Grail was exactly as she'd described it, a roughly turned wooden cup that looked as though it had been made on some ancient lathe, which it probably had; the Egyptians had used bow lathes a thousand years before the birth of Christ. Easy enough to find on the archaeological black market.

The Crown of Thorns was made of old rusted iron, a common torture device used by the early Romans. The cloth part of the device was long gone but the intent was still clear: a sack was fitted over the head coming down to the eyebrows in front and to the mid-neck at the back, covering the ears. Heavy iron chain was sewn into the hem with the chain just above the eyes, around the ears and down to the middle of the neck at the back.

The purpose of this was to weigh the sack and produce eight to ten pounds of downward pressure. Inside the cloth at the eye line and going all around were inward-facing, slightly downward-pointing thorns of iron. The weight of the chain pulled the iron thorns into the flesh of the head, and sometimes even through the skull and into the brain. The device was used well into the Middle Ages and was a favorite of the Spanish Inquisition.

The Ring of Christ was just as impossible to date for authentication as the chalice and the crown. It was a simple bronze ring, justifiably tarnished with age and with a coinlike upper surface. The Romans and the people they conquered in the Holy Land were very likely to have worn rings just like it in the first century.

The design on the coin on the upper surface showed the Chi-Rho X-shaped symbol that was the combination of the first two letters of Christ's name in Ancient Greek. Between the arms of the X were the symbols for alpha and omega, the beginning and the end. Together the Chi-Rho symbol was used as a sigil, or magic seal, by early Christians. The ring seemed terribly familiar and Holliday suddenly remembered seeing one almost exactly like it in a little museum at Kourion on the Island of Cyprus.

Meg Sinclair saved the best for last, reverently removing the shroud, which was actually nothing more than a large shred of rotting cloth. Holliday grinned.

He had no doubt that if tested the cloth would show remnants of human tissue and various organic stains, and if dated would show it to be contemporary with the time of Christ. The cloth was almost certainly byssus, the fine white linen typically used for the wrappings of late Pharaonic era Egyptian burials. Taken altogether the relics were a tour de force. Meg glanced into the box one last time and pulled out something else: two interlocking pieces of wood, probably imported cedar from the mountain slopes of Syria. Jean de

Saint-Clair's Instrument of God, the early Jacob's Quadrant, that had allowed him to navigate his way to the Farther Shore and an exact copy of the one he'd found in the ancient vizier's tomb in Libya the year before.

Meg turned to him, smiling, and then she winked. Holliday paled as the truth sank in. Meg had known about the navigation instrument from the very beginning. That meant that Bernheim, the French naval historian, had been in Rex Deus's pocket well before they'd met in La Brasserie Malakoff in Paris.

And it was Bernheim who'd pointed him toward Brother Morvan and inevitably to his meeting with Meg Sinclair in the chapel on Mont Saint-Michel. He cursed himself for a fool. He'd been set up from the start and he hadn't seen it, even though part of him *must* have known that the meeting at the island fortress was too much of a coincidence, the first of many, in fact. Now it was going to cost him his life as well as Peggy and Rafi's.

Operation Assyrian began just like Byron's poem described – like a wolf coming down on the fold, the sheep in this instance being the members of Rex Deus. The only warning was the cracking triple bark of the Galil mounted grenade launchers and the shattering sound of breaking glass. By instinct Holliday dropped to the floor, squeezing his eyes shut and covering his ears. He had a pretty good idea of what was coming.

Three heavily armed soldiers clad in black armored vests, black balaclava ski masks and dark goggles rolled through the ruptured stained-glass windows, following the three grenades that were still spinning down the length of the refectory table.

Two of them were flash-bang stun grenades and the other was smoke. The flash-bangs went off first, blinding everyone at the table as every retinal receptor short-circuited along with an eardrum-rupturing blast of disorienting 180-decibel sound. A split second later the smoke grenade went off and the room began to fill with thick yellow smoke.

There were moans and screams all around Holliday as he climbed to his feet and peered into the smoke. People blindly stumbled into him as he struggled to find the door. There was a crashing sound and the door into the room burst open and he heard a loud voice bellowing, 'Sa'al Holliday, to me!'

Sa'al was Israeli for Lieutenant Colonel. Holliday fought his way to the door along with the rest of the dazed, blind and deafened members of Rex Deus who were still standing.

One of them was the Pentagon general. Holliday elbowed him in the throat and the heavyset man went down. The only thing between him and the door was the reeling figure of Miles Bainbridge, the cash or credit card televangelist who was rubbing at his tear-stained cheeks and moaning. Holliday cocked his fist and punched him in the mouth as hard as he could, feeling the expensive capped teeth shattering beneath his knuckles. Finally he made it to the door.

A black-suited figure gripped him by the arm. 'Colonel Holliday?'

'Yes.'

'Long time no see, sir. Please come with me and hurry, the clock's ticking.'

The man in black virtually dragged him out of the room. Holliday noticed a silenced Glock 17 in his hand. One of Katherine Sinclair's heavies was slouched on the floor, his own Glock on the floor beside him and his brains leaking on to the wall.

'He drew down on me,' said the man in black.

They rushed down the corridor to a narrow set of stairs leading down. 'We have to hurry, sir, please.' They clattered down the stairs with other black-suited soldiers close behind them.

'You're Shaldag? Unit 5101?' Holliday asked, referring to the Israeli Special Forces group. Shaldag was supposedly responsible for marking the target for Operation Babylon, the destruction of the nuclear reactor at Osirak in Iraq.

'We don't exist, sir,' answered the man, gripping his arm again. They stepped out into the big commercial-style kitchen in the basement of Poplar Hill. 'And we were never here, sir.' The man's voice was familiar but Holliday couldn't quite place it. They reached the tunnel leading to the stables. Holliday saw another of Katherine Sinclair's guards sprawled across the floor. The results of those strange ethereal coughing sounds Holliday had heard.

'He draw down on you, too?' Holliday asked.

The man led him into the stone-lined tunnel.

'No, sir,' said the man. 'He fired on me. We don't fire unless absolutely necessary, but we always fire back when fired upon.'

'That sounds like something I might have said,' Holliday said and grinned.

'You did, sir. Roman Military Tactics 301, sir. Boom, Ah, USMA-Rah-Rah, USMA-Rah-Rah, Ooh, Rah, Ooh, Rah . . . sir.' The West Point Rocket cheer. Who *was* this kid in the black balaclava helmet? They reached a set of stone steps and raced up them to exit in the stables.

'Do I know you?' asked Holliday. They ran across the garage side of the stables and out into the sheeting rain. Visibility was almost zero but the man in black seemed to know where he was going.

They ran into a grove of poplars and down a narrow, almost invisible path. He could hear the sound of gunfire behind him. He turned and looked back over his shoulder. There were a dozen black-suited men behind him.

They reached a clearing. Two UH-1 Iroquois helicopters stood in the clearing, rotors spinning. Surprisingly the choppers sported the red and white livery of the Franklin County Sheriff's Office. The sliding doors of the helicopters were open, a black-balaclava-wearing soldier standing beside each one.

'This way,' said the man at Holliday's side, grabbing his arm in an iron grip again. Holliday, his shepherd and six others crowded into the vehicle. Even before the door slammed shut they were in the air. A man seated beside the pilot turned and slipped off his headphones. His face was darkly tanned, lined and worn by too much sun and too much worrying.

'We lose anyone, Menzer?' asked the older man.

'No, sir. All present and accounted for.'

'Excellent,' said the older man. His caretaker pulled off his balaclava.

'Misha?' Holliday said, dumbfounded. 'Misha Menzer?' The thick eyebrows, pointy chin and the beak of a nose were a dead giveaway, although the Menzer he'd known had a face spotted with pimples and wore heavy plastic glasses. His ex-student grinned.

'That's me, sir. Thayer Hall, sir. Class of oh-five. You told me I'd wind up in the car wash at a base motor pool if I didn't pull up my socks.' Menzer had been one of his exchange students back in the day. A better sense of humor than soldierly aptitude, he'd thought at the time.

'Nothing I like better than being proven wrong,' said Holliday. He reached out and clapped his ex-student on the shoulder. 'Especially when I get my ass pulled out of the fire.'

'My pleasure, sir,' said Menzer. 'Pulling asses is our business, sir. They needed someone who'd recognize you. I volunteered. Orders from the boss.' He nodded toward the man beside the pilot and said something in Hebrew to the other men on the chopper and they laughed. Holliday glanced out the window. He was vaguely aware of flying over hills and forest land but that was about it. He tapped the man in the front seat on the arm. The older man turned and slipped off his headphones.

'They said they'd kill my cousin and her husband if I didn't cooperate. We have to get them before it's too late,' Holliday said urgently, yelling over the whickering clatter of the rotors and the roar of the big turbine.

'No need,' yelled back the man. 'We got a heads-up that they were going to be snatched, from the Vatican of all places. A man named Father Thomas Brennan, of all people. Head of the Vatican Secret Service,' said the older man. Sodalitium Pianum. Holliday had butted heads with Brennan once before, also about a kidnapping.

'What happened?' he asked.

'We snatched them first,' said the man in the co-pilot's seat. 'They're safe and sound. We've got them at Ramat David Air Base up near Haifa in the north, waiting to fly over here and meet you.'

Holliday felt his heart swell with relief.

'Thank you,' he said gratefully.

'*Tsu gezunt,*' said the older man. 'You're welcome.'

'I take it you're Mossad,' said Holliday. 'Misha wouldn't say.'

'Misha is a good boy, a good shot, too,' said the older man. 'We had a man infiltrating Quince's group. Turns out they're an outsourcing operation the CIA uses for black bag operations in so-called friendly countries. Our man GPS-tagged your shoes and the Sinclair woman's cell phone with data-pulling chips. We've been following you ever since.'

'That doesn't answer the question.'

'Some questions shouldn't be asked,' said the older man.

'You don't exist.' Holliday smiled.

'You catch on quickly, my boy.' The older man smiled back, and they flew on through the falling rain.

33

Peggy Blackstock, her husband, Rafi, Doc Holliday and Arnie Gallant were fishing with hand lines in the placid waters of Bedford Basin at the inner end of Halifax Harbour. It was a perfect summer day, bright sun shining from a cloudless blue sky. Gallant had provided the dory, obscurely named the *Geoffrey G.*, and an endless stream of local lore, out-and-out fabrications and tall tales and an equally endless monologue on the best method of bait fishing. It was R & R for everyone, but especially for Peggy, who'd had a miscarriage, almost certainly brought on by recent events.

'What exactly are we fishing *for*?' asked Peggy.

'Bull fish and mackerel mostly,' said Gallant. 'Eels, maybe.'

'Gross,' said Peggy.

'Can you eat them?' Rafi asked.

'The mackerel, I s'pose,' Gallant said and

shrugged. 'The bull fish if you were desperate. Eels if you like that sort of thing.'

'What does bull fish taste like?' Peggy asked.

'Whatever its last meal was,' said Gallant.

'What does it eat?' Rafi asked.

'Mostly *chaetognatha Sagitta elegans*,' responded Gallant.

'Elegant spear,' said Holliday abstractedly. He was staring thoughtfully at absolutely nothing.

'Pardon?' Peggy said.

'*Sagitta elegans*. That's what it means when you translate the Latin.'

'Arrow worms,' said Gallant, jigging his line a little. 'They look like hairy horse penises with a big jaw on the end. And they're slimy.' He nodded toward the placid water. 'There's billions of them down there.'

'And we're fishing here?' Peggy said. 'Eee-ewe. Gross.'

Gallant laughed, then turned to Holliday, who was still staring out across the water. 'A penny for them,' said the lobsterman.

'Rear Admiral Pulteney Malcolm, Royal Navy.'

'And who might he be?'

'Commander of HMS *Royal Oak*, the ship that delivered Major General John Ross and his troops to the shores of Maryland. In August of 1814. Ross went on to rout the Americans at the Battle of Bladensburg. The Americans lost so badly it allowed Ross and his men to march on Washington and burn it to the ground. He was the first person credited with defeating an entire U.S. Army in the field. A month later he was picked off by a pair of teenage snipers. His body was pickled in a barrel of Jamaican rum and the *Royal Oak* took him to Halifax. The *Royal Oak* was probably anchored in Bedford Basin. Somewhere right around here.'

'And what would this have to do with the price of lobster then?' asked Gallant. Peggy and Rafi had stopped concentrating on their fishing and were listening closely. Peggy knew Doc well; there was something in the air and it wasn't the smell of fish. Holliday continued the history lesson.

'There was more on board the *Royal Oak* than Ross's body in a barrel of rum. When he sacked Washington, Ross had three main objectives – the Capitol, the White House and the Treasury. In the treasury they found twenty thousand un-circulated silver dollars and an unknown quantity of ten-dollar gold double eagles.'

'So?' Peggy asked.

'While I was doing research in Scotland I accidentally got into a batch of letters from a young midshipman on the *Royal Oak* named Cameron McLeod. Young Cameron was one of Admiral Malcolm's runners and one of his favorites. In one of the letters home to his mother he mentions that the rear admiral had given him an American gold double eagle as a souvenir of the successful pillaging of Washington. He also mentions the number of gold coins in the hoard on board the *Royal Oak*. Ten thousand.'

'And how much would these little bits of gold be worth on today's market?' Gallant asked shrewdly.

'According to my research,' said Holliday, 'the silver dollars would go for about four million and the gold for about ten.'

'For the lot?' Gallant asked.

'Each,' answered Holliday.

'Mary mother of God,' muttered Gallant, his eyes filled with an entirely unholy lust.

'*Ongeshtopt mit gelt!*' Rafi breathed.

'Holy crap!' said Peggy.

'You've got a bite,' said Holliday, glancing at Gallant's jerking line.

*

Katherine Sinclair sat in the damaged study, her life in ruins as well as her house. After the debacle brought down on them by John Holliday and his godless rescuers nothing could be salvaged. The Edwards bitch had launched an all-out attack on Margaret's credibility and the authenticity of her find, and the chances of her son being elected leader faded with each passing day. The position would fall either to Edwards herself or to that idiot preacher Bainbridge.

She picked up the telephone in front of her and dialed Joseph Patchin's private number at the CIA. He answered on the second ring.

'Yes,' he said.

'You know who this is?'

'Yes.'

'Initiate Ironstone immediately. We have no other choice now.'

'I understand,' answered Patchin. The line went dead. Katherine Sinclair hung up the phone. There was no turning back now. The United States of America would never be the same again.

Read on for the first
chapter from Paul
Christopher's new thriller

The Templar
Conspiracy

Available from Penguin in
July 2012.

It was Christmas Day in Rome, and it was snowing. Snow was a rare occurrence here, but he was ready for it. He had kept his eyes on the weather reports for the past ten days. It was always best to be prepared.

The name on his American passport was Hannu Hancock, born of a Finnish mother and an American father in Madison, Wisconsin, where his father taught at the university and his mother ran a Finnish craft store. Hancock was forty-six, had attended East High School, followed by a bachelor's and then a master's in agronomy at the University of Wisconsin, Madison. His present job was as a soil-conservation biologist and traveling soil-conservation consultant with the US Department of Agriculture. Hancock had been married for three years to a young woman named Janit Ferguson, who had died of lung cancer. He was childless and had not remarried.

Not a word of this was true. Not even the people who hired him knew who he really was. He traveled under a number of passports, each with a different name and fully detailed biography to go along with it. The passports, along with a great deal of money, were kept in a safety-deposit box at Banque Bauer in Geneva. As an alternate he kept several more passports and a secondary nest egg tucked away in a bank in Nassau, the Bahamas, where he also owned a relatively small house in Lyford Cay – Sir Sean Connery was his closest neighbor – as well as a self-storage locker on the Carmichael Road on the way to the airport. The Bahamas house was his usual destination after doing a job. It would be his eventual destination again, but he'd been told to remain available for another assignment in Rome sometime within the next six days.

Not for a minute did he consider failing, nor did he think about the enormity of the initial act he'd been hired to complete. He never failed; he never made mistakes. Remorse was an emotion that was unknown to him. Some people would have called him a sociopath, but they would have been wrong. He was simply a man with a singular talent, and he practiced it with enormous efficiency. He left the motive and morality of his task entirely in the hands of his employers. In his own mind he was nothing more than a technician – a facilitator of the needs of the people who hired him.

Hancock made his way down the Corso Vittorio Emanuele II in the lightly falling snow. He glanced at his watch. It was six thirty in the morning, and it was still dark. Sunrise would be in an hour and four minutes. He still had plenty of time. He was wearing a white ski jacket purchased in Geneva, blue jeans from a vintage clothing store in New York, and high-top running shoes from a store in Paddington, London. He had a pale gray backpack slung over his shoulder and tucked under his arm was a long, Christmas-paper-wrapped box of the kind usually used for long-stemmed roses. On his head, covering his dark hair, he wore a white balaclava ski hat rolled up into a watch cap.

He'd seen virtually no one on his walk, except for a few taxi drivers, and the steel shutters were pulled down over the entrances to the cafés, bars and small pizzerias along the way. Partly it was the unfamiliar snow on the ground, and partly it was the day. Most people would be at home with loved ones, and the more pious would be preparing breakfast before heading out to St Peter's Square for the Apostolic Blessing from the Pope, scheduled for noon.

Hancock reached the Via Dei Filippini and turned into the narrow alley. Cars were angle-parked along the right-hand side, the only spaces available for the large nineteenth-century apartment block on the left. Hancock's own little DR5 rental was where he'd left it the night before. He continued down the alley until he reached an anonymous black door on the right. Using the old-fashioned key he'd been provided, he unlocked the door and stepped inside.

He found himself in a small, dark foyer with a winding iron staircase directly in front of him. He began to climb, ignoring several landings, and finally reached the top. A stone corridor led to the right, and Hancock followed it. The passage took several turns and ended at one of the choir lofts.

He looked down into the central part of the church, eighty or ninety feet below. As expected, it was empty. Most churches in Rome, big and small, would be vacant this morning. Every worshipper in the city was hurrying to St Peter's in time to get one of the good spots close to the main loggia of the church, where the Pope made his most important proclamations.

There was a narrow door at the left side of the choir loft. Opening it, Hancock was faced with a steep wooden staircase with a scrolled banister. He climbed the steps steadily until he reached the head of the stairs and the small chamber at the top. The floor of the chamber was made of thick Sardinian oak planks, black with age, and the walls were a complex mass of curving struts and beams of the same wood, much like the skeletal framework of a ship from the Spanish Armada, which was not surprising since the framework was built by the best Italian shipwrights from Liguria in the late sixteenth century.

The framework supported the heavy outer masonry dome and allowed the much lighter inner dome to be significantly taller than was normally seen in churches built at that time. A simple wooden staircase with banisters on both sides soared upward, following the dome's curve and ending at the foot of a small round tower steeple that capped the dome.

Hancock climbed again, reaching the top of the dome, and then went up a narrow spiral staircase into the tower. He checked his watch. Still forty minutes until the sun began to rise. He dropped the heavy parcel and shrugged off the backpack. The trip from the outer door on Via Dei Filippini to the tower had taken him eleven minutes. By his calculations the return journey would take no more than seven minutes since he would be going down rather than up and he'd no longer be carrying the extra weight.

Before doing anything else, Hancock took out a pair of surgical gloves and snapped them on. He opened the flap on the backpack and took out a wax-paper-wrapped fried-egg sandwich and ate, quickly and methodically making sure that no crumbs fell on the stone floor at his feet. As he ate, he looked out over the city. The snow was coming down more heavily now, easily enough to cover his tracks down the alley to the access door but not so heavily as to obscure vision. He finished the sandwich, carefully folded the waxed paper and slipped it into the pocket of his ski jacket.

He set the alarm on his watch for eleven thirty, pulled the masklike balaclava over his face to conserve heat and slid down to the floor. Within three minutes he had fallen into a light, dreamless sleep.

The alarm beeped him awake at exactly eleven thirty. Before standing up, he opened the backpack again and took out a loose-fitting white Tyvek suit, which covered him from chin to ankles. It took him only a few moments to slip it on. The snow was still falling lightly, and in the suit and the white balaclava, he would be invisible against the dull blur of the Christmas sky.

Hancock crouched over the backpack and removed a device that looked very much like a digital video camera. He stood up, and with the viewfinder up to his eye, he scanned the northwestern skyline on the far side of the Tiber River. The range was still exactly 1,311.64 yards, but he'd wanted to check the windage. He'd guessed from the straight fall of the snow that there was virtually no breeze, but the Leupold range finder was sophisticated enough to account for hidden air currents, as well as plot a ballistic line that computed the differential in height between him and the target. This was important since the Chiesa Nuova and its tower steeple were more than three hundred meters higher than the target, which lay across the river from the Plain of Mars.

Hancock bent down and returned the range finder to the backpack. He then began to undo the Christmas wrapping, carefully folding the red-and-gold paper and sliding it into the backpack. He lifted the top of the box, revealing the basic components of an American Cheytac Intervention .408 caliber sniper rifle, which was to Hancock's mind the greatest weapon of its kind ever made. He screwed on the stainless-steel muzzle brake and suppressor, slipped the US Optics telescopic sight on to its rails and slid the integral shoulder rest out of the stock. Finally, he fitted the seven-round box magazine into its slot in the forestock.

The rifle was immense by most standards – fifty-four inches, or almost five feet long, when assembled. The weapon had a built-in bipod toward the front of the rifle and a telescopic monopod at the rifle's point of balance. Hancock chose neither. Instead he took a custom-made sand-filled rest from the backpack and placed it on the capstones of the chest-high wall of the tower.

By kneeling on one leg, he could bring the target to bear almost exactly. He looked at his watch. Five minutes to twelve. It would be soon now. He took his handheld Pioneer Inno satellite radio out of the backpack and plugged in the earbuds.

The radio was tuned to CNN, which was carrying the Apostolic Blessing live, something the network did every year on Christmas Day.

According to the commentator, more than sixty thousand people were gathered in St Peter's Square to hear their sins being forgiven. Based on the last four *Urbi et Orbis* blessings, Hancock knew that he had no more than a minute and ten seconds to find the target and take the shot. At two minutes to twelve, a huge cheer went up in the square. Hancock tossed the radio into the backpack and rose to his firing position, placing the barrel just behind the suppressor on the sand pillow. He turned the knob on the telescopic sight two clicks, and the target area jumped into view: the central loggia, or balcony, of St Peter's Basilica.

There were eight other people on the long balcony with His Holiness: two bishops in white vestments and miters; two priests in white cassocks with red collars; a sound man with a boom microphone; a cameraman; the official Vatican photographer, Dario Biondi; and a senior cardinal who held the large white-and-gold folder containing the blessing.

In the middle of it all was the Pope himself.

He seated himself on a red-and-gold throne with a golden crozier, or shepherd's crook, held in his left hand. He was dressed in white-and-gold vestments and a matching white-and-gold silk miter. Behind the throne, barely visible in the shadows of the doorway, Hancock could see several darkly suited members of the *Vigilanza*, the Vatican City security force.

At last, through the sight, he saw the Pontiff's lips begin to move as he started the short blessing: *Sancti Apostoli Petrus et Paulus: de quorum potestate et auctoritate confidimus ipsi intercedant pro nobis ad Dominum.*

A papal banner draped over the balcony lifted slightly in a light wind, and Hancock adjusted the sight minutely. Below the balcony, unseen and unheard, the enormous crowd gave the obligatory response in unison: *Amen.*

Fifteen seconds gone.

Hancock wrapped his latex-gloved finger around the trigger as the Pope began the second line: *Precibus et meritis beatæ Mariae semper Virginis, beati Michaelis Archangeli, beati Ioannis Baptistæ, et sanctorum Apostolorum Petri et Pauli et omnium Sanctorum misereatur vestri omnipotens Deus; et dimissis omnibus peccatis vestris, perducat vos Iesus Christus ad vitam æternam.*

Twenty-five seconds gone.

The field of vision clear: a three-quarters profile – not the best angle for the job but good enough.

The crowd responded once again: *Amen.*

Thirty seconds gone. Through the telescopic sight Hancock saw the Pope visibly take a breath before beginning the third line of the blessing. His last breath.

Hancock fired.

The 2.75-inch, missile-shaped, sharp-nose round traveled the distance between Hancock and the target at a muzzle velocity of 3,350 feet per second in just a fraction over 1.5 seconds.

Hancock waited until he saw the impact, striking the pontiff in center mass, ripping through the chest wall and tipping the throne backward into the doorway of the balcony. Sure of his primary kill, Hancock then emptied the six-round magazine in an arc across the balcony, his object to create mayhem and as much confusion as possible. He succeeded.

With the task completed, he took the rifle down, laid it on the stone floor of the tower and took a few moments to clean up his brass and strip off the Tyvek suit. He put the shell casings into the pocket of his ski jacket, stuffed the Tyvek suit into his backpack and headed downward.

He had overestimated the time it would take for the return journey. Five minutes after beginning the downward trip, he reached the alley, locking the anonymous black door behind him. At six minutes, ahead of schedule, he climbed into his rental car and headed for the Rome Termini, the main railway station.

As he drove, he heard siren after siren heading for the Vatican, but no one paid him the slightest bit of attention. He arrived at the train station eleven minutes after the assassination and caught one of the frequent Leonardo Express trains to Fumincino Airport, where he caught a pre-booked flight to Geneva on the oddly named Air Baboo, a short-haul company that used Bombardier Dash Eight turboprops.

The elapsed time from kill to takeoff was fifty-four minutes. By that time neither the Vatican Police nor the State Police had even established the direction the onslaught had come from, let alone any clue as to the identity of the assassin.

The job was done. The Pope was dead.

'Ironstone' had begun.

He just wanted a decent book to read ...

Not too much to ask, is it? It was in 1935 when Allen Lane, Managing Director of Bodley Head Publishers, stood on a platform at Exeter railway station looking for something good to read on his journey back to London. His choice was limited to popular magazines and poor-quality paperbacks – the same choice faced every day by the vast majority of readers, few of whom could afford hardbacks. Lane's disappointment and subsequent anger at the range of books generally available led him to found a company – and change the world.

'We believed in the existence in this country of a vast reading public for intelligent books at a low price, and staked everything on it'
Sir Allen Lane, 1902–1970, founder of Penguin Books

The quality paperback had arrived – and not just in bookshops. Lane was adamant that his Penguins should appear in chain stores and tobacconists, and should cost no more than a packet of cigarettes.

Reading habits (and cigarette prices) have changed since 1935, but Penguin still believes in publishing the best books for everybody to enjoy. We still believe that good design costs no more than bad design, and we still believe that quality books published passionately and responsibly make the world a better place.

So wherever you see the little bird – whether it's on a piece of prize-winning literary fiction or a celebrity autobiography, political tour de force or historical masterpiece, a serial-killer thriller, reference book, world classic or a piece of pure escapism – you can bet that it represents the very best that the genre has to offer.

Whatever you like to read – trust Penguin.

read more
www.penguin.co.uk